PAUL TEMPLE
AND THE
VANDYKE AFFAIR

Francis Durbridge

WILLIAMS & WHITING

Applications for performance or other rights should be made to The Agency, 24 Pottery Lane, London W11 4LZ.

Cover design by Timo Schroeder

9781912582952

Williams & Whiting (Publishers)
15 Chestnut Grove, Hurstpierpoint,
West Sussex, BN6 9SS

Titles by Francis Durbridge published by Williams & Whiting

Also published by Williams & Whiting:
Francis Durbridge : The Complete Guide
By Melvyn Barnes

Titles by Francis Durbridge to be published by Williams & Whiting

Breakaway – The Family Affair
Breakaway – The Local Affair
Johnny Washington Esquire
Murder On The Continent (Further re-discovered serials and stories)
One Man To Another – a novel
Operation Diplomat
Paul Temple and the Alex Affair
Paul Temple and the Canterbury Case (film script)
Paul Temple and the Conrad Case
Paul Temple and the Geneva Mystery
Paul Temple and the Jonathan Mystery
Paul Temple and the Lawrence Affair
Paul Temple and the Margo Mystery
Paul Temple: Two Plays For Radio Vol 2 (Send For Paul Temple and News of Paul Temple)
The Man From Washington
The Passenger
Tim Frazer and the Salinger Affair
Tim Frazer and the Mellin Forrest Mystery

INTRODUCTION

Those not familiar with all aspects of the multi-faceted career of Francis Durbridge (1912-98) might welcome a brief résumé. He began in 1933 as a writer of sketches, stories and plays for BBC radio, mostly light entertainments, but a talent for crime fiction became evident in his early radio plays *Murder in the Midlands* (1934) and *Murder in the Embassy* (1937). The *Radio Times* (11 February 1938) mentioned that Durbridge had by then written some one hundred radio pieces, and Charles Hatton commented in *Radio Pictorial* (28 October 1938) that "He is one of the very few people in this country who have succeeded in making a living by writing for the BBC."

Although Durbridge continued to write plays and serials for BBC radio for many years, using his own name and the pseudonyms Frank Cromwell, Nicholas Vane and Lewis Middleton Harvey, his future had already been assured when he created the dream team of novelist/detective Paul Temple and his wife Steve. In fact the audience reaction to his 1938 radio serial *Send for Paul Temple* led to sequels over several decades that cemented his impressive UK and European reputation. So following *Send for Paul Temple* in 1938, Durbridge responded later the same year with *Paul Temple and the Front Page Men* and continued with many more. From 1939 to 1968 there were another twenty-six Paul Temple cases, of which seven were new productions of earlier broadcasts.

Then in 1952, while continuing to write for radio, Durbridge embarked on a run of BBC television serials that attracted huge viewing figures until 1980. And additionally, from 1971 in the UK and even earlier in Germany, he became known for intriguing stage plays that were not simple whodunits but more in the style of Frederick Knott's *Dial M for Murder* or Ira Levin's *Deathtrap*.

Paul Temple and the Vandyke Affair was first broadcast on the BBC Light Programme in eight thirty-minute episodes from Monday 30 October to Monday 18 December 1950, and the episodes were repeated on Friday each week. With Temple played by Kim Peacock (1901-66), it was the thirteenth outing for Temple and Steve. Although Peacock had a long run in the role, beginning in 1946 with *Paul Temple and the Gregory Affair* and ending in 1953 with the one-hour play *Paul Temple and Steve Again*, he was replaced by Peter Coke (1913-2008) for *Paul Temple and the Gilbert Case* (1954). Coke then made Temple his own in ten subsequent serials until the concluding *Paul Temple and the Alex Affair* in 1968.

Marjorie Westbury (1905-89), as Steve Temple, partnered both Peacock and Coke in all their appearances, and before Peacock she had played Steve opposite Barry Morse in *Send for Paul Temple Again* (1945) and Howard Marion-Crawford in *A Case for Paul Temple* (1946). In total she was Steve on twenty-two occasions until the final serial *Paul Temple and the Alex Affair* (1968) – which coincidentally was a new production of her first appearance as Steve in the 1945 *Send for Paul Temple Again*. But mention must also be made of Lester Mudditt, who played Sir Graham Forbes of Scotland Yard on nineteen occasions from the original serial in 1938 until *Paul Temple and the Spencer Affair* (1957-58).

A new production of *Paul Temple and the Vandyke Affair* was broadcast on the BBC Light Programme from Thursday 1 January to Thursday 19 February 1959, with episodes repeated on Saturday each week. By this time Peter Coke was well established in the role of Temple, this being his fifth appearance, and of course Marjorie Westbury played Steve. For the first time, Richard Williams appeared as Lester Mudditt's successor in the role of Sir Graham Forbes. An interesting point about Peter Coke, incidentally, is that in the original 1950 production of *Paul Temple and the Vandyke Affair* he had played Terry Palmer (one of the suspects!).

Recordings of this serial were marketed by the BBC. The original 1950 production was included in the CD box set *Paul Temple: The Complete Radio Collection: The Early Years 1938-1950* (BBC, 2016); while the 1959 production was firstly issued in two audiocassettes and five CDs (BBC, 2004) then later included in the CD box set *Paul Temple: The Complete Radio Collection: The Fifties 1954-1959* (BBC, 2016).

Turning to Temple's popularity on the Continent, the Dutch radio version was *Paul Vlaanderen en het Vandyke mysterie* (30 September to 18 November 1951, eight episodes), translated by J.C. van der Horst and produced by Kommer Kleijn, with Jan van Ees as Vlaanderen and Eva Janssen as Ina; the German radio version was *Paul Temple und der Fall Vandyke* (12 September to 30 October 1953, eight episodes), translated by Marianne de Barde and produced by Eduard Hermann, with René Deltgen as Temple and Annemarie Cordes as Steve; and the Danish radio version was *Vandyke-mysteriet* (23 June to 11 August 1961, eight episodes), translated by Else Faber and produced by Sam Besekow, with Frits Helmuth as Temple and Ghita Nørby as Steve.

The Temples also proved popular with cinemagoers - played by Anthony Hulme and Joy Shelton in *Send for Paul Temple* (1946, based on the original 1938 radio serial); John Bentley and Dinah Sheridan in the two films *Calling Paul Temple* (1948, based on the 1945 radio serial *Send for Paul Temple Again*) and *Paul Temple's Triumph* (1950, based on the 1939 radio serial *News of Paul Temple*); and John Bentley and Patricia Dainton in *Paul Temple Returns* (1952, based on the 1942 radio serial *Paul Temple Intervenes*). These movies have been preserved by Renown Pictures, are shown regularly on Talking Pictures TV, and were collected as the DVD box set *The Paul Temple Collection Limited Edition* (Renown Pictures, 2011).

Unlike many of Durbridge's radio and television serials, *Paul Temple and the Vandyke Affair* has never been novelised – so this volume presents a welcome opportunity for today's readers to see the original script in print.

Melvyn Barnes
Author of *Francis Durbridge: The Complete Guide* (Williams & Whiting, 2018)

This book reproduces Francis Durbridge's original script together with the list of characters and actors of the BBC programme on the dates mentioned, but the eventual broadcast might have edited Durbridge's script in respect of scenes, dialogue and character names.

PAUL TEMPLE
AND THE
VANDYKE AFFAIR

A serial in eight episodes
By FRANCIS DURBRIDGE
Broadcast on BBC Radio
30 October – 18 December 1950
CAST:

Paul Temple . . . . Kim Peacock
Steve, his wife . . . . Marjorie Westbury
Charlie . . . . .Michael Harding
Sir Graham Forbes . . . . Lester Mudditt
Mary Desmond . . . . Joan Hart
Terry Palmer . . . . Peter Coke
Sergeant Digby . . . . . . .James E Thompson
Bill McCall . . . . .Tommy Duggan
Inspector Eden . . . . Donald Gray
Roger Shelly . . . . Richard Hurndall
Philip Droste . . . . Roger Delgado
Vanessa Droste . . . . Grizelda Hervey
Charles Marett . . . . .Raf de la Torre
Louis Franz. . . . . Olaf Olsen
Luke . . . . .Charles Richardson
Marian Faber . . . . Susan Buret
Railway porter . . . . James E Thompson
Dr Foy . . . . Robert Alban
Telephone Operator . . . . . .Betty Baskcomb
Other parts played by
Pat Jamblin, Janet Morrison
Alun Owen, David Peel,
Gladys Spencer and Lewis Ward

NEW PRODUCTION
Broadcast on BBC Radio
1 January – 19 February 1959
CAST:

Paul Temple . . . . Peter Coke
Steve, his wife . . . . Marjorie Westbury
Charlie . . . . James Beattie
Sir Graham Forbes . . . . .Richard Williams
Inspector Eden . . . . .Frederick Treves
Terry Palmer . . . . Peter Wilde
Mary Desmond . . . . .June Tobin
Queenie Edwards . . . . . . Armine Sandford
Madame Flaubert . . . . . .Catherine Salkeld
Bert Walters . . . . .Haydn Jones
Roger Shelly . . . . .Richard Hurndall
Bill McCall . . . . John Scott
Sergeant Digby . . . . David Spenser
Philip Droste . . . . Simon Lack
Vanessa Droste . . . . .Grizelda Hervey
Charles Marett . . . . John Bryning
Newsvendor . . . . .Rolf Lefebvre
Luke .Jon Farrell
Telephone Operator . . . . . Betty Baskcomb
Receptionist . . . . .Beatrice Ormonde
Waiter . . . . .David March
Louis Franz . . . . .Rolf Lefebvre
Dr Foy . . . . John Graham
Marian Faber . . . . .Betty Hardy
A porter . . . . .James Thomason

EPISODE ONE

THE SITTER-IN

OPEN TO:	The sound of a piano. PAUL TEMPLE is playing, with one finger only, a rather garbled version of one of the hit tunes from Oklahoma. The piano continues for some little time …
STEVE:	(*Finally exasperated*) Oh, Paul, do stop that awful noise!
TEMPLE:	(*Surprised*) What do you mean – awful noise!? It's out of Oklahoma!

The piano stops.

STEVE:	Not when I saw it! (*A pause: thoughtfully*) Paul, I've been thinking about this Desmond case …
TEMPLE:	(*Faintly irritated*) Steve, I don't want to talk about the Desmond case! I've been thinking about it all day. I want a rest.
STEVE:	Well, why don't you read a book or have a bath or something …
TEMPLE:	(*Indignantly*) A bath? Why on earth should I have … (*On reflection*) You know, that's not a bad idea, Steve!

TEMPLE bangs the piano and closes the lid.

| TEMPLE: | (*Calling*) Charlie! |

A door opens.

CHARLIE:	(*Briskly*) Yes, sir?
TEMPLE:	(*Proudly*) I'm going to have a bath, Charlie.
CHARLIE:	O.K., sir.
TEMPLE:	Run the water – and make sure it's hot.
CHARLIE:	Yes, sir.
TEMPLE:	Oh, and I'd like the bath salts. The ones from Paris – the expensive ones – the ones you like, Charlie.
CHARLIE:	Very good, sir.

STEVE: You'll find a bath towel in the airing cupboard, Paul. Oh, and darling, don't sing, remember the neighbours don't like it.

TEMPLE: Do you like opera, Charlie?

CHARLIE: Yes, sir.

TEMPLE: Good. I'm going to sing the complete score of La Traviata. You'll be enchanted, Charlie.

CHARLIE: (*Dubiously*) I hope so, sir.

The sound of the flat buzzer.

CHARLIE: That's someone at the door! Excuse me, Mrs T.

STEVE: It's all right, I'll answer it! You run the water, Charlie. (*Crossing to the door*)

CROSS FADE to STEVE opening the front door.

STEVE: (*Pleasantly surprised*) Why, hello, Sir Graham!

FORBES: Hello Steve! Is Temple in?

STEVE: (*Laughing*) Yes, as a matter of fact he's just going to have a bath. Come along in, Sir Graham!

The door closes.

FORBES: I think you've met Inspector Eden, Steve.

STEVE: Yes, of course! How are you, Inspector?

EDEN: I'm very well, thank you, Mrs Temple. (*The INSPECTOR is a well-spoken man of about fifty; at the moment he is in a very serious mood*)

STEVE, SIR GRAHAM and the INSPECTOR enter the drawing room.

EDEN: I'm afraid we've dropped in at an awkward moment.

STEVE: No, that's all right. I'll tell Paul you're … Oh, here he is!

TEMPLE: (*Faintly exasperated*) Darling, it's the most extraordinary thing but whenever I decide to take a bath our so-called hot water system …

4

	(*He stops speaking: surprised*) By Timothy, Sir Graham!
FORBES:	(*Laughing*) Hello, Temple! Sorry if we've got you out of the bath!
TEMPLE:	You arrived just in time! Five minutes later I should have been a human icicle! My word, you look happy, Eden! What's on your mind?
EDEN:	We're very worried about the Desmond case, sir.
TEMPLE:	I'll bet you are!
EDEN:	I've never known such a case! Even the American papers are full of it!
TEMPLE:	I don't know about the American papers. I know Steve's full of it. She won't let me talk about anything else.
FORBES:	Do you know how many letters we've had since this case started?
TEMPLE:	No.
FORBES:	Twenty thousand …
TEMPLE:	By Timothy!
FORBES:	… and we're still getting nearly two thousand a day.
STEVE:	Why, that's fantastic!
FORBES:	(*Clearing his throat*) I – er – understand you've seen Mrs Desmond, Temple?
TEMPLE:	Yes, she phoned me shortly after the baby disappeared. She's been phoning and writing ever since. (*Suddenly*) Look here, Sir Graham, I'm interested in this case but frankly I'd like to hear your side of the story.
FORBES:	(*Quietly*) Go on, Eden …
TEMPLE:	Let me have the facts: assume I know nothing whatever about the case, Inspector.

5

EDEN:	Well, a young widow called Desmond – Mrs Mary Desmond – has a flat in Westchester House; that's a large block of flats on the Edgware Road.
TEMPLE:	Yes, go on …
EDEN:	One evening, about a week ago – a week last Tuesday to be precise – Mrs Desmond had a dinner date in Town – here – in the West End. Actually she'd been invited out to dinner by a young fellow called Terry Palmer.
FORBES:	Palmer's an old friend: they go out together quite a lot.
EDEN:	Mrs Desmond has an eighteen month old baby and since the death of her husband, which was just over two years ago, both she and the baby – Susan – have lived at Westchester House. When she has a date in Town or wants to pop down to the local cinema she employs a sitter-in.
FORBES:	It's always the same sitter-in: an elderly spinster by the name of Miss Millicent.
EDEN:	There seems to be very little doubt that Miss Millicent is a perfectly ordinary and responsible person: she's been acting as a sitter-in for Mrs Desmond for almost a year.
STEVE:	(*Intrigued*) Go on, Inspector …
EDEN:	Well, last Tuesday week when Mrs Desmond had this date with Palmer she phoned Miss Millicent and the old girl agreed to sit in as usual. Miss Millicent turned up at the flat at about 6.30 and Mrs Desmond met Terry Palmer at The Commodore Club in Brook Street just after 7.15.
TEMPLE:	Go on …

6

FORBES: Mrs Desmond and Palmer stayed at The
             Commodore until about 10.45. When Mrs
             Desmond arrived back at the flat, which was
             just after 11.15, there was no sign of either
             Miss Millicent or the baby.

EDEN: (*Slowly: significantly*) Both the child and the
             sitter-in had completely disappeared.

FORBES: Now there's one interesting point, Temple.
             Although Mrs Desmond is distressed –
             obviously deeply distressed – by what's
             happened, she certainly doesn't blame Miss
             Millicent; in fact she's quite convinced that the
             sitter-in has had nothing whatever to do with it.

TEMPLE: (*Thoughtfully*) I see.

EDEN: Well, those are the facts, sir. Now tell us how
             you fit into the picture.

TEMPLE: I'm afraid I don't, Inspector – at least, not
             officially. I've received several letters from
             Mrs Desmond and this morning Terry Palmer
             phoned me. He seemed very anxious that I
             should have a talk to Mrs Desmond.

EDEN: And did you?

TEMPLE: Yes, Steve and I drove down to Westchester
             House shortly after breakfast. (*START FADE*)
             When we arrived at the flat Terry Palmer was
             there. He was rather a different sort of person
             from what I'd expected …

COMPLETE FADE.

*FADE UP of TERRY PALMER. PALMER is a well-educated
man of about thirty-seven or eight. His manner is slightly
hesitant and nervous: he gives the impression that he is not
really very sure of himself.*

PALMER: Mr Temple?

7

TEMPLE: Yes.

PALMER: It's awfully good of you to come like this. I really must apologise for phoning but – (*Noticing STEVE*) Oh, I beg your pardon!

TEMPLE: This is my wife.

PALMER: Oh, how do you do, Mrs Temple? It's awfully nice of you both to come, I … Do come in, Mrs Temple.

PALMER opens a door.

MARY: What is it, Terry?

MARY DESMOND is about thirty-two: an emotional type of person.

PALMER: It's Mr and Mrs Temple, Mary.

MARY: (*Very surprised*) Oh!

TEMPLE: You seem surprised, Mrs Desmond – weren't you expecting us?

MARY: You said in your letter that you were too busy to see me, so I thought …

PALMER: (*Interrupting MARY*) That was over a week ago, Mary. I – I spoke to Mr Temple again this morning. He's changed his mind.

TEMPLE: Only to the extent of having a chat with you, Mrs Desmond. Frankly, I doubt very much whether there's anything that I can do.

MARY: (*A note of irritation in her voice*) Then why did you come?

TEMPLE: Mr Palmer telephoned me. He said that you were desperate and that you wanted to see me.

MARY: (*Tensely: near to tears*) Well, I've seen you. I'm quite sure you're right and there's nothing you can do for me. Please go …

PALMER: (*Embarrassed*) Mary, please!

STEVE: (*Quietly*) Is this a photograph of your little girl?

PALMER: Yes. Yes, that's Susan.

STEVE:	She's awfully pretty, isn't she? How old is she, Mrs Desmond?
MARY:	She's just eighteen months.
STEVE:	Is she walking?
MARY:	(*Hesitantly*) Yes, she started to walk when she was twelve months. (*Distressed*) She's … very advanced for her age.
TEMPLE:	(*Quietly*) I suppose you don't happen to have a photograph of Miss Millicent?
MARY:	No, but the police have. I believe they got it from Miss Edwards.
STEVE:	Who's Miss Edwards?
PALMER:	That's Queenie Edwards: she lives with Miss Millicent.
TEMPLE:	Where?
MARY:	Miss Millicent rents a small house on the Finchley Road.
TEMPLE:	And you say this Miss Edwards – Queenie Edwards – lives with her?
MARY:	Yes. She's a sort of P.G. I understand they've been together for years.
TEMPLE:	I see. Mrs Desmond, I'm quite prepared to do anything which might help the police to find your baby, on the other hand …
MARY:	The police! They'll never find Susan! All they do is ask a lot of stupid and ridiculous questions.
PALMER:	My dear, you've got to have patience.
MARY:	Patience! It isn't a question of patience! I don't know how you can be so calm about things, Terry! (*Distressed*) It's over a week since Susan disappeared.
TEMPLE:	(*Quietly*) Yes, well … Let's see if I've got the facts right, Mrs Desmond. On Tuesday of last

9

	week you and Mr Palmer had dinner at the Commodore Club: you arrived there at about …
PALMER:	About half past seven …
TEMPLE:	… and you got back to the flat at about …
MARY:	It was about a quarter past eleven.
TEMPLE:	What happened when you arrived at the flat?
MARY:	Well, I rang the bell and there was no reply. Naturally, I was surprised but I came to the conclusion that Miss Millicent had fallen asleep – she did that once before, didn't she, Terry?
PALMER:	Yes – yes, she did.
TEMPLE:	Go on …
MARY:	Well, when I realised that Miss Millicent didn't intend to answer the door I let myself in. The flat looked perfectly all right: there was a large piece of coal on the fire, the radio was playing, the curtains were drawn – it all looked perfectly normal. And then …
TEMPLE:	You discovered that the flat was empty.
MARY:	Yes.
STEVE:	What did you do when you realised that Miss Millicent and the baby were missing?
PALMER:	Well, for a moment, quite frankly, we just didn't know what to do. We were stunned.
STEVE:	But what did you do – eventually?
PALMER:	I phoned Miss Edwards to see if, by any chance, Miss Millicent had returned home. Of course she hadn't.
TEMPLE:	Was Miss Edwards surprised when you told her what had happened?
PALMER:	Yes, of course – awfully surprised. She seemed awfully upset, I thought.
TEMPLE:	Go on …

MARY:	Well, there's nothing else to tell. No one had seen Miss Millicent or Susan – no one in the block, I mean. I made Terry telephone for the police …
TEMPLE:	You said just now that when you entered the flat the radio was playing.
MARY:	Yes.
TEMPLE:	Can you remember what it was playing?
MARY:	It was dance music but just what sort of dance music I'm afraid I can't remember.
TEMPLE:	I see.
PALMER:	You haven't told Mr Temple about the telephone message, Mary.
MARY:	Miss Millicent had rather a bad memory so if anyone rang up I used to make her jot the message down on a pad – it really didn't matter then if she forgot to tell me about it.
STEVE:	Was there a message then – on this particular night?
MARY:	Yes. It was scribbled on the pad by the telephone. What was it, Terry? What did it say?
PALMER:	The message, which was in Miss Millicent's handwriting, said: "A Mr Vandyke telephoned – he left no message".
TEMPLE:	Mr Vandyke?
PALMER:	Yes – and the funny thing is Mary doesn't know anyone called Vandyke. Neither do I if it comes to that.
TEMPLE:	M'm …
STEVE:	Mrs Desmond, I read something in one of the papers about a doll?
MARY:	Oh, yes. Susan had a doll: a little Dutch girl in a blue dress. Terry bought it for her. The doll

	doesn't appear to be in the flat: she must have taken it with her.
STEVE:	There's nothing else missing?
MARY:	No, nothing.
TEMPLE:	When did you first meet Miss Millicent?
MARY:	About a year ago. I advertised for a sitter-in in the local paper and Miss Millicent answered the advertisement. You know, Mr Temple, if anything's happened to Susan I'm quite sure Miss Millicent hasn't had anything to do with it. She's a terribly nice person, isn't she, Terry?
PALMER:	She's a poppet, and she's awfully fond of Susan – awfully.
TEMPLE:	How well do you know this friend of hers – Queenie Edwards?
MARY:	Oh, hardly at all. Miss Millicent brought her to the flat one night about six months ago and I suppose I've spoken to her about half-a-dozen times on the telephone.
STEVE:	Is she about the same age as Miss Millicent?
MARY:	Good gracious, no! She's about thirty. She works at Madame Flaubert's, the milliners in Mount Street.
TEMPLE:	(*START FADE*) I see. Well, thank you, Mrs Desmond. Now don't worry! And remember, the police may seem to be asking a lot of unnecessary questions but in the long run …

FADE SCENE.

FADE UP of SIR GRAHAM FORBES …

FORBES:	(*FADE IN*) Yes, she told us about the phone call, Temple – also about the doll – but it doesn't seem to have got us anywhere …
TEMPLE:	Did you check the call, Inspector?

EDEN: Yes. There was a call all right. It went through the exchange at about nine o'clock.

FORBES: So Miss Millicent and presumably the baby must have been in the flat up till about nine.

TEMPLE: (*Thoughtfully*) Yes. I'll tell you a point in Mrs Desmond's story that struck me as being rather odd. Why did she ring the bell instead of simply letting herself into the flat? After all, Miss Millicent wasn't a servant remember – she was a sitter-in.

EDEN: Yes, that's quite a point. What do you make of this Vandyke business, Temple? Do you think Mrs Desmond's telling the truth when she says she doesn't know anyone called Vandyke?

TEMPLE: Yes, I think she is.

STEVE: Perhaps Miss Millicent got the name wrong?

FORBES: I don't think so, Steve. We've checked on all the people of a similar sounding name who might have telephoned Mrs Desmond.

EDEN: (*Suddenly*) What's your opinion of Palmer, sir?

TEMPLE: I'm not awfully impressed by him, Inspector – not awfully.

EDEN: (*Smiling*) I see what you mean.

FORBES: I think Palmers all right: of course he's in a rather difficult position, isn't he?

STEVE: Is he <u>very</u> friendly with Mrs Desmond?

FORBES: I don't know. It's difficult to say, Steve. He used to be a great friend of her husband: the three of them used to go on holidays together.

STEVE: What does he do?

EDEN: That appears to be something of a mystery, Mrs Temple. He calls himself a freelance journalist.

FORBES: (*Curious*) What happened this morning, Temple – after you saw Mrs Desmond?

13

TEMPLE:	I sent Steve along to Madame Flauberts. I wanted her to take a good look at Queenie Edwards.
FORBES:	Did you take a good look at her, Steve?
STEVE:	Yes – we had quite an interesting chat.
FORBES:	(*A grim chuckle*) I'll bet you did!
STEVE:	What do you mean, Sir Graham?
FORBES:	Go on, Steve. Tell us what happened …
STEVE:	(*START FADE*) Well, as soon as I walked into Madame Flaubert's I spotted Queenie Edwards. I don't know how I was able to recognise her because I'd never seen her before and I'd never even seen a photograph of her, nevertheless I knew instinctively that the tall, rather good looking girl, was Queenie Edwards …

COMPLETE FADE.

FADE UP.

STEVE:	Good morning!
QUEENIE:	Good morning, madam. (*QUEENIE EDWARDS has a very slight cockney accent: the accent becomes more pronounced when QUEENIE is excited*)
STEVE:	You've got a rather nice little hat in the window. The one with the feather. Do you think I could try it on?
QUEENIE:	Yes, of course, madam. Excuse me a moment, I'll get it for you.

STEVE casually hums to herself as QUEENIE EDWARDS gets the hat from the window.

FLAUBERT:	Are you being attended to, madam? (*MADAME FLAUBERT is a sophisticated French woman in her late forties*)
STEVE:	Yes, thank you.

14

A moment.

QUEENIE: Is this the one?

STEVE: Oh, yes! That's it! Oh, it's dark blue – I thought it was black.

QUEENIE: No, madam – dark blue.

STEVE tries on the hat.

STEVE: (*Looking in the mirror*) I rather like it …

QUEENIE: It suits you, madam.

STEVE: I don't quite know about the feather …

QUEENIE: We could take the feather off for you, but I think it would spoil it.

STEVE: (*Still staring in the mirror*) Yes. Yes, I think you're right. It is nice, isn't it? What a pity it's blue …

QUEENIE: Did you particularly want black, madam?

STEVE: Yes, I did. (*Thoughtfully*) Still, it's very nice … How much is it?

QUEENIE: It's twelve and a half guineas, madam.

STEVE: (*Pleasantly*) Oh, dear, that's rather a lot, isn't it?

QUEENIE: It's a model, you see. I'm afraid most of our hats are models, madam.

STEVE: Yes, all right, I'll take it.

QUEENIE: Thank you, madam.

STEVE: Here's my card – would you send it to that address, please?

QUEENIE: Yes, certainly, Mrs – (*She stops: a change of attitude: tense and a little unfriendly*) Mrs Temple?

STEVE: (*Pleasantly*) Yes.

QUEENIE: Is that – Mrs Paul Temple?

STEVE: Yes, that's right. (*Smiling*) You're Queenie Edwards, aren't you?

QUEENIE: (*A note of tenseness in her voice*) Yes.

15

STEVE:	I was talking to a friend of yours this morning, or rather a friend of a friend of yours – Mrs Desmond.
QUEENIE:	(*Haltingly*) I've only met Mrs Desmond once.
STEVE:	She's terribly distressed about her baby and your friend Miss Millicent.
QUEENIE:	Yes, I know.
STEVE:	(*Friendly: endeavouring to arouse QUEENIE's interest*) What do you think happened, Miss Edwards? Do you think your friend …
QUEENIE:	(*Interrupting STEVE*) I don't know what happened!
STEVE:	I see. (*A moment*) When was the last time you saw Miss Millicent?
QUEENIE:	(*Coldly*) I saw her the night she went to Mrs Desmonds. We had tea together. She was in quite good spirits: I'm sure she never dreamt that anything like this would happen.
STEVE:	(*Watching QUEENIE*) What do you think has happened?
QUEENIE:	(*Tensely*) I've told you, I don't know. (*Complete change*) Would you like this hat in a box, madam, or shall I ask one of our assistants …
STEVE:	(*Quietly; interrupting QUEENIE*) Miss Edwards …
QUEENIE:	Yes, madam?
STEVE:	My husband has promised Mrs Desmond to find out what's happened to her baby and your friend Miss Millicent. Now I'm not suggesting that you know anything, but …
QUEENIE:	(*A shade defiantly*) But what, Mrs Temple?
STEVE:	Why do you resent being questioned, surely you realise that …

QUEENIE: (*Overwrought*) I've been asked far too many questions! First the police, then the reporters, and now – you come snooping around! You didn't want that hat! You only came in here because you wanted to ask me a lot of questions … Because you wanted to pry … and push your nose into things which don't concern you. Now go away! Leave me alone! For God's sake leave me alone! (*She starts to cry*)

STEVE: (*Softly*) Miss Edwards, please!

FLAUBERT: (*Alarmed*) Is anything the matter, madam?

STEVE: No, it's quite all right.

FLAUBERT: Queenie, what is it? What's the matter with you?

QUEENIE: (*Sniffing into her handkerchief*) I'm sorry, Madame Flaubert.

FLAUBERT: Really, Queenie! You'll have to pull yourself together, my dear. We can't go on like this, you know. (*To STEVE*) I'm so sorry, madam. She's a little overwrought. She's had a great deal of worry just recently and …

STEVE: That's all right. It's quite all right. I understand, perfectly …

FLAUBERT: Is there anything I can show you, madam?

STEVE: No. No, if you don't mind I'd like to talk to Miss Edwards.

A pause.

QUEENIE: I'm sorry. I'm sorry I blew off steam like that.

STEVE: That's all right. Do you feel better?

QUEENIE: Yes.

STEVE: You wait till my husband hears what I've paid for this hat – he'll blow off steam all right. He'll blow the roof off.

QUEENIE laughs.

STEVE: Queenie – you don't mind if I ask you one or two questions now, do you?

QUEENIE: No. No, go on …

STEVE: Did Miss Millicent work for anyone else besides Mrs Desmond?

QUEENIE: She didn't work at all. I mean, not properly.

STEVE: No, I mean – did she act as a sitter-in for anyone else?

QUEENIE: Oh, yes – one or two people.

STEVE: Who, for instance?

QUEENIE: Well, I just can't remember, not off hand. But Mr Shelly would know – why don't you ask Mr Shelly?

STEVE: Who's Mr Shelly?

QUEENIE: He runs a Mother's Help Bureau in Hampstead. I think he calls himself Shelly's Services. You know the kind of thing: they provide sitters-in, mother's help, arrange dinner parties …

STEVE: And Miss Millicent worked for Shelly's Services?

QUEENIE: She was on their books. I think she did about two nights a week for them. She didn't get Mrs Desmond through Shelly, that was a private arrangement.

STEVE: How well did you know Miss Millicent?

QUEENIE: Oh, ever so well. We've been together for years. She was an old school friend of mother's. She's an old maid but she's not the stuffy type, quite broadminded. I mean if I want to take a boyfriend home for supper I take him home, there's no nonsense.

STEVE: Queenie, have you heard of anyone called Vandyke?

18

QUEENIE: Vandyke? No, not that I know of. But it's funny you should ask me that. The police asked me that very same question. I told them I've never heard of anyone called Vandyke. I'm sure Miss Millicent hadn't either. Who is this Mr Vandyke anyway?

STEVE: He telephoned Mrs Desmond the night your friend disappeared. (*Friendly; almost a confidential manner*) What's your opinion about all this, Queenie?

QUEENIE: (*START FADE: thoughtfully, a note of tenseness in her voice*) I don't know … I've thought about it … I've laid awake every night thinking about it … But I don't know what could have happened to her … I just don't know – and that's the truth, Mrs Temple.

COMPLETE FADE.

FADE UP of SIR GRAHAM FORBES …

FORBES: Well, you certainly got a great deal more out of Queenie Edwards than we did, Steve.

EDEN: Yes, we seemed to get off on entirely the wrong foot. It was quite a while before she even told us about Shelly.

TEMPLE: Did you see this fellow Shelly?

EDEN: (*Significantly*) We did.

FORBES: Have you seen him, Temple?

TEMPLE: Not yet, but I intend to.

EDEN: What a character! Queenie Edwards was right. He runs a sort of Mother's Help Agency. To look at him you'd think he'd walked straight out of the chorus. But he's got his head screwed on all right. I shouldn't be surprised if he isn't a pretty shrewd bird.

FORBES: I'm quite sure he is.

STEVE: Was he any help, Sir Graham?

FORBES: Well, he gave us the names and addresses of two other people that have used Miss Millicent as a sitter-in. Unfortunately they couldn't help us. (*With a sigh*) I don't have to tell you why we're here, Temple. We shall need all the help we can get over this case. It's a pretty tough assignment.

TEMPLE: Yes, and a pretty expensive one too by the look of things.

EDEN: What do you mean, sir?

TEMPLE: Twelve guineas for a hat! By Timothy!

STEVE laughs.

FADE UP of music: the music is gay and swift.

FADE DOWN of music.

STEVE: (*Quietly*) Paul …

TEMPLE: (*His thoughts elsewhere*) Yes, darling?

STEVE: What are you thinking about?

TEMPLE: I was thinking about Terry Palmer. He's either a very good freelance journalist or …

TEMPLE is interrupted by the opening of the door.

TEMPLE: Yes? What is it, Charlie?

CHARLIE: If you want a bath the water's o.k. now, sir.

TEMPLE: Well it wasn't o.k. half an hour ago when Sir Graham was here! I should have been frozen to death.

CHARLIE: It's all right now. I've hotted it up.

TEMPLE: Yes, all right, Charlie.

The door closes.

TEMPLE: (*Yawning*) Gosh, I'm tired. I don't know whether to have a bath or not. What time is it, Steve?

STEVE: It's just gone nine.

TEMPLE: Where did you say that towel was – in the airing cupboard?

STEVE: Yes, darling. Paul, what were you saying about Palmer?

TEMPLE: Oh, I was saying – he's either a very good freelance journalist or he's got a private income. Did you notice the suit he was wearing and the gold cigarette case?

STEVE: Yes. You know, that name strikes a bell – Terry Palmer. I'm sure I've seen it somewhere quite recently or ... (*Suddenly*) Just a minute! Where's that magazine – the one you bought this morning?

TEMPLE: (*Suddenly, remembering*) By Timothy, you're right! There's an article in it by Palmer. Where's the magazine? It should be here with the Radio Times, Steve ...

STEVE: Here it is!

STEVE turns the pages of the magazine.

TEMPLE: Yes. Yes, that's it ...

STEVE: Science and the Modern Criminal by Terry Palmer.

TEMPLE: M'm – it appears that Mr Palmer's interested in criminology.

STEVE: Have you read the article?

The telephone rings.

TEMPLE: No. I started to read it, but ...

STEVE: It's all right, I'll take it. (*She lifts the receiver: on the phone*) Hello?

QUEENIE: (*On the other end of the phone: tense*) Hello? Who is that, please?

STEVE: This is Mrs Temple speaking.

21

QUEENIE: Oh, this is Queenie – Queenie Edwards. Do you remember me? We met this morning in Madame Flauberts.

STEVE: (*Pleasantly*) Yes, of course I remember you! What is it, Queenie? Is anything the matter?

QUEENIE: (*Tensely*) I want to talk to your husband. Is he there, Mrs Temple? Please – it's very important.

STEVE: Yes, just a minute. (*Quietly; aside to TEMPLE*) It's Queenie Edwards – she wants to talk to you. I think there's something the matter.

TEMPLE: (*Quietly*) I'll take it in the bedroom – you hold on, Steve.

STEVE: (*On the phone*) Just a minute, Queenie. My husband's coming …

QUEENIE: (*Tensely*) He won't be long will he, Mrs Temple?

STEVE: No, no, of course not. Is anything wrong, Queenie?

QUEENIE: I've got to see your husband, Mrs Temple. It's important. Terribly important.

There's a click as TEMPLE picks up the receiver in the bedroom.

TEMPLE: Hello?

QUEENIE: Is that you, Mr Temple?

TEMPLE: Yes. What can I do for you, Miss Edwards?

QUEENIE: I've got to see you. It's important. Terribly important. I've got to see you tonight.

TEMPLE: Well, what is it you want to see me about?

QUEENIE: About Miss Millicent. Listen – there's something I've got to tell you. Please believe me, Mr Temple, it really is important.

TEMPLE: All right, I'll see you. You've got my address.

QUEENIE: No, no, I don't want to come to the flat. Not tonight – I don't think that would be wise. Could you – meet me somewhere?

TEMPLE: Well, where would you suggest?

QUEENIE: I'm at Marlow. I'm catching the 9.28. Could you meet me at Paddington?

TEMPLE: Yes, all right.

QUEENIE: The train gets in at 10.45. I think it's platform 6.

TEMPLE: Yes, all right, Miss Edwards. Don't worry – we'll be there.

QUEENIE: Thank you. (*Suddenly, remembering, slowly*) Oh – in case I don't see you, Mr Temple … I've posted you a letter …

QUEENIE replaces her receiver.

TEMPLE: (*Surprised*) What do you mean you've posted … Miss Edwards! Hello! Hello!

STEVE: She's rung off, Paul.

TEMPLE: Yes. (*He replaces his receiver*)

STEVE replaces her receiver.

FADE.

Quick FADE UP.

TEMPLE: (*A note of excitement in his voice*) Did you hear what she said, Steve?

STEVE: Yes.

TEMPLE: What do you make of it?

STEVE: I don't know. I wonder what she's doing out at Marlow?

TEMPLE: Marlow – that's on the Thames, isn't it – near Maidenhead?

STEVE: Yes.

TEMPLE: (*Thoughtfully*) Paddington … 10.45. (*A decision*) I'm going down to get the car, darling.

FADE UP of music.,

FADE DOWN of music.
FADE UP background noises of Paddington Railway Station.
FADE UP of carriage doors opening and closing: the noise of people leaving the train and crowding onto the platform.
TEMPLE and STEVE are scrutinising the passengers: watching for QUEENIE EDWARDS.

STEVE: I don't see any sign of Queenie …

TEMPLE: No, neither do I!

STEVE: Are you sure this is the Marlow train?

TEMPLE: Yes, of course it is, darling!

STEVE: (*Suddenly*) Is that her over … (*Changing her mind*) No! No, it isn't!

TEMPLE: It doesn't look to me as if she's on the train, Steve.

STEVE: (*Still watching*) No, I'm afraid it doesn't.

TEMPLE: You stay here, darling. I'm going further down …

STEVE: (*Quickly; stopping TEMPLE*) No, wait a minute!

A tiny pause.

TEMPLE: What is it?

STEVE: (*Slowly; peering*) What's that crowd doing over there?

TEMPLE: Where?

STEVE: At the end of the platform.

TEMPLE: I don't see any … (*Noticing the crowd*) Oh, yes! (*Briskly*) Wait here, darling!

FADE UP of platform noises.

*Quick FADE UP the noise of an approaching ambulance: the
ambulance quickly comes to a standstill.*
FADE platform noises down.

FADE UP a distant background of excited voices.

STEVE: (*Tensely*) Paul, what's the matter?

TEMPLE: (*Quietly; his thoughts elsewhere*) She <u>was</u> on
            the train, only …

STEVE: Only what, darling? (*A moment*) Paul, what's
            happened?

TEMPLE: (*Tensely*) She's been beaten up, Steve.
            Someone must have gone into her compartment
            and … Her face was battered to pieces … My
            God, Steve, she looked awful!

STEVE: (*Shocked*) Oh, Paul!

TEMPLE: Thank God, she was unconscious! (*A moment*)
            They've taken her to the hospital, darling.
            There's nothing we can do. Come along, let's
            go back to the flat.

STEVE: Yes, all right.

FADE UP of platform noises.

A long pause.

STEVE: Paul, what are you thinking about?

TEMPLE: (*Thoughtfully*) I wonder if we shall get that
            letter tomorrow morning?

FADE UP of music.

FADE DOWN of music.
*FADE UP the noise of an electric razor: PAUL TEMPLE is
shaving. The bathroom door opens.*

STEVE: Good heavens, Paul, haven't you finished
            shaving yet?

TEMPLE: I'm nearly finished. Has the post arrived?

STEVE: Not yet darling. It should be here any minute now. (*Turning away*) Breakfast is ready.

TEMPLE: All right. I'm coming.

The sound of a telephone ringing is heard in the background.

STEVE: (*Calling*) Paul, there's the phone!

TEMPLE: (*Calling back to STEVE*) It's all right, Steve – I'll take it!

TEMPLE crosses to the phone and lifts the receiver.

TEMPLE: (*On the phone*) Hello?

EDEN: (*On the other end of the phone*) Hello, who is that? Is that you, Temple?

TEMPLE: Yes, speaking …

EDEN: This is Eden …

TEMPLE: Oh, good morning, Inspector!

EDEN: (*Seriously*) Temple, listen. I thought you'd like to know about that girl – Queenie Edwards.

TEMPLE: (*Quietly*) What's happened?

EDEN: She's dead. She died at four o'clock this morning.

TEMPLE: (*Depressed*) Oh. Oh, I'm sorry about that. Did you see her, Inspector?

EDEN: Yes, I was at the hospital when it happened.

TEMPLE: Did she talk?

EDEN: No, unfortunately the poor girl never regained consciousness.

TEMPLE: (*Thoughtfully*) Oh, I see.

EDEN: I understand you were at Paddington last night?

TEMPLE: Yes, I had a phone message from Queenie Edwards asking me to meet her there. I'll tell you about that later.

EDEN: Yes, all right. (*Suddenly*) Well, I thought I'd let you know, Temple.

TEMPLE: Yes, thanks for ringing.

EDEN: Goodbye.

TEMPLE: Goodbye, Inspector.

TEMPLE replaces the receiver.

STEVE: (*Apprehensively*) What's happened, Paul? Is it Queenie Edwards?

TEMPLE: Yes.

STEVE: She isn't …?

TEMPLE: Yes, darling, I'm afraid so.

STEVE: Oh, Paul! (*Distressed*) What a dreadful thing …

The door opens.

TEMPLE: Darling, don't upset yourself … (*A moment: turning*) What is it, Charlie?

CHARLIE: It's the post, sir.

TEMPLE: (*Quickly: taking the letters*) Oh, thank you, Charlie!

CHARLIE: There's rather a lot this morning, sir.

STEVE: Has the letter arrived?

TEMPLE: (*Sorting the letters*) I don't see an envelope with the Marlow postmark, unless … Oh, yes, here it is!

TEMPLE tears open the envelope.

STEVE: (*After a moment: quietly, surprised*) Paul, what's the matter? Isn't there a letter inside?

TEMPLE: No … No, there's just this ticket.

STEVE: What is it? What's it for?

TEMPLE: (*Thoughtfully*) It's a cloakroom ticket … (*Reading*) Commodore Club … Number 94 …

STEVE: But why should Queenie Edwards send you a cloakroom ticket?

TEMPLE: (*Thoughtfully*) There must be a coat or something at the Commodore that she wants me to collect. (*Suddenly*) We'll go there tonight, darling. It's no good going there this morning. We'll only arouse suspicion.

27

STEVE: (*Suddenly*) Paul …

TEMPLE: Yes, Steve?

STEVE: Who do you think murdered Queenie Edwards?

TEMPLE: I don't know. But … By Timothy, I intend to find out! (*START FADE*) Come along, darling, let's have breakfast …

COMPLETE FADE.

Slow FADE UP the noise of a car: the car draws to a standstill. The engine ticks over.

STEVE: Is that the Commodore Club?

TEMPLE: Yes. Yes, that's the place over on the right.

TEMPLE opens the car door.

STEVE: Have you got the ticket?

TEMPLE: Yes, it's here …

STEVE: What happens if it turns out to be for the Ladies Cloakroom?

TEMPLE: I shall make a dignified exit and hand the ticket over to you, darling.

STEVE: Don't you think it would be much simpler if we both went into the club together, then if it is for the Ladies Cloakroom I could …

TEMPLE: No, I don't want to do that, Steve. I want you to wait here in the car. I shan't be long.

STEVE: Yes, all right. (*Stopping TEMPLE*) Oh, Paul …

TEMPLE: (*Turning*) Yes?

STEVE: (*A moment: seriously*) Take care, darling …

FADE SCENE.

Slow FADE UP background noises of the foyer of the Commodore Club. A dance orchestra can be heard playing in the distant background.

FADE noises slightly.

BERT WALTERS is a middle-aged cockney.

BERT:	(*Pleasantly*) Good evening, sir!
TEMPLE:	Good evening! You seem very quiet tonight.
BERT:	Yes, it is a bit on the quiet side. Probably liven up later …
TEMPLE:	(*Feeling in his pockets*) Now where on earth did I put that ticket …?
BERT:	Always a game with these 'ere tickets, isn't it, sir?
TEMPLE:	(*Suddenly*) Oh, here we are!
BERT:	(*Taking the ticket*) Thank you, sir. (*He moves back into the cloakroom: he is searching the pegs and whistling softly to himself. A pause*) What is this for, sir – an overcoat?
TEMPLE:	(*Hesitating*) I think it's …
BERT:	(*Interrupting TEMPLE*) Just a minute! Number 94 … This is the attaché case, isn't it? The one that was left 'ere a couple of days ago.
TEMPLE:	(*Quickly*) Yes, it belongs to a friend of mine – he asked me to pick it up for him.
BERT:	Oh! I wondered when he was goin' to collect it. (*Picking up the case*) 94 … Yes, this is it all right … Here we are, sir. One attaché case.
TEMPLE:	(*Taking the case*) Thank you.
BERT:	(*Accepting a tip: pleasantly surprised*) Oh, thank you, sir!
TEMPLE:	(*Suddenly: an apparent afterthought*) Oh, this friend of mine, Mr – er –?
BERT:	(*Hesitantly*) Palmer, wasn't it, sir?
TEMPLE:	Oh, yes – Mr Palmer. He didn't leave anything else, did he?
BERT:	No, sir. It would 'ave been marked on the ticket if he'd left anything else, sir.
TEMPLE:	Oh, I see. Goodnight.
BERT:	Goodnight, sir. Thank you, sir!

FADE UP noises from the foyer and the distant dance orchestra.

FADE DOWN.

CROSS FADE to the sound of approaching footsteps, the noise of a car engine being started and the car door opening.

STEVE: Everything all right, darling?

TEMPLE: Yes.

TEMPLE climbs into the car.

STEVE: Did you get … (*Surprised*) Oh, it's an attaché case! Is that what the ticket was for?

TEMPLE: Yes. It was left at the cloakroom by Terry Palmer.

STEVE: (*Surprised*) How do you know?

TEMPLE: The attendant told me. Apparently Palmer left it there two days ago. (*Suddenly*) Switch the engine off, Steve. Let's see what's inside the thing.

The car engine is switched off.

STEVE: Is the case locked?

TEMPLE: Yes.

STEVE: (*Suddenly*) Darling, wait a minute!

A moment.

TEMPLE: What are you doing? What are you listening for? (*Suddenly, laughing*) Oh, it's all right, I've already done that! Don't worry, Steve – it won't blow up! (*An afterthought*) I hope.

STEVE: How are you going to get it open – force it?

TEMPLE: No, I've got some keys here somewhere … Ah, here we are! (*Taking keys from his pocket*) I think one of these might fit … (*He is examining the keys*) This looks a possibility … (*Trying to open the case with a key*) No, I'm afraid it's too … Just a minute! Yes, that's done it! (*He opens* the case) By Timothy! Steve, look! Look what's in the case!

STEVE: (*Amazed*) It's the doll! Paul, it's the doll!!!

FADE UP of music.

Slow FADE DOWN of music.
The sound of a key in a lock is heard: the door opens.
TEMPLE and STEVE enter their flat.

TEMPLE: Is Charlie out?

STEVE: Yes, he went out soon after we did. Paul, what are you going to do – about the doll, I mean?

TEMPLE: I'm going to phone Sir Graham. I want this doll examined. I want to know if there's anything inside it. (*Thoughtfully*) I'd like to tear the thing to pieces myself but I suppose the Yard wouldn't like it.

STEVE: Well, it looks a perfectly ordinary doll to me.

TEMPLE: Yes, I think it is. In which case why did Palmer put it in an attaché case and deposit it at The Commodore?

STEVE: Well, if Palmer was responsible for the kidnapping of Miss Millicent and the baby – and frankly, I don't see how he could have been – then obviously he'd want to get rid of the doll.

TEMPLE: Why?

STEVE: Well, he probably thought it was incriminating.

TEMPLE: Then surely the obvious thing to do would be to destroy it.

STEVE: Yes. (*Thoughtfully*) It doesn't make sense, does it?

TEMPLE: I wonder if, by any chance, the cloakroom attendant … (*He stops: after a moment*) What is it, Steve?

31

STEVE: (*Puzzled*) There's a note here – on the pad by the telephone. Charlie must have written it.

TEMPLE: Yes, of course. (*A pause*) Well – what does it say?

STEVE: (*Slowly; bewildered*) It says "A Mr Vandyke telephoned ... he left no message" ...

FADE UP of music.

END OF EPISODE ONE

EPISODE TWO

THE MARLOW INCIDENT

OPEN TO:

STEVE: ... If Palmer was responsible for the kidnapping of Miss Millicent and the baby — and frankly, I don't see how he could have been — then obviously he'd want to get rid of the doll.

TEMPLE: Why?

STEVE: Well, he probably thought it was incriminating.

TEMPLE: Then surely the obvious thing to do would be to destroy it.

STEVE: Yes. (*Thoughtfully*) It doesn't make sense, does it?

TEMPLE: I wonder if, by any chance, the cloakroom attendant ... (*He stops: after a moment*) What is it, Steve?

STEVE: (*Puzzled*) There's a note here — on the pad by the telephone. Charlie must have written it.

TEMPLE: Yes, of course. (*A pause*) Well — what does it say?

STEVE: (*Slowly; bewildered*) It says "A Mr Vandyke telephoned ... he left no message" ...

TEMPLE: (*Surprised*) Vandyke!

STEVE: (*Quickly*) Wasn't that the man that phoned Mrs Desmond the night that Miss Millicent and the baby disappeared?

TEMPLE: (*Thoughtfully*) Yes. Yes, it was. (*Quickly*) Let me have a look at that note, Steve.

A moment.

STEVE: It's Charlie's handwriting ...

TEMPLE: Yes ... (*Slowly*) I wonder what time this man telephoned.

There is the sound of the front door being opened.

35

STEVE:	Well, we left the flat at about half-past eight so it must have been after … (*Suddenly*) Here's Charlie!

CHARLIE enters. He is in a perky moody: whistling to himself.

TEMPLE:	Hello, Charlie! I thought you'd gone out for the evening!
CHARLIE:	Coo, so did I! Beryl stood me up. Blimey, she isn't 'alf getting temperamental these days.
TEMPLE:	(*Quietly; casually*) Charlie, we've just seen this note. What time did this man telephone?
CHARLIE:	Soon after you left – I suppose it'd be about half past eight.
STEVE:	You're sure you got the name right?
CHARLIE:	Yes, course I'm sure. As a matter of fact I … (*He stops: having noticed the doll*) Hello, what's this?
TEMPLE:	(*Casually; quickly*) Oh, it's only a doll, Charlie.
STEVE:	(*Dismissing the subject*) I bought it for a little girl I know.
TEMPLE:	Charlie, I'm very interested in this telephone call. Now tell me, what happened exactly?
CHARLIE:	(*Puzzled*) What do you mean?
TEMPLE:	Well, what did he say – this Mr Vandyke?
CHARLIE:	He didn't say anything, at least not much. The phone rang, I picked it up, and a voice said: "Can I speak to Mr Temple, please?" I said: "I'm sorry but he's out – any message?"
TEMPLE:	And then what happened?
CHARLIE:	The voice said: "No message. Just tell him a Mr Vandyke telephoned."
TEMPLE:	And that's all.
CHARLIE:	That's all.
TEMPLE:	What did he sound like, this – Mr Vandyke?

CHARLIE: Oh, quite a pleasant sort of chap.

TEMPLE: Was it an educated voice?

CHARLIE: Yes. Yes, I suppose it was.

TEMPLE: Would you recognise it again?

CHARLIE: (*Thoughtfully; uncertain*) Well, I don't know … I don't know about that.

The front door buzzer sounds.

TEMPLE: (*Dismissing CHARLIE*) Yes, all right, Charlie. See who that is.

CHARLIE: Very good, sir.

CHARLIE crosses and opens the front door. We hear the voices of TERRY PALMER and MARY DESMOND.

MARY: (*In the background*) Good evening. Could we see Mr Temple, please?

CHARLIE: (*Hesitating*) Well –

PALMER: Would you tell Mr Temple that Mrs Desmond and Terry Palmer would like a word with him.

CHARLIE: (*In the background*) Very good, sir. Just a moment, please.

STEVE: (*To TEMPLE*) It's Mrs Desmond.

TEMPLE: Yes. (*Quickly*) Put the doll behind that cushion – quickly, Steve! (*Raising his voice; pleasantly*) Come in, Mrs Desmond! Hello, Palmer!

MARY: (*Overwrought: faintly apprehensive*) I do hope we're not interrupting your dinner, Mr Temple, but …

TEMPLE: No, of course not! We finished ages ago …

STEVE: (*Dismissing him*) That's all right, Charlie.

TEMPLE: You look very worried, Palmer. Has anything happened?

PALMER: (*Surprised*) Haven't you seen the evening paper?

TEMPLE: No?

MARY:	(*Distressed*) Queenie Edwards is dead! She's been murdered. Murdered, Mr Temple!
TEMPLE:	Oh. (*Quietly*) Yes. Yes, I knew about that.
STEVE:	What does it say in the paper?
PALMER:	It simply says that she was beaten up and that she died as a result of her injuries. The Tribune points out, not without significance, that she was a friend of Miss Millicent's.
MARY:	Mr Temple, do you think this means that whoever murdered Queenie Edwards has also murdered Miss Millicent and … and …
PALMER:	No, Mary! No! I keep telling you, it doesn't mean anything of the sort. Just because Queenie Edwards has been murdered it doesn't necessarily mean that anything very terrible has happened to either Susan or Miss Millicent. Mary, my dear, I know you've been through a great deal but you've got to pull yourself together.
STEVE:	Mr Palmer's right, Mrs Desmond, you've simply got to get a grip on yourself.
MARY:	What do you think about all this, Mr Temple? What do Scotland Yard think? Do they think that Queenie Edwards was murdered because …
TEMPLE:	Because what, Mrs Desmond?
PALMER:	Mary's got it into her head that Queenie Edwards was murdered because she knew why Miss Millicent and the baby were kidnapped.
TEMPLE:	Always assuming, of course, that Miss Millicent and the baby were kidnapped.
PALMER:	What do you mean?
MARY:	What other possible explanation could there be?

TEMPLE: Mrs Desmond, let's take a good look at the facts in this case. Just over a week ago you and Mr Palmer had a dinner date at the Commodore Club. You left your daughter – an eighteen months' old baby – in the care of a sitter-in – a Miss Millicent. When you returned to your flat both the baby and the sitter-in had completely disappeared. There was a note, in Miss Millicent's handwriting, stating that a Mr Vandyke had telephoned but had left no message. Neither you, nor Mr Palmer, has heard of anyone called Vandyke.

PALMER: That's correct.

TEMPLE: Now Miss Millicent, the sitter-in, has a small house in Hampstead and she shared it with a girl called Queenie Edwards. Last night I received a telephone message from Queenie Edwards – from Marlow near Maidenhead – asking me to meet her at Paddington Station. She told me that she had a very important message for me concerning Miss Millicent adding, as an afterthought, that if by any chance I missed her she'd posted me a letter. Well, I did miss Queenie for the simple reason that on the train from Marlow she was beaten up and received injuries from which, as you now know, she subsequently died.

PALMER: And the letter?

TEMPLE: The letter, Mr Palmer, turned out to be a cloakroom ticket.

PALMER: (*Surprised*) A cloakroom ticket? What for?

TEMPLE: (*Watching PALMER*) For the Gentleman's Cloakroom at the Commodore Club. I took the ticket along this evening and in return for the ticket they handed me an attaché case. (*Slowly*) Would you like to see what was in the attaché case, Mr Palmer?

PALMER: (*Puzzled*) Why, yes, of course.

TEMPLE: (*Quietly*) Remove that cushion, darling!

A moment.

MARY: Terry, look! It's the doll! It's Susan's doll!

PALMER: (*Stunned*) The doll! (*Suddenly*) But where the devil did you get it?

TEMPLE: I've told you, it was in the attaché case.

PALMER: (*Bewildered*) Are you trying to tell me that Queenie Edwards left an attaché case at the Commodore Club containing the doll and then deliberately sent you the cloakroom ticket?

TEMPLE: No, Queenie couldn't have left it at the Club – certainly not without an accomplice. I've already told you it was left in the Gentleman's Cloakroom.

PALMER: Then who did leave it?

TEMPLE: (*Quietly; watching PALMER*) Don't you know, Mr Palmer?

MARY: (*Softly; amazed*) What do you mean?

PALMER: What the devil are you getting at?

TEMPLE: Didn't you leave the doll there – in this attaché case – two days ago?

PALMER: (*Indignant*) Most certainly not! Why, good God, man, are you crazy! Mary, you don't believe that I …

MARY: No, of course not! Mr Temple, who on earth gave you such an idea?

TEMPLE: The cloakroom attendant told me that Mr Palmer deposited the case in the cloakroom a couple of days ago.

PALMER: But that's nonsense!

TEMPLE: Did you leave a case at the Commodore, not this particular one, but another one?

PALMER: (*Indignantly*) No, I didn't. I've never been near the cloakroom. As a matter of fact I've not been near the club, not since – not since that night. That's the truth, isn't it, Mary?

MARY: Yes.

TEMPLE: I see.

MARY: (*Near to tears*) May I … take the doll, please …?

TEMPLE: I'm afraid I shall have to hand it over to the Inspector, Mrs Desmond.

MARY: Just for a moment, please …

A slight pause.

STEVE: (*Quietly*) Is it the same doll?

MARY: (*Softly; moved*) Yes. Yes, it's the same doll all right. I can tell by the skirt. Look, Terry … You see, Mrs Temple, Susan used to put the skirt in her mouth and then pull the fringe down towards … towards … (*She is unable to speak, near to tears*)

PALMER: Mary, darling, don't! (*A pause. Quietly*) Temple, what the devil's behind all this? If what you've told us is the truth then someone must have quite deliberately taken the doll from the child, put it in an attaché case and deposited it at the Commodore.

TEMPLE: Yes.

PALMER: (*Almost aggressively*) But why? Why? For Pete's sake, why?

TEMPLE: I don't know why. (*A moment; watching PALMER*) Not yet, Mr Palmer.

FADE UP of music.

FADE DOWN of music.

FADE UP the noise of the flat buzzer.

STEVE: (*In the bedroom: calling*) Paul, you haven't packed your slippers!

TEMPLE: (*Calling back: near the mike*) I shan't need them, darling!

STEVE: Yes, of course you will! Where's your dressing gown?

The buzzer continues.

TEMPLE: It's at the bottom of the case near ... Steve, isn't Charlie ever going to answer that door?

STEVE: (*Calling*) He's out, darling. He went out soon after breakfast.

TEMPLE: By Timothy, why didn't you say so!

TEMPLE crosses to the front door and opens it.

TEMPLE: Why, hello, Sir Graham!

FORBES: (*Amused*) Sorry if I've got you out of bed, Temple!

TEMPLE: Nonsense, we've been up for hours. Another quarter of an hour and you'd have missed us.

STEVE: (*Calling*) Who is it, darling?

TEMPLE: (*Calling back*) It's Sir Graham!

STEVE: (*Calling*) Hello, Sir Graham!

FORBES: (*Calling*) Hello, Steve!

STEVE: (*Calling*) Would you like some coffee?

FORBES: (*Calling*) No, thanks!

TEMPLE: Come along, Sir Graham!

FADE.

Quick FADE UP.

FORBES: Is Steve packing?

TEMPLE: Yes.

FORBES: Are you going away?

TEMPLE:	Only for the weekend. We're going down to Marlow.
FORBES:	Oh. (*Significantly*) That's not a bad idea, Temple.
TEMPLE:	That's what I thought.
FORBES:	Where are you staying – at the Wordsworth?
TEMPLE:	Yes.
FORBES:	Eden's got one of his men down there – he'll probably look you up.
TEMPLE:	Good.
FORBES:	Well, we've checked the doll. It's a perfectly ordinary doll – nothing unusual about it. It was bought from Harridges in Regent Street.
TEMPLE:	What about the attaché case?
FORBES:	I'm afraid it doesn't tell us a great deal. There were two sets of prints; one quite obviously yours, the other belonging to Bert Walters the cloakroom attendant.
TEMPLE:	Have you seen Walters?
FORBES:	(*Laughing*) We had him out of bed at half-past six this morning. He's not a very reliable type, I'm afraid.
TEMPLE:	I don't expect he would be – not at half-past six.
FORBES:	He now says that he's not absolutely sure that it was Palmer that deposited the attaché case.
TEMPLE:	Well, to give Walters his due he didn't sound a hundred per-cent sure last night.
FORBES:	Do you think it was Palmer?
TEMPLE:	(*Thoughtfully*) I don't know.
FORBES:	Well, if it was Palmer how exactly did Queenie Edwards get hold of the cloakroom ticket, that's what I'd like to know.

TEMPLE: What's more to the point – <u>Why</u> did she get hold of it – and <u>why</u> did she take the trouble to send it to me?

FORBES: I think the answer to that is pretty obvious, Temple. She wanted you to know that Palmer's mixed up in this business – that he's probably responsible for the kidnapping of Miss Millicent and the baby.

TEMPLE: Then why did he leave the doll in the cloakroom of the Commodore Club?

FORBES: Obviously because he wanted to get rid of it.

TEMPLE: That doesn't make sense. He could have destroyed it – he could even have thrown it away. No, Sir Graham. Whoever deposited that doll in the cloakroom did so because they'd received explicit instructions.

FORBES: (*Thoughtfully*) I'm not so sure. I'm not so sure about that, Temple.

TEMPLE: Tell me: did you find out why Queenie Edwards went down to Marlow?

FORBES: No, we didn't. All we know is that she had the afternoon off and she caught the two o'clock from Paddington. Eden's got rather an interesting theory – the only trouble is it doesn't make sense.

STEVE enters.

STEVE: Interesting theories very often don't, Sir Graham!

FORBES: Oh, hello, Steve! Eden thinks that Queenie Edwards went down to Marlow to see Miss Millicent: he thinks, for some peculiar reason, that Miss Millicent and Queenie Edwards were in league with one another. Just exactly what

44

	they were in league about, however, seems to have escaped him.
TEMPLE:	Nevertheless, it is an interesting theory. (*Suddenly*) Sir Graham, you say that Inspector Eden's got one of his men down at Marlow?
FORBES:	Yes, a Sergeant Digby. He's a bright young fellow: you'll like him, Temple. He's staying at The Wordsworth Hotel.
TEMPLE:	Has he discovered anything?
FORBES:	Yes. He discovered that the moment Queenie Edwards arrived at Marlow she went straight to The Wordsworth. She made a telephone call from there at a quarter past nine.
STEVE:	That must have been the one we received, darling. It was about nine-fifteen.
TEMPLE:	Yes.
FORBES:	(*Taking his leave*) Well, I hope you have a pleasant weekend, Temple.
TEMPLE:	Thank you.
FORBES:	It's a delightful spot – Marlow.
TEMPLE:	Yes.
FORBES:	I like it. Always have liked it. Like that stretch of the river. (*Almost a sigh*) It's so peaceful down there.
STEVE:	Let's hope it stays that way, Sir Graham.

FADE UP of music.

FADE DOWN of music.
A door opens.

GEORGE:	(*A pleasant young man with an unfortunate accent: he is carrying a suitcase*) Here we are, sir.
STEVE:	(*Delighted*) Oh, what a lovely room, Paul!

GEORGE: Smashing. Best room in the 'ouse this. Smashing view.

TEMPLE: By Timothy, yes! It is pleasant.

GEORGE: Shall I put the case in the corner, sir?

TEMPLE: (*Turning*) Yes, that'll do nicely. Here we are …

GEORGE: (*Delighted*) Oh, thank you, sir!

The door closes.

STEVE: (*Staring out of the window*) Darling, it's lovely! Just look at the view …

A moment.

TEMPLE: It's such a perfect day.

STEVE: Smashing.

They laugh.

There is a knock on the door.

TEMPLE: (*Calling*) Come in!

The door opens.

DIGBY: Excuse me. Mr Temple? (*DIGBY is about thirty-two or three: he has a pleasant, but not a particularly cultured, voice*)

TEMPLE: Yes?

DIGBY: (*Hesitantly*) May I come in?

TEMPLE: Well –

DIGBY: (*Closing the door behind him: quietly*) My name is Digby, sir. I had a message through from the Yard that you and Mrs Temple …

TEMPLE: (*Interrupting DIGBY*) Oh, hello, Sergeant!

DIGBY: If you're just about to unpack, sir, I'll drop in later.

TEMPLE: No, no, we're in no hurry! Oh, this is my wife, Sergeant. Darling – Sergeant Digby.

DIGBY: Good morning, Mrs Temple.

STEVE: Good morning, Sergeant.

DIGBY: I thought I'd just let you know that I'm staying here under the name of Baker, sir – Room 26.

	If there's anything I can do for you, just let me know.

TEMPLE: That's very nice of you, Sergeant. Tell me: how long are you staying down here?

DIGBY: Well, I did intend going back to Town this afternoon, sir, but – (*Confidentially; a faint note of excitement in his voice*) Well, as a matter of fact, Mr Temple, I think I'm on to something.

TEMPLE: Oh?

DIGBY: (*With quiet enthusiasm*) When Queenie Edwards came down here – to Marlow, I mean – she made a bee line for this hotel. That was about a quarter past four. She ordered tea and she sat in the lounge until about half-past six. Now I've had a talk to one of the waiters – a reliable old boy called Benson – and Benson tells me that it's perfectly obvious that Queenie was expecting someone and that whoever she was expecting never turned up.

TEMPLE: (*Interested*) Go on …

DIGBY: Queenie hung about the hotel until about a quarter past nine then she made a telephone call and caught the 9.28 back to Town.

TEMPLE: I see.

STEVE: I suppose you don't happen to know who she was expecting, Sergeant?

DIGBY: (*A note of excitement in his voice*) No, but I've got a pretty good hunch, Mrs Temple. (*To TEMPLE, confidentially*) Do you, by any chance, know a rather flamboyant individual called Shelly, sir?

47

TEMPLE:	(*Surprised*) Shelly? (*Interested*) Yes … He runs a Mother's Help Bureau at Hampstead – Miss Millicent was on his books.
DIGBY:	That's the gentleman.
TEMPLE:	We've never met, but I know who you mean all right. Go on, Digby.
DIGBY:	Well, Roger Shelly has a bungalow near here …
TEMPLE:	(*Impressed*) Has he, by Timothy!
DIGBY:	It's over on the far side of the river between Marlow and Maidenhead.
TEMPLE:	That's interesting!
DIGBY:	He's supposed to use the place for weekends but so far as I can gather he spends a great deal more time down here than he does in Town. Anyway, to cut a long story short …
TEMPLE:	To cut a long story short you think that Queenie Edwards came down here in order to see Shelly.
DIGBY:	(*Emphatically*) Yes, sir, I do.
STEVE:	Well, that bungalow's certainly a strange coincidence, isn't it, darling?
TEMPLE:	Is Shelly down here at the moment?
DIGBY:	Yes – (*Smiling*) – as a matter of fact that's why I'm staying on.
TEMPLE:	What do you mean?
DIGBY:	I bumped into Shelly last night – here – in the hotel bar. We started talking about the weather, motor cars, you know how it is. Suddenly, I forget how the conversation started, he mentioned this card game we've been hearing so much about – Canasta. He said he was anxious to play it.
TEMPLE:	Well?

48

DIGBY: (*Grinning*) I'm going to teach him. He's invited me out to his bungalow. I'm expected for dinner at eight o'clock.

TEMPLE: Smart work, Digby.

STEVE: (*Amused*) It's a small point, Sergeant, but can you play Canasta?

DIGBY: (*Laughing*) I can't even play Gin Rummy, Mrs Temple.

STEVE: Well, what are you going to do?

DIGBY: I'll get by all right. I certainly ought to, I've been reading about the confounded game since six o'clock this morning. Anyway, I don't intend to spend the entire evening playing cards. I'm rather interested to get Mr Shelly's views on the Desmond case.

TEMPLE: Providing he'll talk about it.

DIGBY: Oh, he'll talk, sir. He's not the reticent type.

TEMPLE: What time do you expect to be back?

DIGBY: Oh, about eleven – certainly no later. I'll drop in on you, sir, if you like – tell you how I've got on.

TEMPLE: Yes, I wish you'd do that, Sergeant.

DIGBY: Very good, sir.

STEVE: (*Curious*) Oh, Sergeant, tell me; what exactly do you hope to get out of Mr Shelly?

DIGBY: Well, just between ourselves, Mrs Temple – promotion.

They laugh.
FADE SCENE.

FADE UP Scene.
From the distant background a clock can be heard chiming: it is half-past one.
TEMPLE and STEVE are in bed.

49

STEVE:	(*Softly; rather sleepy*) Paul …
TEMPLE:	Yes, darling?
STEVE:	Are you awake?
TEMPLE:	(*Faintly amused*) Yes, of course I'm awake.
STEVE:	What time is it?
TEMPLE:	It's just gone half past one.
STEVE:	(*Thoughtfully*) It's very odd about Digby, isn't it? I wonder why he didn't call?
TEMPLE:	(*Thoughtfully*) I don't know.
STEVE:	Of course he may have been late and didn't want to disturb us.
TEMPLE:	(*Jumping out of bed*) Yes, well, I don't like it, Steve!
STEVE:	(*Surprised*) Darling, what are you doing?
TEMPLE:	I'm going round to his room. Where's my slippers?
STEVE:	(*Laughing*) The ones you didn't want me to pack? They're on the floor, darling.
TEMPLE:	(*Finding his slippers*) Oh. (*A moment*) What number did he say the room was – 26?
STEVE:	Yes.
TEMPLE:	(*Surprised*) Steve, what do you think you're doing?
STEVE:	What do you think I'm doing? I'm coming with you, of course. (*Suddenly*) Oh, Lord!
TEMPLE:	What's the matter?
STEVE:	I've forgotten my slippers!
TEMPLE:	(*Laughing at STEVE*) By Timothy, Steve, you are the limit!
STEVE:	Take those off, Paul, and put your shoes on.
TEMPLE:	(*Taken aback*) What?
STEVE:	(*A determined whisper*) You heard, darling, take the slippers off and put your shoes on!

FADE SCENE.

FADE UP of TEMPLE knocking, very softly, on a bedroom door.

STEVE: He's not in, darling.

TEMPLE: No, but wait a minute, Steve!

TEMPLE opens the door.

A pause.

STEVE: He hasn't come back yet, Paul. Look – you can see – the bed hasn't been touched.

TEMPLE: (*Puzzled*) Well, he ought to be back by now surely! Good heavens, it's after half past one.

STEVE: How long would it take him to reach the bungalow?

TEMPLE: I'm not sure exactly where it is, Steve.

STEVE: Of course it's possible I suppose that … (*She stops*)

TEMPLE: What is it, Steve?

STEVE: (*Slowly; after a moment*) Is that the bathroom over there?

TEMPLE: Why, yes, I should imagine so. (*A moment*) Why? (*Curious*) What is it?

STEVE: Oh, nothing.

TEMPLE: What is it, Steve?

STEVE: I'm just imagining things.

TEMPLE: Imagining what?

STEVE: Well – I thought I heard someone in the bathroom, Paul, but I must have been mistaken because …

TEMPLE: We'll soon find out!

TEMPLE crosses and opens the bathroom door.

STEVE: (*A sudden cry of alarm*) Oh, Paul! Paul, look!!! It's Digby, he's standing by the basin; look at him he …

TEMPLE: (*Quietly; alarmed*) My God! Digby!

51

STEVE: (*Desperately shaken; horrified*) Paul, look at his face! Darling, look at his face!

TEMPLE: (*Tensely; a command*) Don't look, Steve! Go back into the bedroom …

STEVE: What's happened? Paul, what's happened to him?

TEMPLE: He's been beaten up … Someone must have used a razor!

STEVE: Oh, Paul!

TEMPLE: (*Under his breath*) The swine! The filthy swine!

DIGBY: (*Hardly about to speak*) Temple … listen …

TEMPLE: (*Tensely; holding DIGBY's arm*) What is it, Digby? What's happened?

DIGBY: (*Trying to speak*) A … A …

TEMPLE: Take it easy … Now what is it, Digby?

DIGBY: (*Slowly gasping*) A … Mr Vandyke … tele … phoned … he … he …

DIGBY gives a final sigh and falls forward bringing down a loose towel rail.

STEVE gives a cry of alarm.

STEVE: (*A cry*) Paul!!!!

A long silence.

TEMPLE: (*Softly*) He's dead … (*A moment, then:*) Come along … Come along, Steve … Let's go back into the bedroom …

They return to the bedroom.

STEVE: Paul, what are you going to do?

TEMPLE: (*Briskly*) Where's the phone? Oh, there it is … (*He crosses and lifts up the telephone receiver*) By Timothy, I only hope there's somebody on at this time of night … (*He flicks the receiver*) Hello! Hello …

McCALL: (*Coming onto the line: an Irish-American: about forty*) Yes?

TEMPLE: (*On the phone*) Who is that?

McCALL: This is the manager – McCall. The night porter's off duty. Can I do anything for you?

TEMPLE: I want to call London, please. It's very urgent.

McCALL: O.K., I'll put you through to the operator.

TEMPLE: (*Suddenly*) Just a minute! Did you say it was the manager speaking?

McCALL: That's right – Bill McCall.

TEMPLE: Well, Mr McCall, when I've finished this conversation would you come up to Room 26, please?

McCALL: (*Faintly surprised*) Yes. Yes, surely. I'm putting you through now.

TEMPLE: Thank you.

There is a click on the line.

OPERATOR: (*Coming onto the line*) Number, please?

TEMPLE: Operator, I want London – Langham 4413 – it's very urgent.

OPERATOR: Langham 4413?

TEMPLE: Yes.

OPERATOR: Hold the line, please.

STEVE: (*Quickly*) Paul, who are you ringing?

TEMPLE: I'm phoning the Inspector. I want Eden to know about Digby before I contact the local people. There's just a chance that Eden might not want me to get in touch with the local police. It's ringing out!

We can hear the number ringing out at the other end.

A receiver is lifted.

EDEN: (*On the line: sleepily*) Hello?

TEMPLE: Is that you, Inspector?

EDEN: Yes. Who is that?

TEMPLE:	This is Temple …
EDEN:	(*Yawning*) Who?
TEMPLE:	Temple … Paul Temple …
EDEN:	For heaven's sake, Temple … this is a fine time to ring up!
TEMPLE:	(*Seriously*) Eden, listen. I'm at Marlow. I'm at The Wordsworth Hotel. (*Slowly, deliberately*) Digby's – been – murdered.
EDEN:	(*Staggered*) What!
TEMPLE:	(*Quietly; urgently*) You heard what I said – Digby's been murdered. Now listen, Inspector. I want to know whether you'd like me to contact the local people first or wait …
EDEN:	(*Aghast*) Temple, have you been drinking?
TEMPLE:	What do you mean?
EDEN:	(*Aggressively*) How the devil can Digby have been murdered?
TEMPLE:	(*Angrily*) I tell you he's been murdered; we found him here, in his room, only five minutes ago!
EDEN:	Temple, listen! Digby left Marlow this morning. He caught the 8.32. I saw him at the Yard at eleven o'clock and I was with him until a quarter past seven this evening.
TEMPLE:	(*Shocked*) You were with Digby until …
EDEN:	Until a quarter past seven this evening!
TEMPLE:	But that's impossible!
STEVE:	(*Tensely*) Darling, what's happened? What is it?
TEMPLE:	(*On the phone*) Inspector, what does he look like – Sergeant Digby?
EDEN:	He's about six foot – rather on the thin side – got a small moustache.

TEMPLE: (*Slowly*) Oh, my God! You're right, Inspector! We've been taken in, we've ... (*Amazed*) Then who the devil is this man? Who is he?

EDEN: (*Emphatically*) I don't know – but he isn't Sergeant Digby!!!

Quick FADE UP of music.

Slow FADE DOWN of music.
FADE UP the sound of breakfast things.

WAITER: Would you like a cereal, madam, or a grapefruit or ...

STEVE: No ... No, nothing, thank you.

TEMPLE: Steve, you've got to eat something!

STEVE: Darling, I don't feel like eating!

TEMPLE: (*Dismissing the WAITER*) That's all right.

WAITER: Thank you, sir.

The door closes.

TEMPLE: You'll feel awfully faint if you don't have any breakfast.

STEVE: Darling, please ... (*A pause*) Paul, I just can't make head or tail of it. If that man wasn't Sergeant Digby then ...

TEMPLE: There's no 'ifs' about it, Steve. The Inspector's seen him – he wasn't Digby.

STEVE: Then why, in heaven's name, did he pretend that he was?

TEMPLE: I don't know. All I know is he certainly got away with it! By Timothy, I never suspected him.

STEVE: Well, who would? All that stuff about Queenie Edwards and Roger Shelly and ...

TEMPLE: (*Interrupting STEVE*) Yes, but you know, Steve, that's the extraordinary part about it. I think that was true. I think he really did have a date with Shelly.

STEVE: Well, if he had a date with him why …

There is a knock on the door.

TEMPLE: Come in!

The door opens.

McCALL: Excuse me. Inspector Eden would like to see you, sir. He's downstairs in the hall.

TEMPLE: Thank you.

McCALL: (*Hesitatingly*) Oh, er – may I have a word with you, Mr Temple?

TEMPLE: Yes, certainly.

McCALL: The Inspector's been asking me a lot of questions. Rather personal questions, I thought. (*A little laugh*) I don't know whether he thinks I'm mixed up in this affair or not.

TEMPLE: It's his job to ask questions, Mr McCall. I shouldn't get worried about that.

McCALL: Yes, I know, but he seems to me kind of suspicious. For one thing, I don't think he believes my story.

TEMPLE: What story?

McCALL: Well, I mean – what happened last night.

TEMPLE: What did happen last night – so far as you are concerned?

McCALL: (*Laughing*) Gee, are you suspicious too!

TEMPLE: (*Smiling*) No. No, I just wanted to get things straightened out.

McCALL: Well, I gave the night porter the night off. He'd got a pretty rotten cold and I told him to pack it in. I stayed on duty myself until about half past one: I was just about to hit the hay when you telephoned down and put the call through to Town. You know what happened after that …

56

TEMPLE:	Did you see Mr Baker at all?
McCALL:	No … (*Suddenly*) Oh, yes, I saw him about half past seven, just before he went out. I didn't see him after that.
TEMPLE:	In other words you didn't see him come back from Mr Shelly's?
McCALL:	No.
TEMPLE:	You knew he had an appointment with Mr Shelly?
McCALL:	Sure. I was in the bar on Friday night when Baker introduced himself.
TEMPLE:	Is Shelly one of your regulars?
McCALL:	Yes – he's in and out pretty regular I guess.
TEMPLE:	What about Baker?
McCALL:	He's a stranger – I'd never seen him before.
TEMPLE:	(*Closing the conversation*) Well, I shouldn't let the Inspector rattle you, McCall. His bark's worse than his bite.
McCALL:	He doesn't rattle me. I just wondered what was at the back of his mind, that's all. (*Suddenly*) Oh, by the way, I suppose there'll be quite a fair amount of publicity over this affair?
TEMPLE:	Yes.
McCALL:	I suppose it'll be in all the papers?
TEMPLE:	I'm afraid so.
McCALL:	(*Amused*) Well, that suits me, I guess.
STEVE:	(*Surprised*) Why, do you want the publicity?
McCALL:	We certainly want something! Business has been terrible!
STEVE:	Yes, but I shouldn't think it'll be very good publicity, Mr McCall!
McCALL:	It'll be publicity, that's all that matters. I know the hotel business. I've been in it a very long time. Believe me, Mrs Temple, a first class

murder never did a hotel any harm! (*Suddenly*) Say, don't tell the Inspector I said that or he will be suspicious!

TEMPLE and McCALL laugh.
FADE SCENE.

FADE UP.

EDEN: Ah, so here you are, Temple!

TEMPLE: I understand you want to see me, Inspector?

EDEN: Yes, I've got Shelly here. Sergeant Bell picked him up at the bungalow about a quarter of an hour ago.

TEMPLE: Oh, good. Where is he – in the manager's office?

EDEN: Yes. Oh, by the way, I've just had a call through from the Yard. They've checked the address – the one that our friend Baker put in the register.

TEMPLE: Well?

EDEN: It's as phoney as his name. It just doesn't exist.

TEMPLE: (*Faintly exasperated*) I wonder who the devil he is, Inspector!

EDEN: I wish I knew, Temple! We've been through his things with a fine tooth-comb.

TEMPLE: Didn't you find anything?

EDEN: Nothing of importance, I'm afraid. (*Suddenly*) Oh, there was this …

TEMPLE: What is it?

EDEN: It's a receipt for a pair of gloves by the look of things …

TEMPLE: (*Examining the receipt*) Hello … They were bought in Paris then?

EDEN: Yes. You see the date – the 26th. That was four days ago.

TEMPLE: (*Reading*) "Charles Marett ... 73 Rue St Lazare ... Paris ... Two thousand and fifty francs" – that's about two guineas ... Yes, I suppose that's about right ...

EDEN: Yes.

TEMPLE: Wasn't there anything else on him – hadn't he a wallet?

EDEN: Yes, there was twenty-two pounds in it – in one pound notes.

TEMPLE: No papers?

EDEN: No, nothing.

TEMPLE: M'm. Well, let's see what Mr Shelly's got to say for himself. (*START FADE*) By the way, does he know about the murder?

EDEN: No. No, not yet ...

TEMPLE: I see.

FADE SCENE.

FADE UP of ROGER SHELLY: he is both annoyed and excited. SHELLY is a theatrical, flamboyant type: about thirty-six or seven.

SHELLY: My dear Sergeant, it's not a bit of use telling me that this is simply a routine measure because quite frankly I don't believe a word you say!

The door opens.

SERGEANT: (*With almost a sigh of relief*) Here's the Inspector, sir. He'll answer your questions.

EDEN: That's all right, sergeant. You can go.

SERGEANT: (*Relieved*) Thank you, sir.

The door closes.

EDEN: Mr Shelly?

SHELLY: (*Indignantly*) Are you Inspector Eden?

EDEN: I am, sir.

SHELLY:	At last! I was beginning to think you were just a figment of the imagination.
EDEN:	I'm real enough, Mr Shelly.
SHELLY:	Well, then, would you mind telling me why precisely I have been dragged out of my bed at this unearthly hour?
EDEN:	It's a quarter past ten, I wouldn't exactly call it an unearthly hour, sir.
SHELLY:	Well, I would! Now what's this all about, Inspector? If it's anything to do with my car then I can assure you that …
EDEN:	(*Interrupting SHELLY*) It isn't anything to do with your car, Mr Shelly. Oh, by the way, this is Mr Temple.
SHELLY:	(*Faintly surprised*) Paul Temple?
EDEN:	Yes.
SHELLY:	Well, what is it you want?
EDEN:	I have reason to believe that you entertained a friend to dinner last night.
SHELLY:	I did. Is that a crime?
EDEN:	What time did your guest arrive?
SHELLY:	About half past seven.
EDEN:	And leave?
SHELLY:	She left about a quarter to ten.
EDEN:	(*Surprised*) She?
SHELLY:	Yes.
EDEN:	We were under the impression that you entertained a Mr Baker?
SHELLY:	Baker? (*Suddenly*) Oh, that line-shooter! No, for some obscure reason Baker couldn't make it. It was all very infuriating. I invited Marian to dinner on the strength of … (*Suddenly, annoyed*) Look here, what is this? What's it all about?

TEMPLE: Supposing you tell us, Mr Shelly.

SHELLY: (*Quietly*) What do you mean?

TEMPLE: Who did you entertain last night – if you didn't entertain Mr Baker?

SHELLY: Entertain is hardly the word! I never spent such a dreary evening – it was dire. I'll tell you exactly what happened. On Friday night I dropped in here for a drink and bumped into a fellow called Baker. He was a terrific line-shooter. Anyway, to cut a long story short, he said he was an absolute wizard at Canasta and he promised to teach me the beastly game.

EDEN: Go on …

SHELLY: Well, I invited him to dinner – that was last night. I also invited a friend of mine, an artist called Marian Faber. Marian has a cottage near Bourne End.

EDEN: Go on …

SHELLY: Well, Marian turned up – and I might add in a frightful mood – and then at about a quarter to eight this wretched fellow Baker telephoned and said that he couldn't make it.

TEMPLE: Did he say why he couldn't make it?

SHELLY: No, he didn't. I was furious.

EDEN: Go on …

SHELLY: What do you mean – go on? There's nothing else to go on about!

TEMPLE: (*Quietly*) Mr Shelly, I understand that you run a sort of Registry Office …

SHELLY: (*Exasperated*) I don't run anything of the sort! I run a Mother's Help Bureau. We provide sitters-in, nursemaids, lady companions. It's quite different from a Registry Office.

TEMPLE:	I see. Hadn't you a Miss Millicent on your books?
SHELLY:	Yes, Miss Millicent was on my books, but for your information I didn't send her to Mrs Desmond. I'd never heard of Mrs Desmond until I read about her in the newspapers.
EDEN:	Did you like Miss Millicent?
SHELLY:	What do you mean, <u>like</u>? She was a very <u>nice</u> person if that's what you mean, Inspector?
TEMPLE:	Mr Shelly, tell me: did anyone else telephone you last night, besides Mr Baker?
SHELLY:	No, no, not that I know of. (*Suddenly*) By the way, is Baker still staying here because if he is I'd like to …
TEMPLE:	Baker's dead. He was murdered.

A pause.

SHELLY:	(*Stunned*) What do you mean – murdered?
EDEN:	(*Watching SHELLY; calmly*) Mr Temple means that he was murdered.

A moment.

SHELLY:	(*Softly; tense*) Is this true?
TEMPLE:	Yes.
SHELLY:	When … was he murdered?
TEMPLE:	Last night.
EDEN:	He was beaten up – his face was slashed with a razor.
SHELLY:	(*Stunned*) My God, that's ghastly … Really ghastly! Who could have done such a terrible thing?
EDEN:	We don't know, Mr Shelly – not yet.
TEMPLE:	Shelly, tell me – was that the first time you'd seen Mr Baker – on Friday night?
SHELLY:	(*His thoughts elsewhere: extremely nervous*) What? Oh, yes … yes …

TEMPLE: You'd never seen him before?

SHELLY: No, never.

TEMPLE: (*Watching SHELLY*) He was a complete stranger to you?

SHELLY: Absolutely. (*Nervously; almost a little frightened*) I say, look here, Temple, I don't want to be tiresome, but …

TEMPLE: But what?

SHELLY: Do you think I could have a drink?

EDEN: (*After a moment*) Yes. I'll ring for the waiter …

SHELLY: I'd – er – I'd like a brandy, Inspector. A double brandy … (*He is obviously very shaken*)

FADE UP of music.

FADE DOWN of music.
FADE UP the ticking over of a car.
The car door opens and closes.

STEVE: Are you going to drive, darling?

TEMPLE: Yes, I'll drive, Steve. (*He climbs into the car*) Where's your hatbox?

STEVE: I thought you put it in the back?

TEMPLE: No, dear, I haven't seen it.

McCALL: (*Pleasantly*) Is this what you're looking for?

TEMPLE: (*Laughing*) Oh, yes! Thanks!

McCALL: Have a pleasant trip back to Town.

TEMPLE: Thank you.

STEVE: It's certainly a nice day.

McCALL: Sure is. Goodbye, Mrs Temple. I hope we shall see you again sometime.

STEVE: Yes, I hope so.

McCALL: It can be very peaceful down here, you know – although I hardly expect you to believe it after the weekend.

STEVE:	Well, it has been rather an unusual weekend, Mr McCall.
McCALL:	Unusual! I'll say it has!
TEMPLE:	(*Changing gear*) Goodbye, McCall!
McCALL:	Goodbye, sir!

FADE UP of the car driving away.
FADE SCENE.

FADE UP of the car: it is travelling quite fast down a country road.

A pause.

STEVE:	(*Thoughtfully*) Paul, I've been thinking about Roger Shelly. Do you think he was telling the truth?
TEMPLE:	About Baker?
STEVE:	Yes.
TEMPLE:	Well, if you don't accept Shelly's story Baker was lying and so was McCall.
STEVE:	What do you mean?
TEMPLE:	McCall said he was in the bar on Friday night when Baker introduced himself to Shelly.
STEVE:	Yes, but for all we know that may have been a put up job.
TEMPLE:	(*Faintly surprised*) A put up job?
STEVE:	Yes. Look, darling. Suppose Baker, or whatever his name is, was told to contact Shelly. He came down to Marlow and arranged to 'accidentally' bump into Shelly in the cocktail bar. Naturally, if McCall was there he'd be convinced, the same as anyone else, that Baker and Shelly were meeting for the first time.
TEMPLE:	(*Interested*) Go on, Steve …

STEVE: Now if Baker did go out to Shelly's, in other words if Shelly was lying when he said that …

TEMPLE: But Shelly wasn't lying: Eden checked with that girl friend of his – Marian Faber. Miss Faber says that she was there when Baker telephoned.

STEVE: But, darling – she may by lying!

TEMPLE: They can't all be lying, Steve! No, darling, the way I figure things is this: when Baker arrived at The Wordsworth Hotel he made a point of …

During the above speech there is a sudden crack, a 'swish', as a bullet strikes across the windscreen and smashes it to pieces.

STEVE: (*Alarmed*) Paul! Paul, what's happened?

TEMPLE: (*Quickly; applying the brakes*) Steve, are you all right!?

STEVE: Yes … Darling, look at the windscreen! Look!

The car draws to a standstill.

TEMPLE: (*Softly*) By Timothy!

STEVE: (*Quickly: alarmed*) Paul, what happened? What was it? What hit the windscreen?

TEMPLE: (*Grimly*) I'll give you three guesses, Steve.

STEVE: (*Tensely*) What do you mean?

TEMPLE: (*Quietly*) It was a bullet …

Dramatic FADE UP of music.

FADE UP of the car: it is drawing to a standstill outside of PAUL TEMPLE's flat. TEMPLE puts the brake on and switches off the engine.

TEMPLE: There we are, darling. Safe and sound.

STEVE: More by luck than judgement!

TEMPLE: By Timothy, I should say so! We were darn lucky, Steve – just look at that windscreen.

The sound of a second car, in the near background, draws to a standstill followed by the opening of the car door.

STEVE: Shall I send Charlie down for the case?

TEMPLE: No, I'll carry it up. You take the hatbox.

STEVE: (*Suddenly*) Paul!

TEMPLE: What is it?

STEVE: Look! There's Terry Palmer and Mrs Desmond!

TEMPLE: Where?

STEVE: Over there – she's getting out of that car!

TEMPLE: By Timothy, yes – and doesn't she look excited!

STEVE: (*Quietly; surprised*) Paul, look! There's a baby in the car ...

MARY DESMOND arrives: she is excited and a little breathless.

MARY: Mr Temple! We were just coming to see you ... I've got some awfully good news ... Susan's back! She's all right ... Perfectly all right ...

TEMPLE: What happened?

MARY: (*Excited*) Terry and I went for a drive ... this morning ... it was just after breakfast ... We drove as far as Richmond and then ... I can't believe it! I just can't believe it!

TEMPLE: Mrs Desmond, please! What happened?

MARY: (*Trying to control herself*) When we got back to the flat ... Susan was there ... She was on the rug near the fireplace ... fast asleep ... (*Laughing, yet near to tears*) I just couldn't believe it ... For a moment I thought I'd gone mad ... I really did, Mrs Temple. I thought I'd gone completely silly ... (*She is crying slightly*)

STEVE: (*Quietly*) Here's Mr Palmer ...

PALMER: (*To MARY; gently, yet with authority*) Go back
             to the car, Mary. I'll talk to Mr Temple.
MARY: (*Softly*) Yes, all right, Terry.

A moment.

PALMER: Hello! What's happened to your windscreen?
TEMPLE: We've had an accident, we … (*Quickly*) Is this
             true, Palmer – about the baby?
PALMER: Yes, perfectly true. It's a most extraordinary
             business, Temple. I just don't understand it. We
             went out for a drive and when we got back to
             the flat – well – there she was.
TEMPLE: Is the kiddie all right?
PALMER: Perfectly all right.
TEMPLE: There was no sign of Miss Millicent, I take it?
PALMER: No, but – you know she must be mixed up in
             this, Temple. In view of what's happened I
             think she must have taken the child away and
             then …
STEVE: Changed her mind?
PALMER: Yes. (*Suddenly*) Look here, Temple. I'm taking
             Mary and the baby down to Eastbourne for a
             few days. If she stays in Town I know exactly
             what'll happen – the reporters will be on her
             doorstep night and day – Frankly, Mary isn't up
             to it – she's in a pretty bad way.
TEMPLE: Yes. Have you contacted the police?
PALMER: I phoned the Yard but unfortunately both Sir
             Graham and the Inspector were out. I left a
             message. Here's our address in Eastbourne in
             case they want to get in touch.
TEMPLE: Yes, all right, Palmer. I'll see to it.
PALMER: Thanks. Thanks a lot. It's awfully kind of you –
             it really is most awfully kind.
TEMPLE: That's all right.

START FADE.
STEVE: Goodbye, Mr Palmer!
PALMER: Goodbye, Mrs Temple!
FADE SCENE.

FADE UP of a door opening.
FADE UP of TEMPLE carrying a suitcase.
TEMPLE: Here's the case, Charlie.
CHARLIE: O.K. I'll take it.
TEMPLE: Put it in the bedroom.
CHARLIE: Yes, sir. What about the car?
TEMPLE: Leave the car for the moment, Charlie.
CHARLIE: O.K., sir.
TEMPLE: (*Calling*) Steve!
STEVE: (*Coming out of the bedroom*) Yes, darling?
TEMPLE: You dropped your glove. It was on the
            pavement. Here we are …
STEVE: (*Taking the glove*) Oh, thanks.
TEMPLE: I thought Mrs Desmond looked terribly … (*He
            stops*) What is it?
STEVE: This isn't my glove, darling.
TEMPLE: Well, it was on the kerb near the car so I
            thought … Oh, Mrs Desmond must have
            dropped it.
STEVE: Do you know where she's staying?
TEMPLE: Yes, give it to me – I'll post it on to her.
STEVE: What were you saying about Mrs Desmond,
            Paul?
TEMPLE: I was saying: she looks to me as if she's
            heading for a first class … nervous …
            breakdown …
STEVE: What are you looking at?
A moment.

TEMPLE: I'm just looking at this glove, Steve. There's a
            tab inside … Do you see where it was bought?
STEVE: No.
TEMPLE: Well – look …
STEVE: (*Reading*) "Charles Marett, … 73 Rue St
            Lazare … Paris …"

FADE UP of music.

END OF EPISODE TWO

EPISODE THREE

INTRODUCING MR DROSTE

OPEN TO:

STEVE: This isn't my glove, darling.

TEMPLE: Well, it was on the kerb near the car so I
            thought … Oh, Mrs Desmond must have
            dropped it.

STEVE: Do you know where she's staying?

TEMPLE: Yes, give it to me – I'll post it on to her.

STEVE: What were you saying about Mrs Desmond,
            Paul?

TEMPLE: I was saying: she looks to me as if she's
            heading for a first class … nervous …
            breakdown …

STEVE: What are you looking at?

A moment.

TEMPLE: I'm just looking at this glove, Steve. There's a
            tab inside … Do you see where it was bought?

STEVE: No.

TEMPLE: Well – look …

STEVE: (*Reading*) "Charles Marett, … 73 Rue St
            Lazare … Paris …" (*Suddenly; astonished*)
            Paul, this is the same address! The one you told
            me about … The one that …

TEMPLE: The one that was on the receipt …

STEVE: Yes. (*Suddenly*) Darling, do you remember –
            the receipt was for a pair of gloves …?

TEMPLE: (*Thoughtfully*) That's just what I was thinking
            …

STEVE: (*Suddenly*) Paul, do you think that these gloves
            are the …

TEMPLE: (*Intrigued, yet exasperated*) I don't know. By
            Timothy, I don't know what to think, Steve!

STEVE: (*Quickly; faintly excited*) Paul, listen! I've got a
            sort of a … a …

73

TEMPLE:	A what?
STEVE:	A sort of an intuition, darling.
TEMPLE:	Oh, by Timothy, not that good old intuition!
STEVE:	(*Seriously*) No, Paul, please!
TEMPLE:	All right … Go on …
STEVE:	Supposing that man – the man that was murdered at Marlow …
TEMPLE:	Call him Baker …
STEVE:	All right. Supposing Baker was murdered because he refused to … to … (*Still thinking about it and gradually losing her enthusiasm*) No, no, that doesn't make sense …
TEMPLE:	(*Quietly*) As a matter of fact, Steve, I think I know why Baker was murdered. Do you remember the last thing he said, darling?
STEVE:	He said: "A Mr Vandyke telephoned …"
TEMPLE:	Yes. Well, before we left the Wordsworth I got Eden to check all the incoming calls. Baker never received a call at the hotel therefore he must either have received the call from Vandyke – or overheard it – somewhere else.
STEVE:	Possibly at Shelly's?

The door opens.

TEMPLE:	Yes, he might have heard it at Shelly's, on the other hand … What is it, Charlie?
CHARLIE:	Excuse me, sir. There was a telephone call for you this morning from a Mr Droste. He wants you to ring him back. I wrote the number down on the pad.
TEMPLE:	Oh. (*Reading from the pad*) Grosvenor 1978.
CHARLIE:	That's right, sir.
TEMPLE:	Mr Droste?
CHARLIE:	Yes – I think that was it. I expect I've spelt it wrong.

74

TEMPLE: Yes, I expect you have, Charlie. Did Mr Droste say what it was he wanted to speak to me about?

CHARLIE: No, sir. He just said would you please ring him back.

TEMPLE: Yes, all right.

CHARLIE: O.K., sir.

The door closes.

STEVE: Mr Droste. Do you know him?

TEMPLE: The name's familiar, Steve.

He picks up the telephone receiver and starts to dial.

TEMPLE: We'll see what it's all about.

After a moment we hear the number ringing out and a receiver being lifted.

GIRL: Good afternoon. Grosvenor 1978.

TEMPLE: Could I speak to Mr Droste, please?

GIRL: Who is it speaking?

TEMPLE: My name is Temple.

GIRL: Oh! One moment, Mr Temple.

A pause.

There is a click as the call is transferred to an extension.

DROSTE: Hello? (*PHILIP DROSTE is a South American: he speaks with a very slight accent and tries, a little too hard, to be essentially English*)

GIRL: Mr Temple is on the line, sir.

DROSTE: Oh! (*Pleasantly*) Mr Temple?

TEMPLE: Yes.

DROSTE: Philip Droste here. How very nice of you to call.

TEMPLE: I understand you telephoned me this morning.

DROSTE: That's quite right, I did. Your man told me that you were out of Town. I trust you had a pleasant weekend, Mr Temple.

TEMPLE: The weather was delightful.

75

DROSTE: Mr Temple, I want to have a chat with you about – about a mutual friend of ours.

TEMPLE: A mutual friend?

DROSTE: Yes – a Mr Walters.

TEMPLE: I'm afraid there's some mistake. I don't know anyone called Walters.

DROSTE: Perhaps "friend" was hardly the right word. You met two or three days ago at the Commodore Club.

TEMPLE: Indeed?

DROSTE: (*Smiling*) He's the cloakroom attendant.

TEMPLE: (*Surprised*) Oh.

DROSTE: (*Brightly*) Could you pop in one evening, Mr Temple? We could have a drink together …

TEMPLE: Which particular evening have you in mind, Mr Droste?

DROSTE: (*A little laugh*) Well, that's up to you, old man. I'm always here. (*Brightly*) Why not tonight?

TEMPLE: (*After a moment*) All right.

DROSTE: Shall we say eight o'clock?

TEMPLE: Yes, that'll do nicely.

DROSTE: I don't know whether you have the address or not. It's 47B Park Lane. It's the top flat. You take the lift right to the top.

TEMPLE: Eight o'clock.

DROSTE: Eight o'clock, old man! Cheerio!

TEMPLE: (*Quietly*) Cheerio …

TEMPLE replaces the receiver.

The flat buzzer can be heard in the background.

STEVE: Who's Mr Droste?

TEMPLE: (*Thoughtfully*) Your guess is as good as mine, Steve.

STEVE: But what does he want?

TEMPLE: (*Still thoughtfully*) Apparently he wants to talk
            to me about the cloakroom attendant at the
            Commodore Club.
STEVE: (*Amazed*) Are you serious?
TEMPLE: Perfectly serious. That's what he said.
The door opens.
CHARLIE: Sir Graham Forbes is here, sir.
TEMPLE: Ah, come in, Sir Graham!
FORBES: Hello, Steve!
TEMPLE: You're just the man I want, Sir Graham!
            (*Aside*) That's all right, Charlie. Sir Graham,
            tell me, do you know a gentleman by the name
            of Droste?
FORBES: Philip Droste? Yes. He owns the Commodore
            Club.
TEMPLE: Oh, does he! That's interesting. What's he like?
FORBES: Well, you hear such extraordinary stories about
            Droste. He has a flat in Park Lane – a sort of
            penthouse.
TEMPLE: Yes, I gathered that …
FORBES: They say he never leaves it from one weekend
            to the next. You certainly never see him about
            the West End.
STEVE: Doesn't he ever visit the Commodore Club?
FORBES: Good heavens, no! You wouldn't get him
            within a mile of the place. He's a very shrewd
            bird is Droste. Before the war he owned the
            Playbox Club in Gradstone Street, the Plaza
            Hotel, and two or three dance halls. I don't
            know whether there's any truth in it but they
            say he's worth the best part of three million.
TEMPLE: Is he straight?

FORBES: Well, we've never had any trouble with him, if that's what you mean. But why are you interested in Mr Droste?

TEMPLE: Apparently he wants to see me. He phoned through this morning while we were at Marlow.

FORBES: I see. (*Suddenly*) Well, I suppose you've heard about the Desmond baby?

TEMPLE: Yes.

FORBES: What do you make of it?

TEMPLE: Well, there's a perfectly simple explanation I suppose, if you're prepared to accept it.

FORBES: What's that?

TEMPLE: Miss Millicent kidnapped the child then thought better of it – or probably got frightened when she read the newspapers.

FORBES: Is that what you think?

TEMPLE: (*A moment*) No.

FORBES: (*Suddenly; irritated*) Temple, I'm worried about this case. Frankly, I'm damn worried. Eden's a good man but he just doesn't seem to be making any headway.

TEMPLE: You can't expect him to make any headway, Sir Graham – not until he really knows what it's all about.

FORBES: What do you mean?

TEMPLE: Have you ever stopped to consider this case? I don't just …

FORBES: (*Irritated*) Of course I've stopped to consider it!

TEMPLE: I don't just mean the various bits and pieces but, well, the case itself. First of all a baby and a sitter-in called Miss Millicent – disappears. That's the beginning of the case. Right. Then a friend of Miss Millicent's – a girl called

78

Queenie Edwards – is brutally murdered. Later we discover that the murder of Queenie is tied up with the disappearance of Miss Millicent and the baby for the simple reason that Queenie leads us, by means of a cloakroom ticket, to the Commodore Club. At the Commodore we find, in an attaché case, a doll belonging to the missing child. Now those are just isolated facts, Sir Graham, but nevertheless …

FORBES: (*Faintly exasperated*) They tie-up! I appreciate that, Temple, but …

TEMPLE: They do more than tie-up, Sir Graham! They add up! But what do they add up to – that's the point!

STEVE: In other words – who is this Mr Vandyke and what's his racket?

TEMPLE: Exactly, Steve!

FORBES: Frankly, Temple, I don't think Vandyke has any – well – racket as you call it. This isn't like the Gregory Affair or the Curzon Case. I think it simply boils down to the fact that we're up against a criminal lunatic.

TEMPLE: I don't agree, Sir Graham. You take this fellow down at Marlow – the man that was murdered. Someone sent him down to Marlow – someone sent him down there for a particular reason. Incidentally, you remember the receipt that Eden found …

FORBES: Yes, I've already contacted the French people about it. The address on the receipt is genuine enough: it's a small shop. They sell gloves; handbags, you know the sort of shop. Paris is full of them.

TEMPLE:	Yes, I rather gathered the address was genuine. Take a look at this glove.

A moment.

FORBES:	(*Amazed*) Where did you get this, Temple?
TEMPLE:	Mrs Desmond dropped it …
FORBES:	Mrs Desmond!
TEMPLE:	Yes.
FORBES:	(*Quickly*) When?
TEMPLE:	About ten minutes ago.
FORBES:	(*Bewildered*) But this is fantastic! Why on earth should Mrs Desmond … you know, Temple, this business just doesn't make sense!
TEMPLE:	It makes sense all right – the trouble is it doesn't make sense to us. (*Suddenly*) Sir Graham, tell me: what do you think the chances are of finding out who that man is – the man that was murdered?
FORBES:	Unless someone comes forward and identifies him I'm afraid the chances aren't very good. We've given the story to the press: there'll be a detailed description of him in the evening papers.
STEVE:	Did Sergeant Digby see him – the real Sergeant Digby, I mean?
FORBES:	No, we've questioned Digby but unfortunately he can't place him. I think Baker, or whatever his name is, must have kept well out of his way.

The telephone commences to ring.

FORBES:	Incidentally, Digby knew nothing whatsoever about Shelly. He didn't even know he had a bungalow at Marlow.

The telephone continues ringing.

STEVE: It's all right. I'll answer it, Paul. (*She lifts the receiver*) Hello?

We hear the sound of button A being pressed and the coins dropping.

PALMER: (*On the other end of the line*) Hello?

STEVE: Who is that?

PALMER: Is that you, Mrs Temple?

STEVE: Yes.

PALMER: Oh, this is Terry Palmer here. Do you think I might have a word with your husband?

STEVE: Yes, I think so.

PALMER: Thanks awfully.

STEVE: (*Aside to TEMPLE*) It's Terry Palmer, darling. He wants a word with you.

TEMPLE: Does he, by Timothy! That's interesting ... I wonder if it's about the glove? (*Quickly and softly*) Sir Graham, I'd like you to listen to this. You take the phone – I'll talk to him on the extension.

FORBES: Yes, all right, Temple.

STEVE: (*On the phone: pleasantly*) Just hold on, Mr Palmer. He's coming.

PALMER: Thanks awfully.

A moment.

We hear the extension receiver being lifted.

TEMPLE: (*Pleasantly*) Palmer?

PALMER: Oh, I'm sorry if I've disturbed you, Temple, but ...

TEMPLE: I thought you were on your way to Eastbourne?

PALMER: (*A little laugh*) We are. Actually I'm in a callbox at the moment.

TEMPLE: Well, what can I do for you?

PALMER:	Temple, do you happen to know if Mary – Mrs Desmond – dropped one of her gloves whilst she was …
TEMPLE:	(*Interrupting PALMER: pleasantly*) Yes, as a matter of fact she did. I've got it here, I was going to post it on to you.
PALMER:	(*With a laugh*) Oh, thank goodness! She was in a state about it! Perhaps you'll post it on then – ?
TEMPLE:	Yes, of course I will. How is Mrs Desmond?
PALMER:	She's still pretty upset, I'm afraid. It's curious, you'd have thought that now she knows Susan's safe she'd be perfectly all right. I suppose she's getting a reaction.
TEMPLE:	Yes. How's the baby?
PALMER:	Oh, Susan's all right, she's crying rather a lot but … (*Suddenly, almost confidentially*) Oh, by the way! Before I forget, I promised Mary I'd speak to you about the doll. Do you remember, the doll you found in the attaché case?
TEMPLE:	Yes, of course I remember!
PALMER:	(*Hesitating slightly*) Well, do you think there's any chance of getting it back? It's an extraordinary thing but Susan's terribly devoted to that doll. You know what kiddies are, you can buy them all sorts of new things but they still seem to cling to their old favourites.
TEMPLE:	Well, so far as I know, Palmer, the doll's still at Scotland Yard. I daresay I could have a word with the Inspector about it.
PALMER:	I wish you would, Temple. (*With a laugh*) Peace at any price – that's my motto! Goodbye, Temple!
TEMPLE:	Goodbye, Palmer.

PALMER: And thanks awfully.
PALMER rings off.
FADE.

FADE UP.
TEMPLE: Did you hear all right, Sir Graham?
FORBES: Yes, every word. Now what the devil is he
             getting at, Temple? Why is he so anxious to get
             hold of the doll? (*Faintly exasperated*) Look
             here, Temple, we've examined that doll from
             head to toe: it's been through every single
             department, not once but a dozen times! I tell
             you frankly, Temple, it's just a perfectly
             ordinary doll.
TEMPLE: I don't doubt it, Sir Graham.
FORBES: Then why does Palmer want it?
TEMPLE: He didn't say that he did: he simply said that
             the baby wanted it.
FORBES: (*Grimly*) Palmer wants that doll – it's perfectly
             obvious that he wants it. The question is –
             why?
STEVE: Of course you may be mistaken, Sir Graham. It
             may not be just a perfectly ordinary doll.
FORBES: But it is, Steve! We know it is. Besides, what
             else could it be?
STEVE: (*Quietly*) A red herring.
FADE UP of music.

FADE DOWN of music.
FADE UP background noises of Park Lane traffic.
FADE UP the noise of a car drawing to a standstill.
TEMPLE: 47B – this is it, Steve …
STEVE: Yes.

TEMPLE:	(*Opening the car door*) I wonder if that's Droste's place?
STEVE:	Where?
TEMPLE:	On the top … those windows …
STEVE:	(*Staring up*) Yes, it looks like it. Sir Graham said it was a sort of penthouse …
TEMPLE:	(*Closing the car door behind him*) I don't expect I shall be long, darling.
STEVE:	Yes, all right, Paul!

FADE traffic noises.
FADE SCENE.

FADE UP the noise of an elevator: it stops and the gates are opened.

EDDIE:	Good evening, sir!
TEMPLE:	Good evening!
McCALL:	(*About to pass TEMPLE*) Excuse me …
TEMPLE:	(*Suddenly*) Why, hello, McCall!
McCALL:	(*Surprised, pleasantly*) Why, hello, there! Say, I didn't recognise you!
TEMPLE:	What are you doing in Park Lane?
McCALL:	(*Laughing*) Just taking a look at the poor – you know how it is! Did you have a nice trip back to Town?
TEMPLE:	If you overlook the fact that someone tried to shoot the daylight out of us we had a delightful trip.
McCALL:	(*Seriously*) No! What happened?
TEMPLE:	About half an hour after we left Marlow a bullet hit our windscreen.
McCALL:	Gee! What d'you know?!
TEMPLE:	Somehow, I don't think it was intended for the windscreen.
McCALL:	But that's terrible! Was Mrs Temple upset?

TEMPLE: She's rather immune to that sort of thing. (*Watching McCALL*) Not that she cares for it, mind you.

McCALL: But that's a dreadful experience! I should have been petrified!

TEMPLE: Just between ourselves, Mr McCall, I was. (*He turns and opens the lift gates*) Do I work this thing?

EDDIE: No, sir, I'll take you up. What floor, sir?

TEMPLE: I believe it's the top.

EDDIE: (*Brightly*) Mr Droste?

TEMPLE: Yes, that's right. (Pleasantly) Goodbye, McCall!

McCALL: Goodbye – and take care of yourself.

TEMPLE: I'll try.

McCALL: (*Calling*) Give my regards to Mrs Temple!

TEMPLE: (*Calling back*) Yes, I will, certainly!

The lift gate closes. EDDIE presses the button and the lift ascends.

A pause.

EDDIE: Been up 'ere before, sir?

TEMPLE: No, I haven't.

EDDIE: Wonderful view. Best view in London, I reckon. Always tell Mr Droste he's got the best view in London.

TEMPLE: (*Thoughtfully*) Really?

EDDIE: Course he's got the windows for it. Wopping big things. He 'ad the old ones pulled out – people thought he was barmy. He wasn't though, he knew what he was doin' all right.

TEMPLE: How long has he been here?

EDDIE: What – Mr Droste? Oh, must be fifteen years now. Yes, must be all of fifteen.

A moment.

85

TEMPLE: That gentleman I was speaking to, Mr –?

EDDIE: Mr McCall.

TEMPLE: Yes, that's right. Does he come here very often?

EDDIE: About once a month: usually on the 15th. I think he works for Mr Droste – don't know what he does exactly.

The lift stops.

EDDIE: Ah, here we are!

The lift gate opens.

TEMPLE: (*Getting out of the lift*) Thank you.

EDDIE: Press that button over there – over on the left. That's it!

TEMPLE presses the button and from inside the flat we hear a soft musical chime.

EDDIE closes the lift gate and the lift descends.

The door of the flat opens.

DROSTE: Mr Temple?

TEMPLE: Yes …

DROSTE: (*Brightly*) My dear fellow, how nice of you to come at a moment's notice. I do appreciate it. It's most considerate of you. May I take your coat?

TEMPLE: Er – thank you.

They move into the hall.

DROSTE: (*Taking TEMPLE's coat*) I've given my man the night off. You know how difficult it is these days – the servant problem.

TEMPLE: I do indeed.

DROSTE: Come along, old man! Come inside. Make yourself at home.

They enter the main room of the apartment.

A pause.

TEMPLE: (*Taking stock*) By Timothy, it certainly is a wonderful view!

DROSTE: (*Laughing*) Yes. On a clear day you can see right across the park …

TEMPLE: (*Impressed*) By Timothy, yes! I can believe it … It's magnificent … (*A moment*) Tell me, what's that building over there – the one with the neon sign?

DROSTE: Oh, that's a restaurant. The Carlos – it's on the corner near the park.

TEMPLE: Oh, yes, of course! A horrible little place …

DROSTE: (*Amused*) Yes …

TEMPLE: What's the joke?

DROSTE: I own it.

TEMPLE: Oh – I beg your pardon.

DROSTE: (*Pleasantly*) That's all right. Now what can I get you to drink, old man? Would you like a dry martini?

TEMPLE: (*Faintly surprised*) Yes, I would.

DROSTE: (*Smiling*) I thought so. (*Mixing drinks*) I once read an article about you in the Saturday Evening Post, Mr Temple. They said you never drank anything except a dry martini.

TEMPLE: A slight exaggeration.

DROSTE laughs.

DROSTE: Here we are …

TEMPLE: Thank you. (*Taking his drink*) Skoal!

DROSTE: Cheerio! (*Suddenly*) Do sit down, old man – sit down.

TEMPLE: (*Sitting down*) Now what is it you want to see me about, Mr Droste – on the telephone you said something about a Mr Walters?

DROSTE: That's right, I did. Bert Walters. He works for me at the Commodore Club.

TEMPLE: Yes.

DROSTE: You remember him?

TEMPLE: Yes, I do. He gave me an attaché case four or five days ago.

DROSTE: That's quite right, he did. (*Pleasantly: a shade casual*) Mr Temple, tell me, how did you manage to get hold of that ticket – the one for the attaché case, I mean?

TEMPLE: Why do you ask?

DROSTE: I'm curious, that's all.

TEMPLE: Well, if you must know it was given to me by a friend of mine.

DROSTE: (*Politely*) Mr Palmer?

TEMPLE: (*Bluntly*) No – not Mr Palmer.

A moment.

DROSTE: (*Laughing*) I feel quite sure that at any moment you are going to tell me to mind my own business. (*Friendly manner*) Now let me explain, old man. Ever since you took that attaché case out of the cloakroom there have been a great many questions asked. Bert Walters, the cloakroom attendant, was dragged out of bed at six o'clock in the morning. Twice, at a moment's notice, he's been taken to Scotland Yard and questioned for the best part of an hour.

TEMPLE: Go on …

DROSTE: Believe me, I'm not, generally speaking, a curious person: but this business intrigues me. (*Slowly*) Why are the police so interested in Bert Walters? Why are they keeping their eye on the Commodore Club?

TEMPLE: Have you asked them why?

DROSTE: No, I haven't.

TEMPLE:	Then why don't you?
DROSTE:	I prefer to ask you, Mr Temple. After all, you presented the ticket – you took the case out of the cloakroom.
TEMPLE:	Yes, but I didn't put it in.
DROSTE:	(*Watching TEMPLE*) How am I to know that?
TEMPLE:	(*Simply*) Ask Mr Walters.
DROSTE:	(*Faintly irritated*) Walters is a most unreliable person. To start with he said he thought that Palmer had deposited the case, later – for some unknown reason – he changed his mind.
TEMPLE:	Does Bert Walters still work for you – at the Commodore?
DROSTE:	Yes, of course.
TEMPLE:	How long has he been there?
DROSTE:	About five months.
TEMPLE:	Isn't that rather a long time – for such an unreliable person?
DROSTE:	(*Evasively: laughing*) Yes, I see what you mean.
TEMPLE:	You know, Mr Droste, you still haven't told me why you're interested in this business?
DROSTE:	But surely that's obvious, old man. I own the Commodore Club. Everything that happens at the Commodore is naturally of interest to me. Besides …
TEMPLE:	Yes?
DROSTE:	I don't want any trouble. I particularly don't want any trouble at the present moment.
TEMPLE:	No?
DROSTE:	No. (*A moment*) Mr Temple, I didn't intend to tell you this, but – I'll let you into a little secret. I intend to apply for naturalisation papers.

	(*Proudly*) It's my wish to become a British subject.
TEMPLE:	And you think that this affair at the Commodore Club …
DROSTE:	(*Confidentially*) Naturally, I don't want any trouble. You know what people say – where there's smoke there's fire. I'm quite sure the Home Office are no exception.
TEMPLE:	You know, Mr Droste, it seems to me that you're making a mountain out of a molehill. Just because you own the Commodore Club it doesn't necessarily mean that you're responsible for everything that happens there. Supposing one of the guests suddenly took it into his head to murder the head waiter …
DROSTE:	… He would have my complete sympathy …
TEMPLE:	(*Laughing*) … You could hardly be held responsible.
DROSTE:	(*Seriously*) I see what you mean, but nevertheless … Look here, old man. I think I'd better put my cards on the table.
TEMPLE:	It might be an advantage.
DROSTE:	Well – I invited you here this evening because – there's something I want to know.
TEMPLE:	Go on …
DROSTE:	I don't expect you to answer my question, but … (*Suddenly*) Oh, I'm so sorry, old man! Let me get you a drink …
TEMPLE:	(*Quietly; yet with authority*) No. No, please! What is it you want to know, Mr Droste?
A moment.	
DROSTE:	(*Slowly: watching TEMPLE*) That attaché case …
TEMPLE:	Yes?

DROSTE:	The one that Walters gave you …
TEMPLE:	Yes?
DROSTE:	(*After a moment*) What was inside it, Mr Temple?
TEMPLE:	(*Smiling*) Do you mean to tell me that you don't know?
DROSTE:	Of course I don't know! If I knew, I shouldn't be asking you. (*Politely*) You refuse to answer my question?
TEMPLE:	Have you asked the police what was inside the case?
DROSTE:	Yes, I asked Inspector Eden.
TEMPLE:	What did he say?
DROSTE:	In diplomatic language he told me to mind my own business. (*Smiling*) Is that your reply, too?
TEMPLE:	No, I'm afraid I'm not quite so diplomatic as the Inspector. As a matter of fact, Mr Droste, I'm rather an accommodating sort of chap. You'll probably find that out if we get better acquainted. Do you remember reading about that baby – the little girl – the one that disappeared?
DROSTE:	The Miss Millicent affair?
TEMPLE:	That's right. Well, the little girl had a doll – a Dutch doll. The doll disappeared when the child was kidnapped.
DROSTE:	Well?
TEMPLE:	(*Quite simply*) That's what I found in the attaché case, Mr Droste. The doll.
DROSTE:	(*Apparently amazed*) Are you serious?
TEMPLE:	Perfectly serious.
DROSTE:	Tell me: was the doll examined at all?
TEMPLE:	It was.
DROSTE:	By the police?

91

TEMPLE: Yes. It turned out to be a perfectly ordinary doll. There was nothing inside it – nothing concealed – if that's what you're thinking.

DROSTE: (*Amused*) Just a doll in fact.

TEMPLE: Exactly.

Suddenly DROSTE starts to laugh: he is greatly amused and laughs for some little time. As the laughter dies down Temple speaks …

TEMPLE: Now, Mr Droste, perhaps you wouldn't mind answering a question or two?

DROSTE: (*Still amused*) I shall be delighted.

TEMPLE: What did you imagine was in the attaché case?

DROSTE: (*Vaguely*) I just didn't know, I … I had a horrible feeling that someone might have stolen something – some jewellery perhaps – and deposited it at the Commodore. It was very stupid of me but I have rather that sort of an imagination.

TEMPLE: I see. Well, I don't think I should worry so much about the Commodore, Mr Droste, as about The Wordsworth.

DROSTE: (*Quietly; serious*) What do you mean?

TEMPLE: Don't you own The Wordsworth Hotel at Marlow?

DROSTE: (*After a moment*) Yes. Yes, I do. (*Suddenly*) Oh, I see what you're getting at, old man! This murder … Well, it's nothing to do with me. You said yourself if someone murders the head waiter it wouldn't be my responsibility. The same thing applies to a guest. Incidentally, how did you know that I own the Wordsworth?

TEMPLE: I didn't. It was simply a guess. (*A moment*) I bumped into McCall.

DROSTE: Oh, I see.

TEMPLE: I suppose he told you what happened: that I discovered the body?

DROSTE: (*Watching TEMPLE*) Yes. Yes, he told me. It must have been most unpleasant for you.

TEMPLE: You don't happen to know who the gentleman is, I suppose?

DROSTE: The man that was murdered?

TEMPLE: Yes.

DROSTE: No. No, I'm afraid I don't.

TEMPLE: I see. (*Suddenly*) Droste, tell me: have you heard of a Mr Vandyke?

DROSTE: (*Taken aback: unable to completely conceal his surprise*) Vandyke – did you say?

TEMPLE: Yes.

DROSTE: Why – why do you ask?

TEMPLE: (*Slowly: watching him*) He telephoned me several days ago; unfortunately I was out. He left no message.

DROSTE: (*Calmly; in control*) I'm sorry, old man. I can't help you. I've never heard of a Mr Vandyke. Now please, let me get you another drink.

The door is suddenly thrown open and DROSTE's wife, VANESSA, enters. She is a smart, sophisticated woman of about forty. At the present moment she is tense and considerably overwrought.

DROSTE: Vanessa!

VANESSA: (*Tensely*) Hello, Philip!

DROSTE: Sweetheart, I didn't expect you back until Thursday …

VANESSA: I know. I had to make up my mind very quickly. It was difficult I – I didn't see anyone until last night.

DROSTE: (*Cutting in: calmly*) You look as if you need a drink, my sweet.

93

VANESSA: No. No, I had something on the plane, I …

DROSTE: Oh, I beg your pardon! This is my wife. Sweetheart, this is Mr Temple – you've heard of Paul Temple, Vanessa. He writes books, you know.

TEMPLE: (*Watching VANESSA very closely*) How do you do, Mrs Droste?

VANESSA: (*Vaguely*) Hello … (*To DROSTE: very offhand*) What did you say – he writes what?

DROSTE: Books, darling. You know, sweetheart – things you read – books! (*Laughing*) Vanessa's always the same after a journey. (*Playfully; patting VANESSA's cheek*) Darling, you are a funny little creature – but it's nice to have you back just the same. Run along, my dear, and powder your nose!

VANESSA: (*Perturbed: almost as if to herself*) Philip, I didn't see anyone until last night and then it was too late for …

DROSTE: (*Laughing at VANESSA*) Yes, all right, darling! All right! There's nothing to worry about, my sweet – run along.

TEMPLE: Have you had a very long journey, Mrs Droste?

VANESSA: No, I've been in Paris for two or three … days … that's all, I …

DROSTE: (*Quickly*) Vanessa, what is it? What's the matter?

VANESSA: You know what it is, Philip, I …

TEMPLE: (*Suddenly*) Look out! She's going to faint!

DROSTE: (*Alarmed*) Vanessa!

As DROSTE speaks VANESSA faints and falls forward: her handbag drops to the ground.

TEMPLE: (*Catching VANESSA*) It's all right, I've got her! You'd better give her a drink! Quickly!

VANESSA: Oh, oh … I … I don't know what happened, I
         …
TEMPLE: It's all right, Mrs Droste …
DROSTE: Here … drink … this …
VANESSA: No, I shall be better … in a moment … I only
         …
DROSTE: Vanessa, don't be a stupid – drink this – please!
A pause.
VANESSA drinks.
VANESSA: (*Finishing the drink*) What – happened?
TEMPLE: You fainted, that's all. It was nothing.
VANESSA: How stupid! I'm sorry, Philip, but you know …
DROSTE: (*Interrupting VANESSA*) That's all right, my
        sweet – you couldn't help it.
VANESSA: I – I think I'd better go and lie down.
DROSTE: Yes, sweetheart, I think you'd better.
VANESSA: (*With forced brightness*) You must have a very
        odd opinion of me, Mr Temple. I don't usually
        do this sort of thing, do I, Philip?
DROSTE: Only on Tuesdays and Fridays.
They laugh.
VANESSA: Oh, dear, how stupid of me! Where's my
        handbag?
DROSTE: Here it is …
VANESSA: Oh, thank you. And my gloves …?
TEMPLE: Here we are, Mrs Droste.
VANESSA: Oh, thank you …
DROSTE: Do you feel better now, my dear?
VANESSA: Yes … I was ill in the plane coming over. I – I
        expect that was the trouble. I'll take some
        aspirin and lie down.
The door opens and closes.
DROSTE: (*Suddenly: a very agreeable manner*) Now, old
        man, let me mix you that drink!

95

TEMPLE: No, no, if you don't mind I think I'd better be making a move.

DROSTE: Well, if you say so! I'm most grateful to you for your information.

TEMPLE: Information?

DROSTE: About the doll.

TEMPLE: Oh, yes.

DROSTE: It was very sporting of you, old man, to take me into your confidence. Believe me, I appreciate it.

TEMPLE: Oh, that's all right. I hope you'll do the same for me sometime.

DROSTE: (*With a little laugh*) Yes, I – I hope so.

DROSTE opens the door.

DROSTE: Goodnight, Mr Temple!

TEMPLE: (*Smiling*) Goodnight, old man.

FADE SCENE.

FADE UP a background of traffic noises in Park Lane.

TEMPLE: (*Very pleased with himself*) Hello, Steve! Sorry I've been so long. (*Opens the car door*)

STEVE: Did you see Droste?

TEMPLE: I did!

STEVE: (*Quickly*) Darling, you're onto something! What's happened?

TEMPLE: (*Excited*) You're dead right I'm onto something! Steve, I'm just beginning to see daylight! Things are beginning to add up!

STEVE: What do you mean?

TEMPLE: Not only did I meet Mr Droste, my beloved, but I met Mrs Droste – and by Timothy what a woman!

STEVE: (*Not caring for this*) What do you mean – By Timothy, what a woman! What's so remarkable about <u>Mrs</u> Droste?

TEMPLE: Shall I tell you?

STEVE: Yes!

TEMPLE: (*A moment: dead serious*) She buys her gloves from the same shop as Mrs Desmond!

Quick FADE UP of music.

FADE DOWN of music.

A door opens.

STEVE: I'm ready now, Paul! Shall I go down to the taxi?

TEMPLE: Yes, darling. I just want to have a word with Charlie.

CHARLIE: I'll carry that down, Mrs Temple.

STEVE: No, it's all right, Charlie. I'll carry the hatbox. (*Calling back*) Don't forget your passport, darling!

The door closes.

TEMPLE: Now listen, Charlie – I want you to take particular note of what I'm saying …

CHARLIE: Yes, sir.

TEMPLE: If anyone rings up – it doesn't matter who they are – I don't want you to say anything about Mrs Temple and me being in Paris. If they ask you where we are just say we're out of Town for two or three days.

CHARLIE: What if it's Sir Graham, sir?

TEMPLE: Sir Graham won't ring; he knows where to get in touch if he wants me. You understand, Charlie?

CHARLIE: Yes, sir. That's o.k., sir. You leave it to me, sir.

TEMPLE: We shall probably be back on Thursday – Friday at the latest.

CHARLIE: Okedoke, sir.

The flat buzzer sounds.

TEMPLE: (*Picking up a suitcase*) Well – goodbye, Charlie!

CHARLIE: Goodbye, sir – 'ave a nice trip.

The flat buzzer sounds again.

TEMPLE: Now who the devil is that?

TEMPLE crosses to the door and opens it.

TEMPLE: (*Surprised*) Oh, hello, Shelly!

SHELLY: (*Also surprised*) Hello, Mr Temple, I … Are you just going out?

TEMPLE: Yes, as a matter of fact I am. I've got a train to catch, I'm rather in a hurry.

SHELLY: Oh, dear! How very tantalising, I did so want to have a word with you.

TEMPLE: I'm sorry, Shelly.

SHELLY: T't – t't – how vexing. Can't you spare me just a moment? It is important …

TEMPLE: (*After a moment's hesitation*) All right! Come in. but you'll have to make it snappy!

The door closes.

SHELLY: (*Curious*) You're not going down to Marlow again, are you?

TEMPLE: Marlow? No – no, we're going to stay with some friends of ours in Hertfordshire. Now what is it, Shelly? What can I do for you?

SHELLY: (*Quietly*) I think perhaps you'd better read this …

TEMPLE: (*Taking a letter from SHELLY*) What is it?

SHELLY: Read it …

TEMPLE: (*Reading*) "… The man you met at Marlow – the man who called himself Baker – was Harry

98

De Wolfe. Let that be a warning, Mr Shelly ..."
(*Looking up*) When did you receive this?

SHELLY: This afternoon. I recognised the handwriting the moment I saw it.

TEMPLE: (*Surprised*) You recognised the handwriting?

SHELLY: Yes.

TEMPLE: Well, whose is it?

SHELLY: Good heavens, don't tell me you don't recognise it! It's Miss Millicent's.

TEMPLE: Miss Millicent's! Are you sure?

SHELLY: Of course I'm sure! I've compared it with the letter she wrote me asking for an interview. I don't profess to be a handwriting expert but there just isn't the slightest doubt that this is Miss Millicent's handwriting.

TEMPLE: (*Watching SHELLY*) Shelly, how well did you know Miss Millicent?

SHELLY: (*Rather offhand*) Hardly at all. She simply wrote to me and I got her two or three jobs as a sitter-in. She seemed a perfectly respectable person: I don't suppose I've spoken to her more than half a dozen times.

TEMPLE: Well, assuming for the moment that you're right and this note was written by Miss Millicent, why did she write to you instead of to Scotland Yard?

SHELLY: That's precisely what I want to know! I've never heard of anyone called Harry De Wolfe.

TEMPLE: M'm – well, Shelly, listen. I want you to take this note to Inspector Eden: tell him I sent you and give him all the details.

SHELLY: (*Interrupting TEMPLE: faintly petulant*) But I don't like Eden! He's a ghastly person! Why

	do you think I brought it to you? Only because I don't want …
TEMPLE:	I'm sorry, Shelly. You'll have to see Eden. In any case, the Yard will want to check on this man De Wolfe.
SHELLY:	I suppose the moment I take this note to Eden he'll get suspicious: he'll probably think that I'm mixed up in this frightful business and wrote the note myself!
TEMPLE:	(*Politely*) Did you write the note yourself?
SHELLY:	(*Horrified*) Of course I didn't!
TEMPLE:	Then there's nothing for you to worry about.
SHELLY:	(*Petulantly*) Nothing for me to worry about? I'm not so sure about that! What does she mean – "Let that be a warning, Mr Shelly"? A warning against <u>what</u> for goodness sake?

FADE UP of music.

FADE DOWN of music.
CROSS FADE to Parisian music: the boulevards of Paris: a background of traffic noises: police whistles, etc. Gay confusion …
SLOW FADE music away.
FADE traffic noises down to the background.
FADE UP the noise of a dilapidated taxi: it is travelling very fast.

STEVE:	Paul, we seem to have been travelling for ages!
TEMPLE:	Yes. (*Peering out of the window*) I don't know where the devil we are.
STEVE:	We're not very far from the Place Pigalle. Do you think he understood you, darling?
TEMPLE:	Of course he understood me! Wait a minute – I'll have another word with the old boy!

TEMPLE opens the partition window.

TEMPLE: I say, driver?
DRIVER: (*Turning*) Monsieur?
TEMPLE: Jusqu'ou devons-nous aller?
DRIVER: Rue St Lazare?
TEMPLE: Oui.
DRIVER: C'est juste au coin, monsieur. Nous y serons tres rapidement.
TEMPLE: Oh. (*To STEVE*) What did he say?
STEVE: (*Laughing*) He says it's on the corner – we shall be there in a minute or two.
TEMPLE: Oh, good. (*To the DRIVER*) Merci …
DRIVER: Merci, monsieur!

TEMPLE closes the window.
FADE UP of traffic noises.
FADE.
FADE UP of the taxi drawing to a standstill.
We hear the taxi door opening and closing.
TEMPLE and STEVE are getting out of the taxi.

STEVE: There it is, Paul!
TEMPLE: Where?
STEVE: Over on the other side of the road. Look – there's a lot of gloves and handbags in the window …
TEMPLE: Charles Marett … Yes, that's the shop all right. (*To the DRIVER*) Combien?
DRIVER: Trois cents vingt francs, monsieur.
TEMPLE: Voici! Gardez le monnais.
DRIVER: Merci, monsieur! Merci …

The taxi drives away.

TEMPLE: Come along, Steve!
STEVE: Darling, be careful – watch the traffic!

FADE UP of traffic noises.

TEMPLE: Come along, Steve, or we'll be here all day!

FADE UP of screeching brakes: police whistles, etc.

TEMPLE and STEVE are crossing the road.

STEVE: (*Alarmed*) Paul, look out!

There is a screeching of brakes.

TEMPLE: (*Laughing*) It's all right, Steve!

STEVE: (*Breathless*) Ye Gods!

TEMPLE: We made it.

FADE traffic noises.

A slight pause.

STEVE: Here we are, Paul … It's rather a nice little
              shop, isn't it?

TEMPLE: Yes. (*Quietly*) Have you got that glove, Steve –
              the one that Mrs Desmond dropped?

STEVE: Yes, it's in my handbag.

TEMPLE: All right. Come on, Steve – let's go inside.

TEMPLE and STEVE enter the shop.

*We hear the sound of the door opening and closing. A bell
tinkles as the door opens and closes.*

FADE traffic to a very distant background.

A moment.

A second door opens.

MARETT: (*Pleasantly*) Good   afternoon,   madame –
              monsieur!

*CHARLES MARETT is a Frenchman: about fifty: he speaks
English but with a distinct accent.*

TEMPLE: Good afternoon …

MARETT: What can I show you, madame?

STEVE: I'm looking for a pair of gloves …

MARETT: Certainly, madame. For evening wear?

STEVE: No, just for …

MARETT: I understand, madame. What size?

STEVE: Six and a half …

TEMPLE: (*Aside*) These are very nice, Steve.

MARETT: They're very smart, monsieur. Tres chic vraiment. They only arrived this morning – they're from Brussels.

STEVE: I don't like the colour, darling. (*To MARETT*) Have you got them in blue?

MARETT: I'm afraid not, madame – in that particular glove there is just the one colour. But one moment, please … (*He pulls out a drawer*) Do you like these?

STEVE: Oh, yes – they're very nice.

MARETT: Expensive – but very good. Try this, madame.

STEVE: (*Pulling on a glove*) It's a little on the tight side …

MARETT: Too tight? Then try this …

A moment.

STEVE: (*Pulling on another glove*) Yes, that's better …

MARETT: Very nice. Looks very smart on you, madame.

TEMPLE: How much are these?

MARETT: Those are … Trois mille sept cents francs … three thousand seven hundred francs, monsieur.

STEVE: That's very expensive.

MARETT: (*Laughing*) Expensive, yes – but very good.

STEVE: (*Suddenly*) Have you got them in blue?

MARETT: Ah, no, madame! There are just the three colours … Black – red – and grey. You particularly want blue?

STEVE: Yes. Yes, I'm afraid I do.

MARETT: Oh. (*Suddenly*) Ah, one moment! Excuse me …

MARETT moves to the rear of the shop.

MARETT: I think I know what you will like, madame.

A slight pause.

TEMPLE: (*Quietly; to Steve*) Have you looked at these gloves – there isn't a tab or a name on any of them.

STEVE: (*Quietly*) Yes, I noticed that.

A moment.

MARETT: (*Returning*) Now, madame …

STEVE: Oh, these are very nice!

MARETT: Tres, tres chic, madame.

STEVE: How much are they?

MARETT: (*Looking at the price tab*) Quatre mille deux cents francs.

STEVE: Four thousand two hundred?

MARETT: Oui, madame. Expensive – but very good.

STEVE: (*After a pause: hesitating*) They're very nice, but, I wanted something a little darker if possible.

MARETT: These are very dark, madame!

TEMPLE: A friend of ours bought a pair of gloves from you – I just forget when she bought them. My wife was awfully taken with them. As a matter of fact that's why we came here.

MARETT: Oh? Well – what were they like, monsieur?

STEVE: They were blue and they had a small band of lace round …

TEMPLE: (*Interrupting STEVE*) Didn't you bring one with you, darling?

STEVE: Why, yes, of course! Of course I did! (*Laughing*) How stupid of me! It's in my handbag. (*She opens her handbag*) Here we are …

TEMPLE: That's the sort of glove we're looking for …

A long pause.

STEVE: Well?

MARETT: (*Slowly; seriously: watching both TEMPLE and STEVE*) I did not realise that you wanted a pair like this, I thought … You'll have to go to

the Boulevard Seminaire ... 29 Boulevard
Seminaire ...

TEMPLE: (*Quietly: facing MARETT*) Is that a shop?

MARETT: No, no, monsieur – it's an apartment ... you go
upstairs to the second floor ... (*A moment*) You
understand me?

TEMPLE: (*Nodding*) Yes, I understand.

MARETT: I would suggest tonight, monsieur, if that is
convenient?

TEMPLE: Yes, that's convenient.

MARETT: Eleven o'clock.

TEMPLE: Eleven o'clock. 29 Boulevard Seminaire.

MARETT: Ask for Mr Palmer ...

STEVE: (*Stunned*) Palmer ...?

Quick, dramatic FADE UP of music.

END OF EPISODE THREE

EPISODE FOUR

BOULEVARD SEMINAIRE

OPEN TO:

MARETT: (*Slowly; seriously: watching both TEMPLE and STEVE*) I did not realise that you wanted a pair like this, I thought … You'll have to go to the Boulevard Seminaire … 29 Boulevard Seminaire …

TEMPLE: (*Quietly: facing MARETT*) Is that a shop?

MARETT: No, no, monsieur – it's an apartment … you go upstairs to the second floor … (*A moment*) You understand me?

TEMPLE: (*Nodding*) Yes, I understand.

MARETT: I would suggest tonight, monsieur, if that is convenient?

TEMPLE: Yes, that's convenient.

MARETT: Eleven o'clock.

TEMPLE: Eleven o'clock. 29 Boulevard Seminaire.

MARETT: Ask for Mr Palmer …

STEVE: (*Stunned*) Palmer …?

MARETT: The name is familiar, madame? Perhaps your friend mentioned it – the lady with the glove?

STEVE: Yes. (*A little laugh*) Yes, I think she must have done.

TEMPLE: Is that Mr Terry Palmer?

The shop door opens and closes, the sound of a bell tinkling as it does so.

MARETT: (*Watching TEMPLE*) Just ask for Mr Palmer – I'm afraid that is all I can tell you. (*Pleasantly*) Will you excuse me, please?

TEMPLE: Yes, of course. (*Quietly*) Come along, darling.

MARETT: (*Pleasantly*) Bonjour, madame! Bonjour, monsieur!

TEMPLE: Bonjour!

The door opens.

MARETT:	(*In the background*) Bonjour madame! Que puis-je vous-montrer ce matin?
LADY:	Que lest le prix de ce sac marron? – Celui de la vitrine avec fermoir argent.
MARETT:	Le marron vaut six mille sept cent cinquante francs.

FADE SCENE.

FADE UP of traffic noises: TEMPLE and STEVE are strolling down the Rue St. Lazare.

STEVE:	(*Puzzled*) Paul, I just don't understand it! The last time we saw Palmer he was on his way to Eastbourne with Mary Desmond.
TEMPLE:	Darling, that's nothing to go by – he could be here in a matter of hours. In any case, I'm not at all sure that our friend was referring to Palmer – not the Palmer that we know at any rate.
STEVE:	Oh, darling, it's too big a coincidence – it must be Terry Palmer.
TEMPLE:	Well, whether it's Terry Palmer or not we've got to watch our step, Steve.
STEVE:	Why do you say that? Aren't you going to keep that appointment?
TEMPLE:	Of course I'm going to keep it, but I'm not so sure about you.
STEVE:	(*Seriously*) What do you mean – you're not so sure about me?
TEMPLE:	This is Paris, darling, remember – not London.
STEVE:	Exactly!
TEMPLE:	And what does that mean?
STEVE:	It means I can't think of a better reason for not letting you out of my sight.

TEMPLE: That's all very well, Steve, but this can be a very tough city. You don't know what we might bump into tonight.

STEVE: Whatever it is – I'm right behind you, Paul! Now cut out the corny heroics, darling, and let's get down to facts. What do you think will happen tonight?

TEMPLE: (*Thoughtfully*) I don't know, Steve. Let's go back to the hotel and talk about it over a drink.

STEVE: Yes, all right.

TEMPLE: Here's a taxi!

A car draws into the kerb.

LUKE: Do you want a cab?

TEMPLE: Yes. Take us to the Hotel Crillon.

LUKE: (*An American: about thirty-seven: pleasantly tough*) O.K. Jump in!

The car door slams.

The taxi accelerates away.

FADE.

FADE UP of the car drawing into the kerb opposite the hotel.

The car door opens and closes.

TEMPLE: How much do you want?

LUKE: It says two hundred francs on the meter – but who cares about the meter anyway?

TEMPLE: (*Amused*) Here we are.

LUKE: Thanks.

TEMPLE: (*Curious*) Are you an American?

LUKE: That's right. Well, don't look so surprised, bud. I'm not the only American in Paris.

STEVE: I'll bet you're the only one driving a cab.

LUKE: You've got something there, lady!

TEMPLE: (*Laughing*) How did this happen?

111

LUKE:	How did <u>what</u> happen? How did I get stuck with this chariot?
TEMPLE:	Yes.
LUKE:	It's a long story, brother. Way back in 44 I received a pressing invitation from a guy called Adolf Hitler. Hitler was a pushover but there was a gal called Louise … (*He whistles*) There was no meter on that baby but she certainly took me for a ride.
TEMPLE:	(*Laughing*) O.K.! Keep the change.
LUKE:	Thanks. (*Suddenly*) Say, how long are you staying over here?
TEMPLE:	Oh – two or three days maybe.
LUKE:	Well, you can always pick me up round the corner. I park near the Madeleine. Like to take you around sometime.
TEMPLE:	Yes, all right. (*A sudden thought*) Oh, by the way – where's the Boulevard Seminaire?
LUKE:	Seminaire? That's near the Place de l' Étoile – quite a step from here.
TEMPLE:	Well, we've got a date there tonight, at eleven o'clock. Do you think you could pick us up?
LUKE:	Sure! I'll be here about 10.45. O.K.?
TEMPLE:	Fine.
LUKE:	(*Brightly*) Be good! (*To himself*) Listen who's talking! The guy with the '57 Citroen …

FADE SCENE.

FADE UP noise of the hotel vestibule.

TEMPLE:	Could I have my key, please? Room 109 …

RECEPTIONIST: Certainly, monsieur! (*Suddenly*) Oh, Mr Temple!

TEMPLE: Yes?

RECEPTIONIST: There's a gentleman would like to see you, sir – he's waiting for you upstairs – Room 604.

TEMPLE: (*Surprised*) To see me?

RECEPTIONIST: Yes, sir. (*Suddenly*) Oh, here is the gentleman ...

STEVE: (*Suddenly*) Paul!

TEMPLE: (*Turning*) What is it, darling?

STEVE: Look who's here! It's Sir Graham!

SIR GRAHAM arrives.

FORBES: Hello, Steve!

STEVE: Hello, Sir Graham! What are you doing in Paris?

FORBES: (*Laughing*) I'll give you three guesses – and don't mention the Folies Bergere! (*Aside: seriously*) I'm in rather a hurry, Temple, I've got a luncheon appointment but I want to have a chat with you. Let's go up to my room.

TEMPLE: Yes, all right, Sir Graham.

FORBES: It'll be quieter up there.

START FADE.

STEVE: When did you get here, Sir Graham?

FORBES: I flew over last night, Steve. I got here about 12.30.

COMPLETE FADE.

FADE UP of TEMPLE.

TEMPLE: ... He said 29 Boulevard Seminaire, ask for Mr Palmer. Whether he was referring to Terry Palmer or not we don't know. We

113

	shall probably know tonight. Well, that's our story up to date. Now what about yours, Sir Graham?
FORBES:	After you left London Shelly came along to the Yard with that note …
STEVE:	The one he was supposed to have received from Miss Millicent?
FORBES:	Yes. Oh, he received it from Miss Millicent all right: we checked the handwriting. As soon as we knew that the note was genuine we got to work on the information, Well, to cut a long story short, Temple, the man that impersonated Digby, the fellow that was murdered, was the man the note mentioned – Harry De Wolfe.
TEMPLE:	I see. Had De Wolfe a police record?
FORBES:	So far as we were concerned – no. But partly because of the receipt we found on him and partly because of a hunch Eden decided to contact the Sûreté. We had a detailed report on De Wolfe within an hour.
TEMPLE:	Go on …
FORBES:	It appears that De Wolfe was at one time a prominent member of a ring trafficking in dangerous drugs. He left France in 1946 and was last heard of officially in Boston, Massachusetts in May '47. Since then both the Sûreté and the F.B.I. appear to have lost track of him.
TEMPLE:	… And then suddenly, quite out of the blue, he turns up at Marlow.
FORBES:	(*Thoughtfully*) Yes.

114

STEVE: Sir Graham, are you suggesting that De Wolfe and Miss Millicent and possibly Shelly are all mixed up in …

FORBES: (*Interrupting STEVE*) I'm not suggesting anything, Steve. I'm simply giving you the facts. I do know that, for some considerable time now, the Sûreté and the Bureau of Narcotics in Washington have been perturbed by the fact that heroin, the most vicious of all the opium derivatives, is getting into the illicit market from a new source. Whether that source is controlled by Shelly or Palmer or even Miss Millicent I wouldn't like to say.

STEVE: But you're convinced that, in some way or other, the disappearance of Miss Millicent and the kidnapping of the Desmond baby are tied up with the murder of De Wolfe.

FORBES: Yes, I am.

TEMPLE: I agree, Sir Graham.

STEVE: Well, tell me: did you examine that note, the note that Miss Millicent sent to Shelly?

TEMPLE: (*Amused*) Of course they examined it, Steve! What are you getting at?

FORBES: There's nothing we can't tell you about that note, Steve. We can tell you what sort of paper it was written on, the kind of ink that was used, we even know the make and model of the pen it was written with …

STEVE: Can you tell when it was written?

FORBES: Yes – it was written about twenty-four hours before Shelly received it.

STEVE: So, unless something's happened to Miss Millicent during the past day or so, she's still alive?

FORBES:	Yes.
TEMPLE:	You seem surprised, Steve?
STEVE:	I am surprised! I've had a funny sort of feeling about Miss Millicent, a sort of intuition.
TEMPLE:	Oh, darling, not that good old intuition!
STEVE:	You can laugh, Paul, but – I don't think she did write that note, I don't think she is alive …
TEMPLE:	Well, look – supposing Miss Millicent isn't alive: supposing someone did forge that note …
STEVE:	Shelly himself for instance …
TEMPLE:	All right, Shelly himself. What's the point?
STEVE:	What's the point if the note wasn't forged and Miss Millicent did write it? Why should she want to warn Shelly, and what exactly is she warning him against?
TEMPLE:	It's pretty obvious isn't it, darling? You saw what happened to Queenie Edwards, you saw what happened to De Wolfe.
FORBES:	In other words the note simply said – "Keep your mouth shut, Mr Shelly, or it's your turn next."
TEMPLE:	Precisely, Sir Graham.
STEVE:	Well, look, darling – you take the suspects in this affair. Terry Palmer, Roger Shelly, Mary Desmond, Bill McCall, and that man you went to see in Park Lane …
TEMPLE:	Philip Droste.
STEVE:	Yes, Droste. Can you imagine any of those people taking orders from a middle-aged spinster like Miss Millicent? It just doesn't make sense!
FORBES:	Well, what's your opinion of all this, Steve?
STEVE:	I'll tell you, Sir Graham. I think you're right about De Wolfe being mixed up with the

	disappearance of Miss Millicent: I think that in all probability Miss Millicent got caught up, quite innocently, with a drug smuggling ring and they had either to get rid of her – which in my opinion they did – or kidnap her.
TEMPLE:	And Mr Vandyke – how does he fit into the picture?
STEVE:	Vandyke is the leader and the leader, in my opinion, is our effeminate friend Roger Shelly.
TEMPLE:	(*Smiling*) Well, it's a point of view, darling. And how do you account for the disappearance of the doll and the fact that it was left in the attaché case at the Commodore Club? And how did Queenie Edwards know that it was at the Commodre Club and why, incidentally, did she send me the cloakroom ticket?
STEVE:	(*Thoughtfully; puzzled*) I – I don't know why, darling.
FORBES:	You're not the only one who doesn't know, Steve! (*Rising*) Well, I suppose I'd better be making a move.
STEVE:	Why don't you join us for lunch, Sir Graham?
FORBES:	Unfortunately I can't. I'm lunching with Pierre Charbonnel.
TEMPLE:	Charbonnel? That name's familiar. Isn't he the ballistics expert?
FORBES:	He was. He's now attached to the Sûreté Nationale: Charbonnel's an old friend of mine – we've known one another for years.
TEMPLE:	I suppose you'll have to tell him what happened this morning?
FORBES:	I'm afraid so, Temple. But don't worry, Charbonnel won't interfere, he'll let you play it your own way. Incidentally, the French people

did check on that shop you know: apparently Marett's been in the Rue St. Lazare for some time. The police have got nothing on him.

There is a knock and the bedroom door opens.

FORBES: Yes – what is it?

RECEPTIONIST: Pardon, monsieur, but this cable has just arrived for you.

FORBES: Oh, thank you!

RECEPTIONIST: Merci, monsieur.

The door closes.

FORBES: (*To TEMPLE and STEVE: opening the telegram*) Excuse me ...

A pause.

TEMPLE: What is it?

FORBES: It's from the Yard – it's in code.

A second pause.

STEVE: What's the matter, Sir Graham?

FORBES: (*Softly: amazed*) Good God!

TEMPLE: Sir Graham, what is it? What's happened?

FORBES: They've found Miss Millicent: they picked her body out of the Thames at four o'clock this morning.

TEMPLE: (*Quickly*) Where?

FORBES: About two miles from Marlow.

TEMPLE: (*Tensely*) How long had she been dead – do they know?

FORBES: (*Slowly*) Yes. (*A moment*) At least a week ...

TEMPLE: Then Steve was right – she couldn't have sent that note to Roger Shelly!

FADE UP of music.

FADE DOWN of music.
FADE UP of background chatter in a restaurant.
FADE chatter slightly.

TEMPLE: Would you like some more coffee, Steve?

STEVE: No, thank you, darling. What time is it?

TEMPLE: It's nearly a quarter past two. What do you want to do this afternoon?

STEVE: I don't know, darling. I've got some shopping I ought to do but somehow I don't feel very much like doing it.

TEMPLE: You'd better leave it over till tomorrow. I think the best thing we can do is go back to the hotel and have a rest for an hour or so.

STEVE: Yes, all right. (*A moment*) Paul …

TEMPLE: M'm?

STEVE: Are you worried about tonight?

TEMPLE: No, I'm not worried about tonight, darling, but – you know, Steve, there's something about this case I don't understand.

STEVE: There's a great deal I don't understand!

TEMPLE: I don't quite see how Mary Desmond fits into the picture. You see, although her baby disappeared the night that Miss Millicent vanished it … (*He stops*)

STEVE: (*Surprised*) What is it?

TEMPLE: (*Softly*) Well, by Timothy!

STEVE: Paul, what is it?

TEMPLE: Look who's here!

STEVE: Bill McCall!

TEMPLE: It's not only McCall, darling! Look who he's with!

STEVE: Who is that man?

TEMPLE: That's Philip Droste of all people! (*Quietly*) They've spotted us, Steve – they're coming over here.

PHILIP DROSTE and BILL McCALL arrive at the table.

119

DROSTE: (*Pleasantly*) Why, hello, Mr Temple! My dear old chap, this is an unexpected pleasure!

TEMPLE: Hello, Droste! I didn't expect to see you in Paris.

DROSTE: (*Laughing*) It only goes to show – it's a small world, old man! (*Suddenly*) Oh, forgive me if I'm interrupting a tete-a-tete.

TEMPLE: No, no, this is my <u>wife</u>. Darling, this is Mr Droste. I think you know Mr McCall.

STEVE: Yes, of course. We met at Marlow.

McCALL: Hello, there!

STEVE: Hello!

DROSTE: Delighted to meet you, Mrs Temple! What a pleasant surprise! Are you staying in Paris for long?

STEVE: Just two or three days.

McCALL: Where are you staying, Temple?

TEMPLE: We're at The Crillon. And you?

McCALL: We only arrived this morning: had a pretty rough trip. Gee, I don't know about you, Mr Droste, but I can still feel things moving around.

DROSTE: (*Faintly irritated by McCALL*) You want something to eat, my friend – that's your trouble. I told you: never start a journey on an empty stomach!

TEMPLE: Is Mrs Droste with you?

DROSTE: (*After a momentary hesitation*) No. No, this is purely a business trip, old man. (*With sarcasm*) McCall's been having a little trouble with our wine merchant or rather with the shippers. I thought it was about time I came over here and straightened things out.

TEMPLE: The iron hand in the velvet glove!

DROSTE: Yes. Yes, we ought to have had it a long time ago. (*Suddenly*) Well, if you'll excuse us. Goodbye, Mrs Temple. I hope we shall meet again sometime. You must tell your husband to bring you along to the flat one evening. I'm sure Vanessa – my wife – would be very pleased to meet you.

STEVE: Thank you.

TEMPLE: How is Mrs Droste – did she recover from her journey?

DROSTE: (*Quickly: almost effusive*) Oh, yes. Yes, she's much better now, thank you. Much better.

McCALL: Have a good time!

TEMPLE: Thanks.

DROSTE: Goodbye, Mrs Temple. So nice to have met you.

STEVE: Goodbye.

TEMPLE: Goodbye, Droste.

DROSTE: Goodbye, old man.

A pause.

STEVE: (*Slowly: quietly*) I wouldn't trust that man an inch.

TEMPLE: Droste?

STEVE: Yes. (*Watching DROSTE and McCALL*) I wouldn't trust him as far as I could throw him …

TEMPLE starts to laugh.

STEVE: Why are you laughing?

TEMPLE: (*Highly amused*) Oh – nothing.

STEVE: Darling, why are you laughing?

TEMPLE: (*Still greatly amused*) Oh – nothing, Steve. Nothing …

TEMPLE continues to laugh.

STEVE: Paul, why are you laughing?!

TEMPLE:	I'm laughing at what you said.
STEVE:	(*Puzzled*) About Droste?
TEMPLE:	Yes.
STEVE:	About not trusting him?
TEMPLE:	(*Laughing*) Yes, darling.
STEVE:	Well, it wasn't that funny!
TEMPLE:	Wasn't it, dear? I think it was. I think it was very funny. Come on, Steve! Let's go back to the hotel.

TEMPLE continues to laugh.
FADE laughter.
FADE SCENE.

FADE UP noises of the hotel vestibule.

TEMPLE:	Could I have my key, please?
RECEPTIONIST:	Certainly, monsieur! Oh, there's a note for you, Mr Temple. It's from your friend – the gentleman in 604.
TEMPLE:	Oh, thank you.

A pause.
TEMPLE opens the note.

STEVE:	What is it, Paul?
TEMPLE:	It's from Sir Graham. He wants us to meet him for a drink at six o'clock. (*Faintly annoyed*) T't, that's rather a nuisance.
STEVE:	Why?
TEMPLE:	You see what the note says: "Charbonnel would like to have a chat with you." I know what that means. Sir Graham's told Charbonnel about our appointment tonight and ten to one the old boy wants to interfere. He'll probably surround the district with gendarmes.
STEVE:	That might not be a bad idea.

TEMPLE: Yes, but that's exactly what I didn't want, Steve. Still – I suppose there's nothing we can do about it.

STEVE: Where are we meeting them – here?

TEMPLE: No, it says the Café Benoit. Now where the devil's that? (*Raising his voice*) Excuse me.

RECEPTIONIST: Monsieur?

TEMPLE: Do you know the Café Benoit?

RECEPTIONIST: Why, yes, monsieur. It's on the corner of the Rue Pigalle and the Rue Fontaine. You can't mistake it, monsieur, it's right on the corner.

TEMPLE: Thank you.

RECEPTIONIST: Merci, monsieur.

TEMPLE: Come along, darling. Let's go up to the room.

FADE SCENE.

Slow FADE UP of traffic noises.
Hold traffic noises.
TEMPLE and STEVE are approaching the Café Benoit.

TEMPLE: There's the café, Steve – over on the corner.

STEVE: It doesn't say Café Benoit, it says … Oh, yes, it does!

TEMPLE: (*Laughing at STEVE*) You look fagged out!

STEVE: You don't look as fresh as a daisy yourself.

TEMPLE: We should have taken a taxi.

STEVE: Or a helicopter! We shall never cross that road!

TEMPLE: Yes, we shall. Wait a minute!

Whistles blow: the traffic skids to a standstill.

STEVE: What's happened?

TEMPLE: Come on, Steve! Be quick … Now's our chance! Be quick, darling!

TEMPLE and STEVE race across the road.

More sounds of police whistles: the traffic starts again.

STEVE: Phew!

TEMPLE: (*Laughing*) Are you all right, Steve?

STEVE: I shall be when I get my breath back.

TEMPLE: Come on, darling, we're late. It's nearly a quarter past six.

FADE DOWN of traffic noises.

FADE UP of the general chatter of an open-air café.

STEVE: I don't see any sign of Sir Graham.

TEMPLE: (*Looking around*) No, neither do I. You sit down, Steve. I'll have a look inside.

STEVE: Yes, all right.

FADE UP of café noises.

WAITER: Que desirez vous, madame?

STEVE: Oh! Un Dubonnet et un Cinzano!

WAITER: Merci, madame.

A moment.

LOUIS: (*In the background: calling with a distinct accent*) Papers … Daily papers … London papers … (*He arrives at STEVE's table*) Papers?

STEVE: No, thank you.

LOUIS: London papers, all the latest news …

STEVE: No, thank you …

LOUIS: Evening News. Star. Standard?

STEVE: No, thank you.

LOUIS: Postcards? You like to buy some pretty postcards? Tower Eiffel …

STEVE: I've seen the Tower Eiffel, thank you very much.

LOUIS: London papers. Evening News. Star. Standard.

STEVE: Oh, all right! Here we are …

LOUIS: Merci … Ou ést le garçon?

STEVE: Il est dans la salle.

LOUIS: Je vais laisser mes journaux sur la table â coté. Dites-lui que je seral de retour dans un moment.

Slight pause.

TEMPLE returns.

TEMPLE: What did that fellow want?

STEVE: He was selling papers – and pretty postcards.

TEMPLE: He seems to have dumped the papers on the next table.

STEVE: Yes, he'll be back in a moment. (*Laughing*) You do meet some crazy people over here. Did you see Sir Graham?

TEMPLE: No, they're not inside.

STEVE: They obviously haven't arrived yet. I've ordered you a Dubonnet.

TEMPLE: Oh, thanks.

TEMPLE sits down.

STEVE: I like this café, Paul, don't you?

TEMPLE: It's certainly attractive … Bit too near the kerb for my liking.

STEVE: I adore these open-air cafés.

A tiny pause.

STEVE: Paul …

TEMPLE: M'm?

STEVE: I've been thinking about tonight, darling. About the appointment at the Boulevard Seminaire.

TEMPLE: Yes?

STEVE:	If this friend of Sir Graham's ...
TEMPLE:	Charbonnel?
STEVE:	Yes, Charbonnel. If he wants to arrange for ... (*She stops speaking*)
TEMPLE:	What is it?
STEVE:	(*Quietly*) She'll know you again, won't she?
TEMPLE:	Who?
STEVE:	That woman over there – in the corner. She hasn't taken her eyes off you.
TEMPLE:	It's only natural. You don't see many good looking men in Paris.
STEVE:	It looks to me as if she knows you. (*Suddenly*) She's turning away ...
TEMPLE:	(*Curious*) Which woman do you mean, Steve?
STEVE:	The one in the red dress.
TEMPLE:	Where? (*Suddenly; surprised*) Oh!
STEVE:	What's the matter?
TEMPLE:	By Timothy, she does know me!
STEVE:	(*Surprised*) Hello – what's been going on here?
TEMPLE:	Steve, do you know who it is?
STEVE:	No, but she's a good looker! Think fast, Mr Temple!
TEMPLE:	It's Mrs Droste.
STEVE:	(*Seriously; surprised*) What?! Are you sure?
TEMPLE:	Yes. Yes, I'm pretty sure.
STEVE:	(*Quickly*) But Droste said she wasn't in Paris, he said that ...
TEMPLE:	Yes, I know what Droste said all right! But that's his wife or by Timothy I'm ... (*He rises*)
STEVE:	Paul, what are you going to do?
TEMPLE:	(*Suddenly*) Wait here, Steve!

TEMPLE leaves the table and crosses to VANESSA DROSTE.

TEMPLE:	(*Pleasantly*) Hello, Mrs Droste! This is a pleasant surprise!

126

VANESSA: (*Tense: faintly on edge*) I – I beg your pardon?

TEMPLE: (*Smiling*) I saw you looking at me. I couldn't place you at first. It is Mrs Droste, isn't it? (*A pause*) I'm Paul Temple, don't you remember?

VANESSA: Oh, yes. Yes, now I remember. I knew I'd seen you somewhere before.

TEMPLE: Are you alone?

VANESSA: (*Hesitating*) I'm – expecting someone.

TEMPLE: Well, look here – I've got my wife with me. She's over there. I'd rather like you to meet her. Why don't you join us until your friend turns up?

VANESSA: I'd rather not if you don't mind. Please don't think me rude, Mr Temple, but …

TEMPLE: (*Slowly; watching VANESSA*) Mrs Droste, I saw your husband this morning.

VANESSA: (*Surprised and almost a little frightened*) Where?

TEMPLE: In a restaurant: we were having lunch and he came in with Mr McCall.

VANESSA: (*Incredulously*) You mean … you saw him here … in Paris?

TEMPLE: (*Still watching VANESSA*) Yes.

VANESSA: I don't believe you … You couldn't have seen him. Why it's impossible … You're joking … (*With a nervous little laugh*) It's just a joke – isn't it?

TEMPLE: No, I saw him. I spoke to him. He told me that he was over here on business.

VANESSA: (*Tensely*) But my husband's not in Paris. I'm sure he's not unless … (*She hesitates*)

TEMPLE: (*Quietly: taking VANESSA by the arm*) Come along, Mrs Droste. Come and have a drink with us …

FADE.

FADE UP of TEMPLE.

TEMPLE: Steve, this is Mrs Droste.

STEVE: How do you do, Mrs Droste? Do sit down.

VANESSA: Thank you.

TEMPLE: I was just telling Mrs Droste, darling, we saw
            her husband this morning with Bill McCall.

STEVE: Yes, they came into the restaurant while we
            were having lunch.

TEMPLE: How long has McCall worked for your
            husband?

VANESSA: Oh – quite a little while now.

STEVE: We met him down at Marlow four or five days
            ago. He seems a very amiable sort of person.

VANESSA: Yes, I think he is.

TEMPLE: What would you like to drink?

VANESSA: May I have a Dubonnet?

TEMPLE: Yes, of course. (*Calling*) Garçon!

WAITER: J'arrive, monsieur.

VANESSA: (*Hesitating*) Mr Temple …

TEMPLE: Yes?

VANESSA: I wonder if you'd do me a favour?

TEMPLE: Well – what is it?

VANESSA: If by any chance, you see my husband again –
            in Paris, I mean – please don't mention that you
            bumped into me. (*Hesitating*) You see …

TEMPLE: Go on, Mrs Droste.

VANESSA: I think perhaps I'd better be perfectly frank
            with you about this. I've got a friend here – in
            Paris. We've been seeing rather a lot of each
            other just recently and my husband …

STEVE: A boyfriend?

VANESSA: (*Hesitating*) Yes. Oh! I don't want to tire you with a lot of personal details but – well – just recently Philip and I haven't been hitting it off too well. We've been getting on one another's nerves so much that I suggested – two or three days ago – that we separated for a little while.

TEMPLE: I see. (*Suddenly*) This boy friend of yours, Mrs Droste – what's his name?

VANESSA: I'm – I'm sorry. I'd rather not tell you if you don't mind.

TEMPLE: It isn't Marett, by any chance? Charles Marett?

VANESSA: Why, me …

TEMPLE: (*Smiling*) Well, don't look so surprised! You know Marett. He owns the shop in the Rue St. Lazare. The little place where you bought your gloves.

VANESSA: (*Tensely*) I've never heard of anyone called Marett. I – I don't know what you're talking about.

TEMPLE: (*Pleasantly*) Oh, come now, Mrs Droste! You know perfectly well what I'm …

WAITER: (*At the table*) Dubonnet! Cinzano!

TEMPLE: Oh, thank you. Now bring another Dubonnet, please.

WAITER: Another Dubonnet? Certainly, monsieur. (*Suddenly: surprised*) Are those your papers?

TEMPLE: Why, no, of course they're not!

WAITER: Well – who put them there?

STEVE: A man left them – he said he'd be back in a few moments.

WAITER: (*Laughing*) But he can't leave his newspapers like that – on one of our tables!

TEMPLE: (*Amused*) What do you mean, he can't? He has. It's nothing to do with us, old boy.

129

WAITER: I'll take them inside.

TEMPLE: (*Suddenly; seriously*) Just a moment! (*To STEVE*) Did he just put them down here, Steve – on the table?

STEVE: Yes. You saw him, Paul. It was the man I told you about. The man with the postcards.

TEMPLE: But it's very odd that he should leave a bunch of newspapers … (*Suddenly*) No, don't touch them!

WAITER: I'll take them inside.

TEMPLE: Don't touch them!

WAITER: (*Protesting: moving the papers*) We shall need the table, monsieur.

TEMPLE: (*Suddenly: desperately*) Steve, get down! Get down on the floor, darling!!!

TEMPLE pulls STEVE down.

STEVE: What on earth …

TEMPLE: Do as I tell you!

STEVE: Paul, my arm!

TEMPLE: Do as I tell you, get down!

STEVE: Paul, for goodness sake …

TEMPLE: (*Quickly: desperately*) Get down, Mrs Droste! Get down!!!

As TEMPLE speaks there is a tremendous explosion followed by the shattering of glass, the scattering of tables, and a sudden babble of wildly excited voices.

A woman screams: a wild hysterical scream.

FADE UP of noise and excited voices.

FADE UP of VANESSA groaning: she is obviously in great pain.

STEVE: Paul! Paul, look at Mrs Droste!

TEMPLE: (*Tensely*) Steve, are you all right?

STEVE: Yes, but look at Mrs Droste! Oh, Paul, look!

TEMPLE: Get hold of her head! Quickly, darling!

130

STEVE: Give me your handkerchief!
FADE UP of VANESSA groaning.
TEMPLE: She's in a pretty bad way, Steve.
STEVE: (*Excited: overwrought*) I think that man's a
            doctor …
TEMPLE: Where?
STEVE: That man over there … (*Calling*) S'il vous
            plait, voulex vous venir, c'est tres urgent.
TEMPLE: He's coming …
STEVE: (*Puzzled*) Paul, what happened? Were the
            papers placed there deliberately?
TEMPLE: (*Quietly*) Yes, there was a catch-bomb
            underneath – the moment the papers were
            moved the bomb exploded. Ah, here's the
            doctor! (*To the DOCTOR*) Voulex-vous
            examiner cette dame – j'ai peur qu'elle soir
            gravement blesse.
*FADE UP of noises: excited voices: the sound of police
whistles and the sound of approaching ambulances.*
FADE UP of music.

Slow FADE DOWN of music.
A moment.
STEVE: What time is it?
TEMPLE: It's time we were making a move, Steve. I
            expect our American friend's waiting for us.
STEVE: Don't let's go, darling. Not until we've heard
            from Sir Graham.
TEMPLE: Well, he promised to phone through at nine
            o'clock, it's now a quarter to ten. Look here,
            Steve, why don't you stay here – in the hotel –
            tonight?

131

STEVE: (*Interrupting TEMPLE*) No, Paul, please! Don't go into that again. No matter what you say, darling, I'm coming with you.

TEMPLE: All right, Steve. Have it your own way.

STEVE: (*A moment*) Paul …

TEMPLE: Yes?

STEVE: (*Thoughtfully*) You know, I'm sure I'd recognise that man again – the man that planted the bomb.

TEMPLE: You'd probably recognise him if you saw him looking exactly the same, but would you recognise him if he was washed and shaved and all spruced up? That's the point.

STEVE: (*Thoughtfully*) Yes …

TEMPLE: Well?

STEVE: I can't imagine him all spruced up, he was such a disreputable individual.

TEMPLE: Was he a Frenchman?

STEVE: No, I don't think he was. He spoke English with an accent. A very attractive accent, but it seemed to me German or possibly Swiss.

TEMPLE: M'm. You know, Steve, we're up against a pretty tough bunch. Have you stopped to think what really happened this evening? Someone sent us a note – which was supposed to be from Sir Graham – and made a date for us at the Café Benoit. Now it's my bet that whoever sent that note also sent one to Mrs Droste.

STEVE: In other words they intended to kill three birds with one stone?

TEMPLE: Exactly. Now if we can find out from Mrs Droste who precisely she expected to see at the café then obviously …

The telephone starts to ring.

STEVE: It's the phone!

TEMPLE: It's all right. I'll take it. (*He lifts the receiver*)
           Hello?

FORBES: (*On the other end of the line*) Is that you,
           Temple?

TEMPLE: Oh, hello, Sir Graham! Where are you?

FORBES: We're still at the hospital. I'm sorry I'm late
           phoning but things have been pretty hectic.

TEMPLE: How's Mrs Droste?

FORBES: She's in a bad way, I'm afraid.

TEMPLE: Is she still unconscious?

FORBES: Yes. They don't seem to think there's much
           hope, but we're holding on just in case.

TEMPLE: What about Droste? Have you found him yet?

FORBES: No. Goodness knows where he's staying!
           We've contacted all the big hotels and most of
           the travel agencies. (*Urgently*) We've got to
           find him, Temple!

TEMPLE: Well, look here, Sir Graham! There's two
           hotels near the restaurant – the place where we
           had lunch. One's called Hotel Voltaire …

FORBES: We've tried the Voltaire.

TEMPLE: And I believe the other one's called La Corrida:
           it's a small place on the Rue Perronet.

FORBES: I don't think they've tried that one. I'll get onto
           that myself straight away.

TEMPLE: When shall we see you?

FORBES: It depends entirely on Mrs Droste – if she is
           going to regain consciousness I want to be here
           when it happens.

TEMPLE: Yes, of course.

FORBES: How's Steve?

TEMPLE: Obstinate – but apart from that all right.

FORBES: (*Smiling*) Well, take care of yourselves.

TEMPLE: We'll try. Goodbye, Sir Graham!
TEMPLE replaces the receiver.
STEVE: What was that crack about being obstinate?
            You weren't referring to me by any chance?
TEMPLE: (*Casual*) Good heavens, no, darling.
STEVE: Well, you weren't talking about the weather!
TEMPLE: Come on, Steve – let's go down. We're terribly
            late.
FADE SCENE.

FADE UP of traffic noises.
It is nearly ten o'clock and there is very little traffic in the
Place de la Concorde.
LUKE: Hello, there!
TEMPLE: I hope we haven't kept you waiting.
LUKE: No, no, that's o.k.
TEMPLE: Jump in, Steve.
STEVE enters the cab.
LUKE: Where do you want to go?
TEMPLE: Boulevard Seminaire.
LUKE: Oh, yeah, sure. Boulevard Seminaire. (*He puts*
            down the flag) Any idea what number?
TEMPLE: 29.
LUKE: (*Sprightly*) 29 Boulevard Seminaire! O.K., bud.
            Jump in !
The car engine starts.
LUKE sounds the car horn.
FADE UP of the car moving away from the kerb.
FADE.

Slow FADE UP of the cab slowly drawing to a standstill.
The car door opens: TEMPLE and STEVE are getting out of
the cab.
LUKE: Here we are – this is it!

STEVE:	It's a nice looking block, darling!
TEMPLE:	Yes.
LUKE:	Cost you a lot of dough to live in a place like this.
TEMPLE:	How much do you want?
LUKE:	How much have you got?
TEMPLE:	(*Laughing*) Look here, would you like to wait for us? I don't expect we shall be very long.
LUKE:	Sure.
TEMPLE:	We're going up to the second floor. If we're not down in twenty minutes come up and fetch us.
LUKE:	O.K. I'll do that. (*Suddenly*) Oh, Mrs Temple!
STEVE:	(*Turning*) Yes?
LUKE:	You've left your handbag.
STEVE:	Oh, thank you.
TEMPLE:	It's all right, I'll get it. (*He opens the door and picks up the handbag from off the seat*) Here we are, Steve.
STEVE:	Thanks.
TEMPLE:	(*To LUKE*) By the way – how did you know the name?
LUKE:	Haven't you seen the evening paper?
TEMPLE:	No.
LUKE:	You should take a look at it.
TEMPLE:	What do you mean?
LUKE:	There's a photograph of you both on the front page.
TEMPLE:	Oh.
LUKE:	It was taken outside of the Café Benoit – or what's left of the Café Benoit.
TEMPLE:	(*Grimly*) Yes.
LUKE:	That must have been a very nasty 'accident'.
TEMPLE:	Except that it wasn't an accident.

LUKE: (*Pulling TEMPLE's leg*) No? You surprise me
             … Twenty minutes?
START FADE.
TEMPLE: (*Laughing*) That's right. The second floor …
LUKE: O.K.
FADE.

FADE UP of a lift: it stops: its gates opening and closing.
A tiny pause.
STEVE: Is this it, Paul?
TEMPLE: I suppose it must be. There doesn't appear to be
             another door.
STEVE: There's no name on the door.
TEMPLE: No. Is there a bell?
STEVE: If there is I don't see it.
TEMPLE knocks on the door.
A pause.
TEMPLE knocks again.
TEMPLE: There doesn't appear to be anyone in.
STEVE: Try again, darling.
TEMPLE knocks again.
TEMPLE: (*Thoughtfully*) No …
STEVE: Is it locked?
TEMPLE: (*Trying the door*) Yes. (*Suddenly*) Wait a
             minute!
From inside the flat we hear a telephone ringing.
STEVE: What is it?
TEMPLE: The phone's ringing.
A long pause.
The telephone continues to ring.
STEVE: There's obviously no one in.
TEMPLE: Yes.
The telephone stops ringing.
STEVE: What are we going to do?

136

TEMPLE: I'm going to try my keys.

STEVE: What do you mean – try and open the door?

TEMPLE: Yes.

STEVE: Paul, you can't do that!

TEMPLE: Why can't I?

STEVE: Well, supposing someone comes along the corridor?

TEMPLE: We'll have to take that chance. You stand on guard. Stand over there, Steve, near the lift. If you see anyone whistle Rule Britannia.

STEVE: (*Amused*) I'd sooner make it C'est Si Bon.

TEMPLE: I don't know C'est Si Bon.

TEMPLE tries to open the door.

STEVE: (*Softly; calling from the background*) How's it going?

TEMPLE: Not so good! (*A pause*) Steve, here a minute …

STEVE crosses to TEMPLE.

TEMPLE: Darling, hold the handle …

STEVE: What for?

TEMPLE: (*Trying to force the key*) Do … as … I … tell you …

A pause.

STEVE: Won't it work?

TEMPLE: (*Straining on the key*) Well – this usually does the trick, but it looks to me as if … Ah, that's done it!

The door opens.

TEMPLE: Good …

STEVE: (*Quietly*) Shall I close the door?

TEMPLE: Yes, but don't latch it.

They enter the flat.

A moment's pause.

STEVE: Where's the light?

TEMPLE: It's all right, I've got it.

The light clicks on.

STEVE: It's a lovely flat, darling.

TEMPLE: By Timothy, yes! It certainly cost a pretty penny to furnish this place.

STEVE: What a heavenly fireplace!

TEMPLE: Yes.

STEVE: Is that a Dufy?

TEMPLE: Where?

STEVE: Over the piano.

TEMPLE: (*Staring at the picture*) Yes, it looks very much like it.

A moment.

STEVE: I wonder where that door leads to?

TEMPLE: (*Quietly*) It's probably one of the bedrooms. Stay here a moment, Steve.

STEVE: Yes, all right.

A door opens.

TEMPLE goes into the bedroom.

A pause.

STEVE: (*Calling*) Paul, are you all right?

TEMPLE: (*From the bedroom: tense*) Yes.

STEVE: Shall I come in?

TEMPLE: (*Quickly: from the bedroom*) No! No, don't come in here, Steve. Stay where you are!

STEVE: (*Tensely*) Why? What is it? Paul, what's happened? (*Moving towards the bedroom door*) What is it?

TEMPLE returns from the bedroom.

TEMPLE: (*Quietly: very serious*) Steve, listen. I want you to go down to the cab and tell our American friend that …

STEVE: (*Interrupting TEMPLE: tensely*) Paul, what is it? What's happened?

TEMPLE: Darling, listen to what I'm saying! I want you to go down to the …

STEVE: (*Tensely*) Paul, what is it? Darling, please, what's happened?

A moment.

TEMPLE: It's the man we saw this morning, the man in the glove shop. Charles Marett …

STEVE: Well?

A moment.

TEMPLE: (*Softly*) He's been murdered. He looks exactly the same as Queenie Edwards, his face … has … been … slashed … with a razor …

STEVE: (*Horrified*) Oh …

TEMPLE: (*Almost to himself*) My God, he looks awful …

A tiny pause.

STEVE: (*Tensely: very softly*) Paul, there's some blood on your sleeve …

TEMPLE: Yes. Yes, I know. (*A pause, then suddenly pulling himself together*) Steve, now listen! Do as I tell you. I want you to go downstairs –

The telephone starts to ring.

TEMPLE: – and ask our American friend if he'll (*He stops speaking*)

A pause.

The telephone continues ringing.

STEVE: What are you going to do – let it ring?

A long pause.

The telephone continues.

STEVE: (*Tensely*) Paul, what are you going to do?

TEMPLE: Wait a minute … (*After a slight pause he lifts the receiver: on the phone*) Hello?

OPERATOR: Passy Quarante-sept treize?

TEMPLE: I – I beg your pardon?

OPERATOR: Etes vous Anglais, monsieur?

TEMPLE: Yes …
OPERATOR: I said: Are you Passy – 47-13?
TEMPLE: Passy … Just a moment! (*He looks for the number*) Yes. Yes, that's right. Passy 47-13.
OPERATOR: One moment, if you please.
STEVE: (*Tensely*) Who is it?
TEMPLE: I don't know, darling!
OPERATOR: Hold the line, please …
STEVE: Paul, who is it?
TEMPLE: Sh!
OPERATOR: There is a call for you from London – a personal call. Hold the line a moment, please.

A pause.

TEMPLE: Hello?
OPERATOR: Hello … Passy 47-13?
TEMPLE: Yes …
OPERATOR: Hold on a moment.

We hear the sound of distant voices on the exchange.

OPERATOR: Vous etes en ligne. Parlez plus fort s'il vous plait.
TEMPLE: Hello?
OPERATOR: Could a Mr Paul Temple take a personal call from London, please?
TEMPLE: (*Staggered*) What!
STEVE: (*Quickly*) Paul, what is it?
TEMPLE: (*Bewildered*) But that's impossible. No one knows I'm here, why …
OPERATOR: (*Emphatically: faintly irritated*) Avez vous entendi ce que j'ai dit? Can a Mr Paul Temple take a personal call from London, please?
TEMPLE: (*Quickly*) Yes. Yes, speaking.
OPERATOR: Is that Mr Temple speaking personally?
TEMPLE: Yes. (*Tense*) Yes – who is it? Who is it calling?
OPERATOR: It's a Mr Vandyke. One moment, please!

FADE UP of music.

END OF EPISODE FOUR

EPISODE FIVE

ROGER SHELLY MAKES
A SUGGESTION

OPEN TO:

OPERATOR: Hold on a moment.

We hear the sound of distant voices on the exchange.

OPERATOR: Vous etes en ligne. Parlez plus fort s'il vous
plait.

TEMPLE: Hello?

OPERATOR: Could a Mr Paul Temple take a personal call
from London, please?

TEMPLE: (*Staggered*) What!

STEVE: (*Quickly*) Paul, what is it?

TEMPLE: (*Bewildered*) But that's impossible. No one
knows I'm here, why …

OPERATOR: (*Emphatically: faintly irritated*) Avez vous
entendi ce que j'ai dit? Can a Mr Paul Temple
take a personal call from London, please?

TEMPLE: (*Quickly*) Yes. Yes, speaking.

OPERATOR: Is that Mr Temple speaking personally?

TEMPLE: Yes. (*Tense*) Yes – who is it? Who is it calling?

OPERATOR: It's a Mr Vandyke. One moment, please!

TEMPLE: (*Staggered*) Vandyke!

STEVE: (*Excited and puzzled*) Paul, what's happening?
What is it, darling?

TEMPLE: (*Serious: puzzled*) I don't understand it, Steve.
There's a call from London – it's a personal
call for me from a Mr Vandyke.

STEVE: But that's ridiculous, no one knows we're here
except …

TEMPLE: Sh!

OPERATOR: I'm so sorry to keep you waiting, monsieur!

We hear the sound of voices on the exchange.

OPERATOR: T't – t't – what is happening tonight? Speak up
London please, your party is on the line waiting

... (*Faintly exasperated*) Oh mon dieu! Qu'arrive-t-il se soir?

We hear more voices on the line. They are indistinctive.

OPERATOR: Will you please speak up, your party is waiting for you ... (*To TEMPLE*) Un moment s'il vous plait, monsieur.

STEVE: (*Quietly*) Paul ...

TEMPLE: Wait a second, Steve – (*Listening, intently*) – I think they've cleared the line.

We hear more blurred voices on the line.

STEVE: (*Quietly*) Paul, I don't know whether you've noticed it or not.

TEMPLE: (*Still listening on the phone*) Noticed what, Steve?

STEVE: You're standing right in front of the window.

TEMPLE: I'm what? (*Turning*) What did you say?

STEVE: I said: You're standing right in front of the window, darling. It looks to me as if the phone's been moved.

TEMPLE: (*Suddenly taking stock*) Yes. Yes, I think you're right, Steve ...

STEVE: Surely the phone ought to be over here, on this table?

TEMPLE: Yes. This seems a ridiculous place for the telephone to be placed ...

As TEMPLE speaks there is the sound of a distant shot followed by the splintering of glass as a bullet comes through the window.

TEMPLE gives a sharp cry: he has obviously been hit: he drops to the ground.

STEVE: Paul!!!!

TEMPLE: (*Tensely: in pain*) Keep away from the window, Steve!

146

More shots are heard and a succession of bullets smash through the window during the following dialogue.

STEVE: Paul, you're hurt!

TEMPLE: No, Steve … no … I'm all right …

STEVE: (*Alarmed*) Paul, you're hurt! You can't get up!!!

TEMPLE: Yes, I can, darling … (*In obvious pain*) It's only my arm, I …

STEVE: (*Worried*) Oh, Paul … Paul …

TEMPLE: (*Holding his arm: obviously in great pain*) Steve, keep … away … from … the … window! Keep … away!!!!

FADE UP the sound of more shots.
Dramatic FADE UP of music.

Slow FADE DOWN of music.
A door opens.

STEVE: (*Quickly*) Sir Graham, is he all right?

FORBES: (*Surprised*) Hello, Steve! I thought you'd left the hospital ages ago!

STEVE: Yes, I did go back to the hotel, but – (*Anxiously*) Sir Graham, is he going to be all right?

FORBES: (*Faintly amused*) Who? Temple?

STEVE: Yes.

FORBES: (*Laughing*) You'd better ask him yourself.

STEVE: What do you … (*Suddenly*) Paul!

TEMPLE: (*Laughing*) Look out, darling! Look out! Mind my arm! Mind … (*Amused*) By Timothy, Steve, I must do this more often!

STEVE: Paul, your arm – is it serious?

TEMPLE: No, but it might have been. I was lucky.

FORBES: You certainly were lucky!

TEMPLE: If it hadn't been for Steve I should have had it. Incidentally, Sir Graham, where was our sharp-shooting friend – on the roof opposite?

147

FORBES: Yes, I think he must have been, Temple, but the place was deserted by the time we got there.

TEMPLE: By Timothy, I certainly fell for that trick all right! Imagine it, Sir Graham! There I was holding the telephone and standing right in front of the window! What made you think of the window, Steve?

STEVE: I don't know. Somehow I felt that the phone call must be a trick and – well – I suppose the rest was intuition.

TEMPLE: That good old intuition, eh?

STEVE: Sir Graham, I've been meaning to ask you – did you find out about the flat?

FORBES: Yes. It belongs to Marett.

STEVE: Marett? You mean the man from the glove shop – the man that Paul found in the bedroom?

FORBES: Yes.

STEVE: But it was Marett that sent us to the Boulevard Seminaire. Why should he do that? If he'd got anything to say to us why didn't he say it in the shop?

FORBES: (*Thoughtfully*) Yes …

STEVE: And that telephone call: I know it was a trick to get Paul in front of the window but do you think it was a genuine call from London or …

TEMPLE: No, it was a fake, Steve – a particularly clever one but nevertheless a fake. (*A little too sure of himself to be convincing*) As a matter of fact I had my suspicions about that call from the moment …

STEVE: (*Laughing*) Now come off it! You fell for it, brother! Hook, line and sinker!

TEMPLE: (*Laughing*) All right, darling! All right!

FORBES: When are you going back to London, Temple?

148

TEMPLE: We're flying back tomorrow morning. (*Casually*) I hope you don't mind, Sir Graham, but I've sent Inspector Eden a cable.

FORBES: A cable – what about?

TEMPLE: About that doll. Do you remember – Palmer spoke to me about it? He said the little girl was asking for it.

FORBES: Oh, yes, I remember.

TEMPLE: Well, I've asked Eden to send it round to my flat.

FORBES: Why?

TEMPLE: Well – with your permission – I'd rather like to hand it back to Palmer. It isn't much use at the Yard, is it?

FORBES: I can't see it's much use to Palmer.

TEMPLE: (*Smiling*) Well, it's not intended for Palmer, not exactly – it's for the little girl. (*Changing the subject*) What about Marett, Sir Graham? Have the French people any idea who murdered him?

FORBES: No. They've been over the apartment with a fine tooth comb but I'm afraid they've drawn a blank.

STEVE: Yes, well in my opinion they don't have to look very far!

FORBES: (*Faintly surprised*) What do you mean?

STEVE: Isn't it obvious who murdered Marett?

FORBES: Not to me it isn't!

TEMPLE: Who are you thinking of, darling – Droste?

STEVE: Droste or Bill McCall. It's obvious that Mrs Droste's been having an affair with Marett: Droste discovered this and either murdered Marett himself or paid McCall to do the dirty work.

TEMPLE: M'm. How does that strike you, Sir Graham?

FORBES: Well – it's quite a theory.

TEMPLE: So all you've got to do is pick up Droste.

149

FORBES: We've picked him up: he was staying at a small hotel near the Boulevard Hausmann.

TEMPLE: Oh. Where is he now?

FORBES: So far as I know he's here at the hospital with his wife – unless the police have taken him down to headquarters.

STEVE: How is Mrs Droste, by the way?

FORBES: She's still unconscious. I gather it's a fifty-fifty chance.

The door opens and DR FOY enters. He is a middle-aged Frenchman.

FOY: I beg your pardon, monsieur. Mr Droste would like a word with you before he leaves. He's in my office.

FORBES: Oh, thank you, doctor.

STEVE: Is there any change in Mrs Droste?

FOY: She's still unconscious, but I have a feeling that it won't be long now. It's difficult to say why exactly but I feel a little more hopeful.

STEVE: Oh, good.

FOY: How is your arm, monsieur – comfortable?

TEMPLE: Yes, it's quite comfortable, thank you.

FOY: Remember what I told you and don't forget to change the dressing the moment you get back to London.

STEVE: Don't worry, I shan't forget, doctor – if he does!

FORBES: (*Start FADE on this speech*) Come along, Temple! I expect you'd like to have a word with Droste.

TEMPLE: We shan't be long, Steve.

COMPLETE FADE.

FADE SCENE.

FADE UP.

McCALL: (*Surprised*) That arm of yours doesn't look too good, Temple. Did that happen at the café?

TEMPLE: No, so far as the explosion was concerned Mrs Temple and I were very lucky. I picked this up later in the evening.

McCALL: Where?

TEMPLE: In the Boulevard Seminaire. A gentleman of somewhat doubtful ancestry took a pot at me.

McCALL: What do you mean – someone tried to shoot you?

TEMPLE: That was roughly the idea.

McCALL: I say, things happen to you, don't they? You were nearly shot driving back from Marlow.

TEMPLE: You have an excellent memory, Mr McCall. (*Turning*) I'm awfully sorry about your wife, Droste. I hope she'll be all right.

DROSTE: (*Quietly*) Everyone is being most kind: I'm sure there's nothing else that can be done. I wanted to thank you, Sir Graham, for getting in touch with me.

FORBES: We had to get in touch with you, Mr Droste. There were certain questions the police wanted to ask you.

DROSTE: Yes, I know. I've seen them. I've had a chat with M. Charbonnel.

FORBES: Does that mean you don't want to answer any more questions?

DROSTE: Not – just at the moment, old man. I've had rather a tiring day and, if you don't mind, I'd like to get back to my hotel.

TEMPLE: (*Quietly*) Droste …

DROSTE: Yes?

151

TEMPLE: There are certain things which I think, under the circumstances, you ought to know.

DROSTE: (*Puzzled*) What sort of things? What do you mean?

TEMPLE: Well – for instance – my wife thinks that you are responsible for the murder of a certain M. Marett.

DROSTE: Marett?

TEMPLE: Yes. Charles Marett: he has a glove shop on the Rue St. Lazare and an apartment on the Boulevard Seminaire.

DROSTE: I've – I've never heard of anyone called Marett and, without wishing to be rude my dear chap, it's a matter of complete indifference to me what your wife thinks.

TEMPLE: But supposing the police think the same?

DROSTE: What – that I murdered this fellow – Marett?

TEMPLE: Yes.

DROSTE: But why should they think that?

A moment.

TEMPLE: Why did you come to Paris, Droste – in the first place?

DROSTE: I told you why – on business. I – had to see a wine merchant.

McCALL: You can check it if you like. I expect the police will, anyway. Here's the name of the firm:- Renoir et Pierpont, 25 Rue Championnet …

TEMPLE: Mr Droste, I want you to listen, very carefully, to what I'm saying. When I visited your flat several days ago, your wife dropped a pair of gloves. You may remember that she fainted and I …

DROSTE: Yes, I remember.

TEMPLE: Well, I picked up the gloves for Mrs Droste and on the inside of one of the gloves I noticed a

152

small tab. It said: Charles Marett, 75 Rue St. Lazare, Paris. Now, without going into details, that address had a certain significance: it was not, in fact, the first time that I had heard of M. Marett.

DROSTE: Go on …

TEMPLE: This morning my wife and I visited the shop in the Rue St. Lazare and on producing a certain glove – not unlike the one belonging to Mrs Droste – M. Marett directed us to an address on the Boulevard Seminaire. We were told to ask for a Mr Palmer.

DROSTE: (*Surprised*) Palmer?

TEMPLE: Yes. The name strikes a chord, Mr Droste?

DROSTE: Well – wasn't it a Mr Palmer who was supposed to have left an attaché case at the Commodore Club?

TEMPLE: It was. It was indeed. (*Slowly; watching DROSTE*) You see, I'm being perfectly frank with you about all this?

DROSTE: Go on …

TEMPLE: When we arrived at the flat on the Boulevard Seminaire there was no sign of a Mr Palmer but there was however, in one of the bedrooms, the dead body of Charles Marett. It was not, I assure you, a pretty spectacle.

McCALL: (*Blustering*) So what? Mr Droste's already told you that he's never heard of Marett so …

DROSTE: (*Stopping McCALL*) Wait a moment, McCall! (*To TEMPLE: quite pleasantly*) Forgive me, old man, perhaps I am a little dense, but – the significance of your story escapes me. Why are you telling me this?

153

TEMPLE: Because I want you to know the facts. The police haven't finished with you, Droste, there'll be a lot more questions.

McCALL: Mr Droste's not frightened of the police!

DROSTE: Of course not! Why should I be?

TEMPLE: Well, supposing the police say to you: we believe that your wife was in love with Charles Marett: we believe that you discovered this fact and came to Paris with the intention of murdering both your wife and her lover. We believe that your first attempt was at the Café Benoit and then later – having missed Marett at the café – you made a second, and successful, attempt at his flat.

DROSTE: (*Quietly*) Is that what the police really think?

TEMPLE: It's a possibility, Mr Droste, so you've got to face it.

FORBES: What's your answer to such an accusation?

DROSTE: There's only one possible answer!

FORBES: What's that?

DROSTE: The truth, Sir Graham. (*Suddenly: a shade emotional*) You're quite right, Temple, I didn't come to Paris on business. I came to find my wife and to try and reason with her. For weeks now I've suspected that Vanessa …

McCALL: (*Interrupting DROSTE*) Don't be a fool, Droste! Keep your mouth shut!

DROSTE: It's all right, McCall. I know what I'm saying. Look, Temple, you've been very frank with me tonight and now I'm going to be perfectly honest with you. Yesterday my wife told me that she was in love with Marett and that she wanted a divorce. Before I had time to discuss the matter or even think about it she walked out of the flat. I

154

contacted McCall and we decided to come to Paris and – well – try and persuade Vanessa to change her mind.

FORBES: Is that true, McCall?

McCALL: Sure – we came to Paris to find Mrs Droste and shake some sense into this character Marett. If we should have torn him apart – but we didn't for the simple reason that we couldn't find the guy.

TEMPLE: Go on …

McCALL: We went to the shop this morning in the hope of seeing Marett but he must have spotted us because by the time we got into the shop the place was deserted. We spent the rest of the time trying to locate Mrs Droste. So far as the explosion at the Café Benoit is concerned we know positively nothing about it: so far as the murder is concerned we know even less.

TEMPLE: And you didn't visit the Boulevard Seminaire?

McCALL: Why should we?!

FORBES: Isn't that obvious: to see Marett?

McCALL: (*Emphatically*) But we didn't know Marett lived in the Boulevard Seminaire!

DROSTE: We tried to find his private address, Sir Graham, but unfortunately – or fortunately perhaps – we were unsuccessful.

FORBES: I see.

TEMPLE: (*Quietly*) McCall …

McCALL: Yes?

TEMPLE: Tell me: have you seen this before?

McCALL: What?

TEMPLE: This cigarette lighter.

McCALL: I've seen one like it.

DROSTE: It's like yours, McCall.

155

McCALL: Yes – exactly.

TEMPLE: Are you sure it isn't yours?

McCALL: Yes, of course I'm sure. I've got mine here in my pock … (*He stops*)

A moment.

TEMPLE: Well?

McCALL: That's funny! (*Feeling in his pockets*) I could have sworn … Say, can I have a look at that lighter?

TEMPLE: Certainly.

A pause.

TEMPLE: Well?

FORBES: Is it yours?

McCALL: (*Puzzled*) Yes. Yes, it is.

DROSTE: (*Laughing*) I thought it was.

McCALL: Where did you get this?

TEMPLE: I found it.

McCALL: Where?

TEMPLE: (*Quite simply*) I found it in the flat on the Boulevard Seminaire. It was by the body of Charles Marett.

FADE UP of music.

Slow FADE DOWN of music.

TEMPLE: Be careful, Steve! Be careful!

STEVE: Now, Paul, don't be stupid! I've got to get the plaster off your arm.

TEMPLE: Yes, darling – well you don't have to pull it off!

STEVE: That's precisely what I do have to do! The doctor said the best thing for me to do was to get hold of the plaster and give it a very quick tug …

TEMPLE: (*Horrified*) Never mind what the doctor said – it's my arm remember, not the doctor's! Now take it nice and easy …

156

STEVE starts to remove the plaster on TEMPLE's arm. He winces and makes a great deal of noise.

TEMPLE: Oh … Oh … Oh … O … Stop! Stop!!!

STEVE: (*Exasperated*) Well, really, Paul!

TEMPLE: What d'you mean – really, Paul!

STEVE: Darling, I hardly touched you!

TEMPLE: Hardly touched me – ye Gods!

STEVE: If this was in one of your novels the detective would be sitting back with a firm, determined expression on his face and he wouldn't be flinching an inch.

TEMPLE: Yes, well it isn't in one of my novels and I don't feel a bit firm or determined. Now just remove the plaster my sweet, and if you can manage to leave me just a particle of skin I should be very grateful.

STEVE: Now look … (*A moment*) Does that hurt?

TEMPLE: (*Immediately*) Yes.

STEVE: (*Surprised*) But I haven't touched you.

TEMPLE: It's subconscious, darling. Psychological. You've got to be very – very gentle.

STEVE: (*Determined*) Subconscious, my foot! Lean back …

TEMPLE: W-what?

STEVE: Lean back!

TEMPLE: (*Retreating*) No! No! No, Steve!

STEVE has got hold of the plaster.

TEMPLE: No!!! No … Whoa!!!

We hear the sound of the plaster being pulled off TEMPLE's arm.

STEVE: It's off!!!

TEMPLE: (*Gasping*) Oh …

STEVE: You never felt a thing …

TEMPLE: Would you mind passing my dressing gown, Miss Nightingale?

STEVE laughs.

The door opens.

CHARLIE: Excuse me, sir.

TEMPLE: What is it, Charlie?

CHARLIE: Inspector Eden is here, sir.

TEMPLE: (*Raising his voice*) Oh, hello, Inspector! Come in!

EDEN: (*Entering the room*) Thank you, sir.

STEVE: That's all right, Charlie.

The door closes.

EDEN: Good afternoon, Mrs Temple.

STEVE: Good afternoon, Inspector.

EDEN: Did you have a nice trip back, sir?

TEMPLE: My arm was a bit troublesome, apart from that it was excellent.

EDEN: Yes – I was sorry to hear about your arm. I hope it's going along all right?

TEMPLE: I'm in very good hands, Inspector. Tell me: have you heard from Sir Graham?

EDEN: I was on the phone to him about an hour ago, sir. He's due back tonight.

TEMPLE: I suppose he told you all the news?

EDEN: Yes. Incidentally, the French people have released Droste and McCall.

TEMPLE: Oh! I'm surprised to hear that.

EDEN: You thought they'd hold them?

TEMPLE: Yes.

EDEN: Well – apparently the actual time of the Marett murder has been established and both Droste and McCall have produced an alibi. I gather it's pretty foolproof or the French police wouldn't have released them.

TEMPLE: And the cigarette lighter?

EDEN: According to Sir Graham, McCall still can't account for the lighter. (*Suddenly*) Oh, I've brought the doll, sir. I understand you'd like to hand it back to Mrs Desmond.

TEMPLE: Yes, if you've no objection, Inspector.

EDEN: No, we've no objection: we've finished with it at the Yard.

TEMPLE: Good. Now tell me about Miss Millicent.

EDEN: There's not a great deal to tell. One of the Maidenhead people picked her out of the Thames at four o'clock on Tuesday morning. According to Dr Gillespie she's been dead the best part of a week.

TEMPLE: Was she murdered?

EDEN: (*Thoughtfully*) I don't know. Gillespie won't commit himself. There aren't any signs of violence, on the other hand …

TEMPLE: How did she get into the water in the first place?

EDEN: Exactly.

TEMPLE: Who identified the body?

EDEN: Shelly did. He was staying at Marlow and we sent for him as soon as the body was discovered.

TEMPLE: Where was it discovered – near The Wordsworth?

EDEN: No, further down the river. Quite near Shelly's place.

TEMPLE: Oh.

EDEN: Mr Temple, shortly after you left for Paris I had a talk to Roger Shelly. As a matter of fact he came along to the Yard with that note – the one he was supposed to have received from Miss Millicent.

TEMPLE: Yes, I know. I sent him.

EDEN: We checked the note, made the usual tests, and
           quite frankly were convinced that the note was
           genuine: but the fact remains it can't be genuine,
           not if Gillespie's right – and I'm sure he is right
           – and Miss Millicent's been dead the best part of
           a week.

STEVE: Was the note dated?

EDEN: No.

STEVE: Then how do you know that it wasn't written
           before she died and posted later?

EDEN: Because, in the first place, it wasn't posted, Mrs
           Temple, it was delivered by hand and in the
           second place the ink tests show – without any
           shadow of doubt – that the note was written
           about twenty-four hours before Shelly received
           it.

TEMPLE: M'm. (*A moment*) What's your opinion of
           Shelly, Inspector?

EDEN: He's a very excitable type, in some ways
           eccentric, but –

TEMPLE: Would you trust him?

EDEN: I don't know. I should imagine he's quite
           unreliable so far as business is concerned. For
           one thing he's always chopping and changing. In
           the past ten years he's been an actor, a
           professional dancer, and believe it or not a dress
           designer.

STEVE: Does he do very well out of this Mother's Help
           Bureau or whatever he calls it?

EDEN: Well, he must do fairly well. He seems to get
           about quite a lot and he's got this cottage down
           at Marlow. I should imagine he's got a private
           income of sorts.

TEMPLE: Yes.

The door opens.

EDEN: Temple, I've been meaning to ask (*He stops*)

STEVE: Yes, Charlie?

CHARLIE: Mr Palmer's here – and Mrs Desmond. I've popped them into the drawing room. Was that o.k.?

STEVE: Yes, that's all right, Charlie.

EDEN: Were you expecting Palmer?

TEMPLE: Yes – he's called for the doll.

EDEN: Do you mind if I have a word with him? I was going to ask him to drop in the Yard.

TEMPLE: No, of course not. (*START FADE*) Come along, Inspector. (*To STEVE*) Are you coming, darling?

FADE SCENE.

Slow FADE UP of TERRY PALMER speaking.

PALMER: It's awfully decent of you to let us have the doll back, Inspector. Awfully decent.

EDEN: That's all right, sir. We've finished with it at the Yard. There's no reason why the baby shouldn't have it.

MARY: Susan will be delighted when she sees it, won't she, Terry?

PALMER: Oh, thrilled to death!

STEVE: How is your little girl?

MARY: Oh, she's fine. But I'm sure she's been missing this silly little thing.

PALMER: It's awfully funny how some kids get attached to things isn't it?

STEVE: Yes …

PALMER: I remember when I was a kid I had a sort of kangaroo. I used to call it Corky. I had an awful lot of fun out of Corky. Often wondered what happened to it.

161

TEMPLE: I know I've asked you this before, Mrs Desmond, but you're quite sure that this is the same doll?

MARY: Yes, I'm quite sure.

EDEN: The doll was deposited – in an attaché case – in the cloakroom at the Commodore Club: a girl called Queenie Edwards sent Mr Temple the cloakroom ticket.

PALMER: (*Faintly impatient*) Yes, we know, Inspector. We also know how the cloakroom attendant told Mr Temple that I deposited the attaché case.

EDEN: Which you didn't?

PALMER: (*Politely*) Which I didn't, Inspector.

EDEN: Mr Palmer, tell me: do you know Marlow very well?

PALMER: Marlow?

EDEN: Yes – it's on the Thames near Maidenhead.

PALMER: I've been there several times.

EDEN: Recently?

PALMER: No – not recently.

MARY: Isn't that where you found Miss Millicent?

EDEN: Yes.

PALMER: (*Rather annoyed*) Oh, I see. Well, I can assure you that you know a great deal more about the murder than we do, Inspector. We didn't even know that Miss Millicent had been found until we read about it. That's true, isn't it, Mary?

MARY: Yes, of course.

EDEN: It hasn't yet been established that Miss Millicent was murdered.

MARY: What do you mean?

EDEN: Well, she was drowned, of course, but whether …

162

MARY: But of course Miss Millicent was murdered! She must have been murdered, why ... (*She hesitates*)

EDEN: Go on, Mrs Desmond?

MARY: Why – if she wasn't murdered, what else could have happened?

EDEN: (*Watching MARY*) She might have committed suicide.

PALMER: You mean she kidnapped the baby, suddenly realised what she'd done, returned the child and then – committed suicide?

EDEN: Yes.

PALMER: Well – it's a possibility, I suppose.

TEMPLE: Then why was the doll delivered to the Commodore Club, why did Queenie Edwards go down to Marlow and who, precisely, is this mysterious Mr Vandyke?

PALMER: What do you mean – who is the mysterious Mr Vandyke?

TEMPLE: Well, Mrs Desmond received a telephone call from someone called Vandyke the night that Miss Millicent and the baby disappeared. Don't you remember?

PALMER: Yes – but you don't attach any significance to that, surely?

TEMPLE: I attach a great deal of significance to it, Mr Palmer. And there's something else I attach a great deal of significance to as well.

PALMER: What?

TEMPLE: (*Quietly: producing the glove from his pocket*) This glove.

PALMER: (*With a little laugh: quite self-possessed*) Forgive me if I'm a little dense but I'm afraid I don't quite see the point.

163

TEMPLE: Well, you may recall that Mrs Desmond dropped this glove the night that the baby …

MARY: (*Very surprised*) I did?

TEMPLE: (*Turning towards MARY: quietly*) Yes.

MARY: But surely there's some mistake – that's not one of my gloves.

STEVE: What!

TEMPLE: Oh, now, Mrs Desmond, please!

PALMER: When did Mary drop that glove?

TEMPLE: Why the night that the baby was returned! Don't you remember – you saw us outside the flat. We'd just returned from Marlow.

PALMER: (*Quite calmly*) I remember seeing you outside the flat and I remember ringing you up about a glove that Mary had lost – but that's not the one.

TEMPLE: How do you know it isn't?

PALMER: Because shortly after I telephoned you she found her glove: it was in the car all the time, down by the side of the seat.

TEMPLE: Palmer, you – er – don't expect me to believe that?

PALMER: (*Quite pleasantly: unperturbed*) I don't see that it's awfully important whether you believe it or not. It happens to be the truth.

TEMPLE: (*Faintly annoyed*) Look here, Palmer: there's a tab inside this glove – it's got the address of the shop where it was bought from.

PALMER: Well?

TEMPLE: The address is – 73, Rue St Lazare, Paris.

MARY: Well, that proves it can't be mine! I've never been to Paris.

EDEN: (*Significantly*) Have you been to Paris, Mr Palmer?

164

PALMER: Yes, of course I have. Several times. As a matter of fact the last time I was there I stayed in the Rue St Lazare. Hotel Licorne. But I didn't buy Mrs Desmond a pair of gloves, if that's what you're thinking.

EDEN: M'm.

A moment.

TEMPLE: (*Quietly*) Mrs Desmond …

MARY: Yes?

TEMPLE: Would you mind trying the glove on?

MARY: No, of course I wouldn't. Providing I can get it on. It looks very small to me.

A pause.

MARY DESMOND is trying to pull on the glove.

PALMER: Well?

STEVE: It's hopeless …

MARY: (*Laughing: still trying to pull on the glove*) It's miles too small. It just won't go near me …

PALMER: (*Smiling: quite pleasantly*) Well – are you satisfied, Mr Temple?

FADE UP of music.

FADE DOWN of music.

TEMPLE and STEVE are having breakfast.

TEMPLE is rather irritated.

STEVE: Paul, you've spilt some coffee on the tablecloth!

TEMPLE: It's a wonder I haven't spilt it all over my suit! Steve, this bandage is far too tight.

STEVE: The doctor said …

TEMPLE: The doctor doesn't know what he's talking about! I'm taking this wretched thing off this afternoon, Steve – doctor or no doctor!

165

STEVE: (*Laughing*) You really are the most dreadful person when you've got anything the matter with you.

TEMPLE: And there's another thing, Steve. You'll have to sleep in the spare room for a night or two. Last night you were tossing and turning …

STEVE: I was tossing and turning!

TEMPLE: Yes, darling.

STEVE: I like that, I must say! Why, from the moment you got into bed …

TEMPLE: (*Laughing*) You were, Steve – honestly! You kept mumbling to yourself all night.

STEVE: (*Also laughing*) Well, if you must know I had a nightmare.

TEMPLE: And by Timothy, it sounded like one.

STEVE: I was dreaming about those confounded gloves! (*Seriously*) Paul, do you think Mrs Desmond was telling the truth?

We hear the sound of the flat buzzer.

TEMPLE: What do you mean?

STEVE: Do you think that was her glove?

TEMPLE: Yes – of course it was.

STEVE: Then why on earth didn't it fit her?

The flat buzzer sounds again.

TEMPLE: For the simple reason … I say, isn't Charlie in?

STEVE: Yes, darling.

TEMPLE: Then why, for Pete's sake, doesn't he answer the door?

STEVE: He's probably in the kitchen.

TEMPLE: He's probably asleep or reading Forever Amber or something!

STEVE: (*Laughing*) You are in a mood this morning! It's all right – I'll answer it.

STEVE crosses into the hall and opens the front door.

166

ROGER SHELLY is standing at the door.

SHELLY: (*Surprised at seeing STEVE*) Oh! Er – good morning.

STEVE: Good morning.

SHELLY: Is Mr Temple in, please?

STEVE: Yes, he's in, but …

SHELLY: My name is Shelly. (*Anxiously*) Do you think I could have a word with Mr Temple?

STEVE: Well –

SHELLY: I know it's frightfully annoying having callers at this time of the day, but – it is important.

STEVE: Well – won't you come in, Mr Shelly?

SHELLY: Oh, thank you. Thank you very much, Mrs Temple. (*Smiling*) It is Mrs Temple, isn't it?

STEVE: (*Closing the door behind SHELLY*) Well, it had better be at this time of the morning!

SHELLY laughs.

TEMPLE: (*Approaching*) Hello, Shelly! You're up nice and early!

SHELLY: It's very naughty of me to call round at this time I know, but I did so want to have a word with you. (*A moment: surprised*) Hello, have you had an accident?

TEMPLE: What? Oh, yes – yes. My wife bit me. Come along, Shelly. Come and have some coffee and tell me what it's all about.

FADE SCENE.

FADE UP of ROGER SHELLY speaking.

SHELLY: Well, I'm most perturbed, Mr Temple. Most perturbed. I don't know whether the police think I'm a suspicious character or not, but really, the questions they've been asking. Do you know I was at Scotland Yard the other day for two hours – positively two hours.

TEMPLE: (*Pleasantly*) Well, I'm often at Scotland Yard for two hours, Shelly. I very frequently spend the whole day at Scotland Yard: there's nothing for you to worry about.

SHELLY: I don't know. I don't trust the police, they're a suspicious lot of bounders. And my word, aren't they incompetent!

STEVE: (*Laughing*) Well, I wouldn't say that, Mr Shelly!

SHELLY: Well, I would! You know that note I received: the one that was supposed to have been written by Miss Millicent?

TEMPLE: Yes.

SHELLY: Well, they said it was genuine! They actually said it was genuine!

TEMPLE: But you said it was genuine.

SHELLY: Yes, I know, but I'm not an expert!

TEMPLE: I was talking to Inspector Eden about that note, Shelly, and the Inspector …

SHELLY: Eden! Well, really – he's the end! The man's a positive imbecile!

STEVE laughs.

TEMPLE: (*Not amused*) Take my advice, and don't underestimate Inspector Eden. He's a great deal shrewder than you think.

STEVE: You know, Mr Shelly, although that note wasn't written by Miss Millicent you can't dismiss it as being completely unimportant. After all, it did reveal the identity of the murdered man – the man at Marlow I mean.

SHELLY: I don't dismiss the note as being unimportant, Mrs Temple – on the contrary! But why – why for goodness sake was it sent to me?

168

TEMPLE: Isn't it obvious why?

SHELLY: Not to me it isn't!

TEMPLE: The person who wrote that note considered you an important character in this affair, Mr Shelly, so important in fact that they thought it worth their while to send you a friendly warning. What was it the note said: " …The man you met at Marlow – the man who called himself Baker – was Harry De Wolfe. Let that be a warning, Mr Shelly …" …

SHELLY: Yes, but why send me a warning? A warning against what for Pete's sake!? It isn't as if I knew that fellow – the one that was murdered. I'd never set eyes on him until I bumped into him at The Wordsworth.

TEMPLE: Shelly, supposing we get to the point. What, exactly, is it you want to see me about?

SHELLY: (*Hesitating*) Well –

TEMPLE: Go on …

SHELLY: You'll probably think this is rather ridiculous, but – (*He hesitates again*)

TEMPLE: Go on, Shelly.

SHELLY: Well – when I realised that Miss Millicent couldn't have written that note I began to wonder if by any chance the whole thing was some kind of a practical joke.

TEMPLE: Why should it be a practical joke?

SHELLY: (*With a little laugh*) Well, I've got a friend – Marian Faber.

TEMPLE: The artist?

SHELLY: (*Faintly surprised*) Yes. Do you know Marian?

TEMPLE: No, but I've heard of her: she's a well-known portrait painter.

SHELLY: That's right.

TEMPLE: Didn't Miss Faber dine with you the night you invited Baker – or rather De Wolfe – to teach you canasta?

SHELLY: (*Surprised*) Yes, that's right! Marian was at the cottage when Baker telephoned to say he couldn't make it. It's a good job for me she was otherwise I don't suppose our dear Inspector would have believed a word I said.

TEMPLE: Well, go on, Shelly. What about Miss Faber?

SHELLY: Well, I was thinking – Marian's a darling but she really has a more malicious sense of humour and she adores practical jokes.

STEVE: You're surely not suspecting that Miss Faber sent you that note simply as a practical joke?

SHELLY: You don't know Marian, Mrs Temple. It's just the sort of thing she would do. Besides, the little devil knew I was worried about the Miss Millicent business.

TEMPLE: Yes, but look here, Shelly. In the first place, what makes you think that Miss Faber could copy Miss Millicent's handwriting, and in the second place …

SHELLY: (*Interrupting TEMPLE*) Oh, Marian could do that all right! As a matter of fact that's what put the whole idea into my head. You see, Marian used to do that sort of thing at parties – copy people's handwriting, I mean. She really is astonishingly good.

TEMPLE: Yes, but how did she get hold of a sample of Miss Millicent's handwriting in order to copy it, and also …

STEVE: How did she happen to know the identity of the dead man – De Wolfe?

TEMPLE: Exactly, Steve!

170

SHELLY: (*Taken aback*) Oh, dear! Oh, dear, I'm afraid I never thought of that!

TEMPLE: (*Smiling*) Well, I should start thinking about it, Mr Shelly.

STEVE: Where does Miss Faber live – at Marlow?

SHELLY: No. She has a studio in Chelsea but she spends most of her time at Bourne End. She's got a bungalow down there. A lovely place. (*With a sigh*) She's disgustingly rich.

TEMPLE: Have you seen Miss Faber – recently, I mean?

SHELLY: Not for about a week. (*Suddenly*) Now I come to think about it, it was the day before I received the note. I'd just returned from Scotland Yard and we bumped into each other in Regent Street. I told her what a ghastly time I was having.

TEMPLE: You haven't spoken to Miss Faber since you actually received the note?

SHELLY: Why, no.

TEMPLE: Shelly, tell me: what sort of a person is Marian Faber?

SHELLY: Oh, rather the quiet type: she can be charming, on the other hand she can be a perfect little vixen if she wants to be.

TEMPLE: M'm – well, I think it might be a good idea if I had a word with Miss Faber.

SHELLY: I doubt if you'll get much help from her. The only time Marian feels like talking is when she's painting and then, my word, she certainly can natter.

TEMPLE: All right – I'll make an appointment for a sitting. She can paint me and talk to me at the same time.

STEVE: I'm sure you'll make a lovely oil painting, darling – especially with your arm in a sling!

TEMPLE: Oh, Lord, I'd forgotten that!

171

STEVE and SHELLY laugh.

SHELLY: Mr Temple, may … I make a suggestion?

TEMPLE: Yes, of course.

SHELLY: Why not let Mrs Temple see Marian – I feel sure
            that she'd get a great deal more out of her than
            anyone else.

STEVE: Thank you, Mr Shelly!

TEMPLE: (*Thoughtfully*) Yes, do you know, I think you're
            right, Shelly. That's quite an idea. Quite an idea
            …

FADE UP of music.

FADE DOWN of music.

*Slow FADE UP the noise of a railway train: it is drawing into
a small station. The train stops followed by the sound of
carriage doors opening and closing.*

*A whistle blows: then we hear a background of passengers on
the platform.*

LOUIS: (*Pleasantly*) Mrs Temple?

STEVE: Yes?

LOUIS: I'm Miss Faber's chauffeur, Mrs Temple. Miss
            Faber asked me to meet the train.

STEVE: (*Pleased*) Oh, thank you. That's very kind of
            Miss Faber.

LOUIS: Have you any luggage, madam?

STEVE: No.

LOUIS: The car's over there, Mrs Temple, just through
            the gate.

STEVE: Oh, thank you.

A pause.

STEVE and LOUIS are crossing towards the car.

STEVE: How far is it from here?

LOUIS: It's about four miles, but it's rather difficult to
            find if you haven't been down here before.

STEVE: Well, I'm very glad Miss Faber sent the car. I should probably have caught the wrong bus or walked in the opposite direction or something.

LOUIS laughs.

STEVE: That seems to be quite a habit of mine these days.

LOUIS: Here we are, madam. (*He opens the door*) I'll move those parcels off the back seat and then you can …

STEVE: That's all right, I can sit in the front.

LOUIS: Oh, thank you, Mrs Temple.

STEVE: (*Suddenly: pleasantly*) By the way, haven't I seen you before somewhere?

LOUIS: I don't think so, madam.

STEVE: What's your name?

LOUIS: Franz, madam. Louis Franz.

STEVE: That's strange – I could have sworn I'd seen you before somewhere.

LOUIS: (*Suddenly*) Oh, just a moment, madam! Didn't you stay at The Wordsworth Hotel – at Marlow – about a week ago?

STEVE: Yes, that's right. My husband and I were down there for the weekend.

LOUIS: (*Smiling*) That's where you saw me, Mrs Temple. You were sitting in the lounge with Mr Temple. I delivered a message to the manager, Mr McCall.

STEVE: Yes. Yes, I remember. (*Laughing*) I knew I'd seen you before!

LOUIS: (*Amused*) You are one of those people who never forget a face!

STEVE: (*Taking her place in the car*) Oddly enough, it's usually voices I remember, not faces. (*Holding the car door*) How do you close this door?

LOUIS: You have to bang it, madam. Allow me.
LOUIS bangs the door of the car.
STEVE: Oh, thank you.
The car starts.
FADE SCENE.

FADE UP of the car: it is travelling fairly fast.
STEVE: How much further have we got to go?
LOUIS: About a mile and a half.
STEVE: Do we drive by the river all the way?
LOUIS: Yes.
STEVE: It seems a very long four miles.
LOUIS: It's probably nearer five from the station. We
           always reckon about twenty minutes. When we
           get round the next bend you'll see the cottage on
           the top of the hill.
STEVE: The cottage?
LOUIS: Yes, madam.
STEVE: Miss Faber's cottage?
LOUIS: Yes.
STEVE: But I thought she had a bungalow?
LOUIS: (*After a moment*) No, madam – a cottage. It's
           one of those – what do you call it? – Tudor
           cottages with a thatched roof. (*He has difficulty
           over the word "thatched": laughing*) Thatched –
           is that the right word?
STEVE: (*Her thoughts elsewhere*) Yes, that's the right
           word. (*A moment*) How long have you worked
           for Miss Faber, Louis?
LOUIS: Oh – nearly two years now.
STEVE: And before that?
LOUIS: Oh, before that I was all over the place.
STEVE: Abroad?
LOUIS: Yes, abroad. Zurich, Copenhagen, Oslo …

STEVE: (*Significantly*) Paris?

LOUIS: No. No, I've never worked in Paris.

STEVE: Have you been there?

LOUIS: Er – no, no never.

STEVE: (*Quietly*) I think you have.

LOUIS: (*Surprised*) What do you mean?

STEVE: I think you've been to Paris all right. As a matter of fact I think you've been to Paris quite recently.

LOUIS: (*Annoyed*) What are you talking about?

STEVE: I'm talking about the Café Benoit, my friend! Don't tell me you don't remember the Café Benoit!

LOUIS: (*Annoyed and irritated*) I don't understand what you mean, I …

STEVE: Don't you? I'm surprised, Mr Franz! Don't you remember a rather disreputable individual selling newspapers and pretty postcards? Oh, now, surely … Just think … (*A pause*) Well?

LOUIS: (*Tensely*) You recognised my voice?

STEVE: Yes.

LOUIS: (*Angrily*) I knew you would! I told Vandyke you would! I knew damn well you'd recognise my voice!

STEVE: (*Tensely*) Now listen, I don't know what your game is but don't be a fool – stop the car!

LOUIS accelerates.

LOUIS: Take your hands off the wheel!

STEVE: You heard what I said, Louis! Now don't be a fool, stop the car before it's too late!

LOUIS: Take your hands off the wheel!

STEVE: (*Grimly*) I'm going to give you one more chance and if you don't stop the car …

175

LOUIS: (*Losing his temper*) Take your hands off the wheel! D'you hear what I say?

STEVE: Stop it! Stop the car!

LOUIS: You fool! You stupid little fool! All right – you asked for it!

LOUIS strikes STEVE across the face.

STEVE: (*Hurt and intensely angry: losing control of herself*) Why you swine, if Paul were here he'd … (*Throwing herself at LOUIS*) You filthy little swine!!!

LOUIS: (*Alarmed*) Be careful! For God's sake be careful or you'll turn the car over!!!!

STEVE: (*Attacking LOUIS*) You little swine, I'll teach you to lay your hands on me …

We hear the sound of car brakes.

LOUIS: (*Frightened*) Look out!!!! Look out, or you'll turn the car into the river!!!!

STEVE: I'll teach you to lay your hands on me, Mr Franz or whatever your name is!!!!

LOUIS: (*Desperately; trying to defend himself and control the car*) Take your hands off the wheel! Take … Look out!!!! Look out!!!!!

There is a cry of alarm from LOUIS as the car leaves the road and plunges across the embankment towards the river.
The car hits the water.
Quick, dramatic FADE UP of music.

END OF EPISODE FIVE

EPISODE SIX

SUSPECT NO. 1.

OPEN TO:

FADE UP the sound of the car.

STEVE: (*Grimly*) I'm going to give you one more chance and if you don't stop the car …

LOUIS: (*Losing his temper*) Take your hands off the wheel! D'you hear what I say?

STEVE: Stop it! Stop the car!

LOUIS: You fool! You stupid little fool! All right – you asked for it!

LOUIS strikes STEVE across the face.

STEVE: (*Hurt and intensely angry: losing control of herself*) Why you swine, if Paul were here he'd … (*Throwing herself at LOUIS*) You filthy little swine!!!

LOUIS: (*Alarmed*) Be careful! For God's sake be careful or you'll turn the car over!!!!

STEVE: (*Attacking LOUIS*) You little swine, I'll teach you to lay your hands on me …

We hear the sound of car brakes.

LOUIS: (*Frightened*) Look out!!!! Look out, or you'll turn the car into the river!!!!

STEVE: I'll teach you to lay your hands on me, Mr Franz or whatever your name is!!!!

LOUIS: (*Desperately; trying to defend himself and control the car*) Take your hands off the wheel! Take … Look out!!!! Look out!!!!!

There is a cry of alarm from LOUIS as the car leaves the road and plunges across the embankment towards the river.
The car hits the water.
FADE UP the noise of the car hitting the water.
FADE SCENE.

Quick FADE UP of STEVE half-swimming half-struggling towards the bank. She is breathless and obviously overwrought.

LOUIS is also in the water – from the background he can be heard shouting for help.

LOUIS: Help! Mrs Temple! (*Desperately*) Mrs Temple. I can't swim!!! Help!!!! (*Struggling in the water: desperately frightened*) Mrs Temple, help me! For God's sake help me – I can't swim!!! (*Weakly: struggling in the water*) I can't swim!!! Help!!!

FADE UP of STEVE struggling out of the water onto the bank. She is breathless – gasping for breath.

FADE UP the sound of an approaching car: the car quickly brakes to a standstill. Voices are heard as two men hurry down the slope towards STEVE. The two men are PHILIP DROSTE and BILL McCALL.

DROSTE: (*Staggered*) Mrs Temple! McCall, look who it is! It's Mrs Temple!

McCALL: (*Amazed*) Mrs Temple! Why – what d'you know?!

DROSTE: (*Bewildered*) What happened? We saw the car zig-zagging all over the place! Did the steering column break?

STEVE: (*Breathless*) No ... No, it was nothing like that ...

McCALL: Say, just look at that car! For Pete's sake just look at it!!!!

In the background LOUIS is still trying to draw attention to himself.

DROSTE: Who is that in the water? Is that your husband?

STEVE: (*Still trying to get her breath*) No ... No, it's a man called Louis Franz, he was ... trying ... to ...

McCALL:	(*Suddenly: he is watching LOUIS*) Say, he's in trouble over there!
STEVE:	He … can't … swim …
McCALL:	(*Still watching*) You're darn tooting right he can't swim! The guy doesn't know where he is!
DROSTE:	He's in a panic …
McCALL:	He sure is! (*He takes off his jacket*) Watch this jacket! I'm going in there!

McCALL wades into the river.

DROSTE:	Give me your arm, Mrs Temple.
STEVE:	Thank you …
DROSTE:	I think I'd better take you up to my car.
STEVE:	(*Still exhausted*) Yes – yes, all right …
DROSTE:	It's strange that we should bump into you like this.
STEVE:	I'm very glad you did.
DROSTE:	McCall and I were driving down to The Wordsworth. He'd just met me at the station. I think you'd better come back to the hotel with us, Mrs Temple.
STEVE:	(*Bewildered*) Yes, … I think I'd better. I can't go very far like this. How far is it?
DROSTE:	The Wordsworth? It's about two miles from here.
STEVE:	When did you get back from Paris, Mr Droste?
DROSTE:	I came back yesterday but I'm flying back to Paris tonight. (*START FADE*) My wife's still in a pretty bad way, I'm afraid. I shouldn't have left Paris only I had a meeting in Town yesterday afternoon.

COMPLETE FADE.

FADE UP.

DROSTE: But that's a most extraordinary story, Mrs Temple! I can hardly believe it! Are you sure this is the same man?

STEVE: I'm absolutely sure. Quite apart from the fact that I recognised his voice, the moment I mentioned Paris he …

DROSTE: (*Interrupting STEVE*) Here's McCall!

McCALL arrives at the car: he is out of breath.

McCALL: Droste, you'd better drive down to the police station. Mention my name and ask for Sergeant Gorringe.

DROSTE: What's happened?

McCALL: It was no use. He was in such a devil of a state there was nothing I could do. I tried to save him, but he … just … wouldn't … help … me …

DROSTE: Have you tried artificial respiration?

McCALL: (*Shaking his head: trying to get his breath back*) He's dead. He was dead when I got him out of the water. If you want my opinion he died from shock more than anything else …

DROSTE: Yes …

McCALL: I'm sorry, Mrs Temple. I did my best. Was he a friend of yours?

STEVE: No. No, he's not a friend of mine.

DROSTE: Mrs Temple had an appointment with Marian Faber …

McCALL: (*Surprised*) What – the artist?

DROSTE: Yes. That fellow met her at the station and passed himself off as Miss Faber's chauffeur.

McCALL: (*Surprised*) What do you mean – passed himself off? Isn't he Miss Faber's chauffeur?

STEVE: No. (*After a moment*) His name's Franz – Louis Franz. The first time I saw him was in Paris.

DROSTE: According to Mrs Temple he was the man responsible for the bomb outrage.

McCALL: You mean – at the Café Benoit?

STEVE: Yes.

McCALL: You're almost as bad as your husband, Mrs Temple! You two certainly go in for surprises! But say, if this character was responsible for that bomb outrage why did he meet you at the station?

STEVE: I don't know, unless … (*Suddenly: remembering*) By the way, Mr McCall, he said that he knew you!

McCALL: Me?

STEVE: Yes.

McCALL: (*Shaking his head*) I've never seen the man before.

STEVE: He said he delivered a message to you – at The Wordsworth – about a week ago.

McCALL: Not to me he didn't. Now don't look at me like that, Mrs Temple!

STEVE: Like – like what? What do you mean?

McCALL: (*Smiling; but reprimanding STEVE*) You know what I mean! You're looking at me as if you don't believe a word I say!

STEVE: (*Faintly embarrassed*) Oh, I can assure you …

McCALL: (*Laughing at STEVE*) That's o.k.! I don't mind whether you believe me or not. It just happens to be the truth, that's all.

DROSTE: You've never seen him before?

McCALL: (*Smiling*) That's right, Mr Droste. It's as simple as that. I've never seen him before.

FADE UP of music.

FADE DOWN of music.

TEMPLE is knocking on the door of MARION FABER's bungalow.

After a little while the door opens. MARIAN FABER is in her late thirties: a faintly arrogant person.

TEMPLE: Miss Faber?

MARIAN: Yes?

TEMPLE: (*Pleasantly*) My name is Paul Temple. I believe my wife had an appointment with you this afternoon, Miss Faber?

MARIAN: She did. The appointment was for half-past three. The next time your wife makes an appointment and fails to keep it, Mr Temple, I should be grateful if she would have the good manners to telephone me.

TEMPLE: My wife had an accident. Otherwise, I can assure you, she would have been here on time, Miss Faber.

MARIAN: An accident?

TEMPLE: Yes.

MARIAN: (*Arrogantly*) What do you mean – what sort of an accident?

TEMPLE: A gentleman by the name of Louis Franz met my wife at the station: he told her that he was your chauffeur and he offered to drive her …

MARIAN: (*Interrupting TEMPLE*) Why that's sheer nonsense! I haven't got a chauffeur.

TEMPLE: (*Controlling himself*) I appreciate that fact, Miss Faber, unfortunately my wife was under the impression that you had a chauffeur. Now, if you would like to hear what happened this afternoon, I suggest you invite me inside. It's hardly the sort of story I can tell standing on a doorstep.

MARIAN: (*A moment, then.*) I'm sorry. I've been in rather a bad mood all day. Do come in, Mr Temple.

TEMPLE: Thank you.

MARIAN: This morning my work went to pieces and then this afternoon when your wife didn't turn up I …

TEMPLE: I know! (*Laughing*) There's no need to apologise, Miss Faber! I know that sort of day only too well!

FADE.

Slow FADE UP of TEMPLE.

TEMPLE: … Steve went back to the hotel with Droste and Bill McCall. They telephoned through to the flat and I motored down from town.

MARIAN: Where's your wife now?

TEMPLE: She's still at The Wordsworth. I left her there while I called round to have a chat with you.

MARIAN: What was this man like, Mr Temple – the man that pretended to be my chauffeur?

TEMPLE: I understand he was about thirty: tall, dark, good looking. He spoke with an accent.

MARIAN: And you say his name was Louis Franz?

TEMPLE: According to the papers we found on him – yes.

MARIAN: I just can't imagine who he is. I certainly don't know anyone called Franz. (*Amused*) What an extraordinary name!

TEMPLE: It's my opinion that Franz worked for a man called Vandyke. Does that convey anything to you?

MARIAN: No. No, I've never heard of anyone called Vandyke.

185

TEMPLE:	(*Watching MARIAN*) I see. (*Suddenly; pleasantly*) May I offer you a cigarette?
MARIAN:	No, thank you. I don't smoke.
TEMPLE:	Have you any objection if I …
MARIAN:	No, of course not.
TEMPLE:	(*Casually; as he takes out his case and lights a cigarette*) I understand Mr Shelly's a friend of yours?
MARIAN:	Yes. I've known Roger for some time.
TEMPLE:	Didn't you dine with him the night that man – De Wolfe – was murdered?
MARIAN:	Yes, I did.
TEMPLE:	Was De Wolfe a friend of yours?
MARIAN:	Of course he wasn't! I never saw the man.
TEMPLE:	I was under the impression he was a friend of Mr Shelly's.
MARIAN:	That doesn't necessarily make him a friend of mine! In any case, he wasn't a friend of Shelly's. Roger simply bumped into him at The Wordsworth and invited him out to dinner.
TEMPLE:	And you never actually saw him?
MARIAN:	(*Hesitating*) No.
TEMPLE:	Miss Faber, when my wife telephoned and made an appointment to see you, what was your reaction?
MARIAN:	What do you mean?
TEMPLE:	Did you believe that she simply wanted to have her portrait painted?
MARIAN:	Yes. Why shouldn't I? I'm an artist. I paint portraits – and I understand your wife is a particularly good looking woman.
TEMPLE:	Didn't it occur to you that Mrs Temple might be coming down here simply because … (*He hesitates*)

MARIAN: Because what?

TEMPLE: Because I wanted certain information from you?

MARIAN: (*A note of tenseness in her voice*) No. No, it didn't. What information are you talking about?

TEMPLE: (*Smiling*) Mr Shelly tells me that you have a rather unusual sense of humour, Miss Faber.

MARIAN: It depends what you mean by unusual?

TEMPLE: I understand you frequently – what shall we say? – go in? – for practical jokes.

MARIAN: (*Tensely*) Are you suggesting that I played a practical joke on Mrs Temple this afternoon? That I deliberately sent that man down to the station ...

TEMPLE: No! No, I'm not suggesting anything of the sort!

MARIAN: (*A note of anger in her voice*) Well – what are you suggesting?

TEMPLE: I'm suggesting that you sent Mr Shelly a note. A threatening note – a note apparently written by Miss Millicent.

MARIAN: (*Contemptuously*) Well, what if I did? The fool was asking to have his leg pulled. Every time you met him he did nothing else but talk about the Millicent affair. It isn't as if he knew the woman very well. I don't suppose he'd spoken to her more than half a dozen times. I met him in Regent Street one afternoon: he'd just been to Scotland Yard. My God, he was full of it! He said he was worried – desperately worried – but it was painfully obvious that he was enjoying every minute of it. (*Laughing*) Well, we gave him something to worry about!

TEMPLE: We?

MARIAN: Yes. Oh, that note wasn't entirely my idea. A friend of mine and Roger's told me exactly what to write and gave me a letter of Miss Millicent's to copy from.

TEMPLE: Well, your friend seems to have been very well informed. He knew De Wolfe's identity before Scotland Yard did.

MARIAN: (*Thoughtfully; puzzled*) Yes. Yes, I know. I've been worried about that. When I wrote the note I thought the name was just a fictitious name – one my friend had invented to make the note sound authentic – but later I discovered ...

TEMPLE: That it was genuine?

MARIAN: Yes.

TEMPLE: (*Watching MARIAN*) What did you do when you discovered that the dead man really was called De Wolfe?

MARIAN: Well, naturally, I had a word with my friend. I asked him how he happened to know De Wolfe's identity and why he hadn't spoken to the police about it.

TEMPLE: And what did your friend say?

MARIAN: He said he didn't want to get involved with the police and in any case if Shelly went to Scotland Yard with the note they'd very quickly check up on De Wolfe.

TEMPLE: I see. Who is this friend of yours, Miss Faber?

MARIAN: (*Hesitating*) I'm sorry. I can't tell you.

TEMPLE: What do you mean – you can't? You mean you won't tell me – is that it?

MARIAN: Very well, I won't.

TEMPLE: Why?

MARIAN: Because ... I ... don't want to get anyone into trouble.

TEMPLE: My dear Miss Faber, you'll get a great many people into trouble – including yourself! – if you withhold important information from the police. (*Quietly: friendly*) Now don't be stupid about this: who gave you the Miss Millicent letter – who told you exactly what to put in that note to Roger Shelly?

MARIAN: I'm sorry. I can't tell you.

TEMPLE: (*Seriously*) Miss Faber, I don't know whether you realise the seriousness ...

MARIAN: (*Interrupting TEMPLE: angrily*) Mr Temple, please! I've told you, I'm not going to tell you who my friend is. The whole thing was a practical joke – the sooner it's forgotten the better. In any case, I don't doubt the police know all there is to know about De Wolfe without dragging my friend or anyone else down to Scotland Yard!

TEMPLE: (*Curtly*) You may be a very brilliant actress, Miss Faber, but, if you'll excuse my saying so, you're a very stupid young woman.

MARIAN: What do you mean?

TEMPLE: (*Forcefully; with a touch of anger*) Why do you think I'm here this evening? Just because I'm curious about a threatening note sent to an effeminate young man like Roger Shelly? Just because I want to get to the bottom of one of your stupid jokes? No! I'm here, Miss Faber, because I'm determined, at all cost, to find out the identity of the mysterious Mr Vandyke.

MARIAN: (*Tensely*) I don't know what you're talking about. I've already told you, I've never heard of anyone called Vandyke.

TEMPLE: I think you have, Miss Faber! I think you've heard a great deal about Mr Vandyke. I've got a shrewd suspicion that you know a great deal more about the Miss Millicent affair than you would like to admit.

MARIAN: That's absolute nonsense! I'd never even heard of Miss Millicent until I read about the case in the newspapers.

TEMPLE: You know where they found Miss Millicent, don't you? In the river – about two miles from here.

MARIAN: Well – what does that prove? I'm not the only person who lives round here, Mr Temple. There's Shelly for instance; he's got a cottage not far from where they found Miss Millicent. And there's Mr McCall at The Wordsworth – and Mr Droste – he's quite a frequent visitor to these parts.

TEMPLE: For a person who's never heard of Mr Vandyke and knows very little about the Miss Millicent affair you seem to be pretty well acquainted with the principal characters in the story, Miss Faber.

MARIAN: (*Suddenly; with charm*) I can see you're quite convinced I'm a double-dyed villain, Mr Temple. (*Laughing*) Or should I say villainess? I'm sure nothing I can say will convince you otherwise.

TEMPLE: (*Pleasantly*) On the contrary: I just think you're being very stupid, Miss Faber.

MARIAN: Because I won't tell you who my friend is?

TEMPLE: We shall find that out, sooner or later. (*Pleasantly; casually*) Would you mind passing

190

me my cigarette case? I left it on the table over there.

MARIAN: (*Crossing to the table*) I'm sorry to have been so difficult, Mr Temple. I hope that next time we meet you'll be able to take a more favourable view of me.

TEMPLE: I hope so.

MARIAN: (*Returning*) Here's your case.

TEMPLE: Thank you.

MARIAN: (*Suddenly: quite pleasant*) Tell me: just out of curiosity. What's the point of the cigarette case – to get my fingerprints?

TEMPLE: Yes.

MARIAN: (*With charm: almost effusive*) Oh, but you should have asked me! I would have been only too happy to have obliged!

TEMPLE: (*A moment; then laughing*) Obviously you're not so stupid as I thought. Goodbye!

MARIAN: (*Amused*) Goodbye, Mr Temple.

The door opens.

TEMPLE: (*Turning: suddenly*) Oh, by the way …

MARIAN: Yes?

TEMPLE: I did notice the photograph of Mr Palmer in the hall. (*Excessively polite*) You did intend me to notice it, didn't you, Miss Faber?

FADE UP of music.

FADE DOWN of music.
FADE UP background noises of the hotel lounge.

STEVE: Hello, darling!

TEMPLE: (*Surprised*) Oh, hello, Steve! I've been looking all over the place for you! (*Briskly*) Are you ready?

STEVE:	Yes, but I promised we'd give Mr Droste a lift into Town. He's flying back to Paris on the night plane.
TEMPLE:	(*Impatiently*) Well, where is Droste – is he ready?
STEVE:	He will be in a moment or so. Paul, how's your arm?
TEMPLE:	Oh, it's fine, Steve. Absolutely grand – never felt better.
STEVE:	You shouldn't be using it, darling. If the doctor knew you were driving a car he'd be furious.
TEMPLE:	Nonsense! It felt better the moment I took it out of the sling. (*Suddenly*) Ah, here's Droste!
DROSTE:	Hello, old man! I'm sorry if I've kept you waiting.
TEMPLE:	That's all right. I've only just arrived.
DROSTE:	Did you see Miss Faber?
TEMPLE:	Yes. Apparently she's never heard of Franz: at any rate he certainly wasn't her chauffeur. I understand you want a lift back to Town, Droste?
DROSTE:	Yes, if it's not causing you too much trouble.
TEMPLE:	No, of course not. Are you ready?
DROSTE:	Yes, I'm ready now.
TEMPLE:	Good.
STEVE:	Wait a moment, darling! Here's Mr McCall.
McCALL:	(*Breathless*) Excuse me …
DROSTE:	What is it, McCall?
McCALL:	There's a call for you from Paris. I gather it's urgent – they've been trying to get you at the flat.
DROSTE:	Oh! (*Quickly*) Excuse me!
McCALL:	(*Hurrying away, with DROSTE*) Take it in my office, it's quicker …

A moment.

STEVE: (*Thoughtfully*) A call from Paris – I wonder if it's about his wife?

TEMPLE: Yes. (*Suddenly*) How are you feeling now, Steve – any better?

STEVE: I certainly feel better than I did. I had a wonderful bath, darling! Both Droste and McCall have been awfully decent …

TEMPLE: Good …

STEVE: You look excited about something, Paul – what's happened?

TEMPLE: I saw Miss Faber and although she apparently knew nothing about the chauffeur she certainly knew something about that note.

STEVE: The one that Shelly received?

TEMPLE: Yes.

STEVE: (*Surprised*) Did you ask her about it?

TEMPLE: I did, and she confirmed what Shelly suspected – that she sent it to him as a practical joke.

STEVE: But who told her about De Wolfe, and how was she able to copy Miss Millicent's handwriting?

TEMPLE: The same person that told her about De Wolfe supplied her with a letter of Miss Millicent's.

STEVE: Did she tell you who that was?

TEMPLE: No, she didn't but I've got a pretty shrewd idea. (*Impatiently; glancing at his watch*) It's eight. I wish Droste would hurry up.

STEVE: Darling, you are impatient! Why are you in such a hurry?

TEMPLE: Because when I've dropped you at the flat I want to drive out to Roehampton.

STEVE: You're not driving anywhere, my sweet! If you want to go to Roehampton I'll take you there. But why Roehampton for goodness sake?

TEMPLE: Because that's where Terry Palmer lives – when he's not with Mrs Desmond – and I want to have a confidential chat with that young man.

STEVE: (*Surprised*) Do you think it was Palmer then that ... (*She stops*)

TEMPLE: What is it?

STEVE: Here's Droste. Something's happened, Paul!

DROSTE: (*Very quietly*) There's no need for you to take me back to Town, Temple. I'm going back with McCall.

TEMPLE: Oh.

DROSTE: (*His thoughts elsewhere*) We've had a spot of trouble at the Commodore, the manager's been taken ill. I want McCall to take charge there, for the time being at any rate.

TEMPLE: I see.

STEVE: Is there any news from Paris?

DROSTE: (*Softly*) Yes.

A moment.

TEMPLE: What is it, Droste? Have you had bad news?

DROSTE: (*After a slight pause*) My wife died ... this ... afternoon ...

STEVE: Oh. Oh, I am sorry, Mr Droste.

TEMPLE: Did she regain consciousness?

DROSTE: No. No, apparently not. Now will you excuse me? I've ... got one or two arrangements to make and ... I don't want to miss the plane ...

TEMPLE: Yes, of course. (*Watching DROSTE*) Goodbye, Droste.

DROSTE: Goodbye. Goodbye, Mrs Temple.

STEVE: Goodbye, Mr Droste.

TEMPLE: Come along, Steve!

FADE UP background noises.

FADE background noises.
FADE SCENE.

FADE UP the noise of a typewriter. The doorbell starts to ring. The typewriter stops.
A door opens.

PALMER: (*Pleasantly surprised*) Why, hello, Temple! I never expected to see you, not at this time of night!

TEMPLE: May I come in, Palmer?

PALMER: Yes, of course!

TEMPLE enters the room.
The door closes.

TEMPLE: Am I disturbing you?

PALMER: Not a bit. I've finished an article and I was just going to help myself to a whisky and soda. Will you join me?

TEMPLE: Well – thanks very much. It sounds an excellent idea.

In the background PALMER mixes drinks.

PALMER: Would you prefer water?

TEMPLE: No, I'd like soda if you've got it.

PALMER: Yes, certainly.

We hear the sound of a syphon.

TEMPLE: How's Mrs Desmond?

PALMER: She's not awfully good, I'm afraid. She still seems awfully on edge. This Miss Millicent business has certainly played the very devil with her nerves. I've got a shrewd suspicion she's not sleeping too well.

TEMPLE: Is she still down at Eastbourne?

PALMER: No, she came back to Town this morning, although I believe the baby's still there. (*Handing TEMPLE his drink*) Here we are.

195

TEMPLE:	Oh, thanks.
PALMER:	(*Raising his glass*) Cheers!
TEMPLE:	Skoal! (*A moment*) Palmer …
PALMER:	Yes?
TEMPLE:	Do you mind if I ask you a rather personal question?
PALMER:	No, of course not. Fire ahead, old boy.

A moment.

TEMPLE:	What exactly is your relationship with Mrs Desmond?
PALMER:	(*After a slight hesitation*) We're very good friends.
TEMPLE:	Is that all?
PALMER:	Yes, at the moment, that's all – unfortunately. (*Smiling, but with just a suggestion of annoyance*) Is there anything else you'd like to know?
TEMPLE:	Look, Palmer, I don't want you to get the wrong impression about this. I'm not interested in your private life as such. Your relationship with Mrs Desmond, and anyone else for that matter, is entirely your own affair. I asked you the question simply because, in my opinion, it might quite possibly have a bearing on this Vandyke case.
PALMER:	How can my private life possibly have any bearing on the Vandyke case?
TEMPLE:	(*Watching PALMER*) Let me be the judge of that, Mr Palmer.
PALMER:	(*Quietly*) I met Mary several years ago – when her husband was alive. I fell in love with her the first time I saw her. When John Desmond died I did everything for Mary, everything I possibly could. Since then I've made a point of

	proposing to Mrs Desmond twice a week – usually on Thursdays and Fridays. She rejects my proposals with monotonous regularity.

TEMPLE: I should try Mondays and Wednesdays, Mr Palmer – you might have better luck. However, I didn't come here to talk to you about Mrs Desmond.

PALMER: (*Faintly annoyed*) What did you come to talk to me about?

TEMPLE: I came because I wanted to ... (*Suddenly; disarming*) Do you think I could have a little more soda in this drink?

PALMER: Er – yes, of course.

We hear the sound of the syphon again.

TEMPLE: Thank you. Now, what was I saying?

PALMER: You were saying that you didn't come here to talk to me about Mrs Desmond.

TEMPLE: Ah, yes! Yes, of course. Palmer, tell me: how long have you known Marian Faber?

PALMER: (*Taken aback*) Marian Faber!

TEMPLE: Yes. (*Politely*) You do know Miss Faber, don't you?

PALMER: Why, yes, of course, but ...

TEMPLE: Well – how long have you known her?

PALMER: (*Embarrassed*) I – I should say about two years, that's all.

TEMPLE: Is <u>she</u> a very good friend of yours?

PALMER: (*Faintly aggressive*) What do you mean?

TEMPLE: (*Quite simply*) Well, is she a very good friend of yours?

PALMER: (*Tensely*) No. No, she's not. She's not a friend of mine at all.

TEMPLE: Oh, really? You've known her for two years but – she's – not a friend of yours?

197

PALMER:	That's right.
TEMPLE:	Now that surprises me, Palmer – really surprises me.
PALMER:	(*Irritated*) Why should it surprise you?
TEMPLE:	I don't know whether you've been to her bungalow recently or not, but …
PALMER:	(*Quickly*) No, I haven't!
TEMPLE:	Well, if you go, Palmer, you'll see your photograph – in the hall – opposite the door. You can't possibly miss it.
PALMER:	(*Surprised*) My photograph?!
TEMPLE:	That's right. It's a very good one. You're wearing a blue suit and …
PALMER:	I know the photograph you mean all right!
TEMPLE:	Did you give it to Miss Faber?
PALMER:	Yes.
TEMPLE:	When?
PALMER:	About – two – years ago.
TEMPLE:	Well, she must have been a very good friend of yours then – judging from the inscription. "To Marian, with all my love."
PALMER:	Why are you interested in Marian Faber?
TEMPLE:	For a variety of reasons. But I can give you one very good reason, Palmer.
PALMER:	Well?
TEMPLE:	Miss Faber admits that she sent a note to Roger Shelly. The note was written exactly as Miss Millicent would have written it.
PALMER:	What do you mean?
TEMPLE:	I mean that Miss Faber copied Miss Millicent's handwriting.
PALMER:	But how on earth was she able to do that?
TEMPLE:	Well, apparently, someone provided Marian with a letter of Miss Millicent's.

198

PALMER: Oh, I see.

TEMPLE: The same person dictated the contents of the note.

PALMER: And you think I'm that person?

TEMPLE: Well, aren't you?

PALMER: Look here, before we discuss anything else let's get my relationship with Marian Faber straightened out. Two years ago I did a series of articles on modern art. Frankly, it's a subject I know very little about, that's probably why the magazine commissioned me to do the series. Anyway, I got a friend of mine to introduce me to Marian Faber. I knew she was a well known portrait painter and had got pretty definite views on contemporary art. Well, Marian was awfully good – she helped me no end so far as the articles were concerned but unfortunately …

TEMPLE: Well?

PALMER: Unfortunately she turned out to be a rather possessive type of person and – Well, damn it all, Temple, you're a man of the world, I don't have to explain.

TEMPLE: (*Quietly*) I see. When was the last time you saw Miss Faber?

PALMER: Oh, about six or seven months ago.

TEMPLE: And you haven't seen her since?

PALMER: Not to speak of. I saw her in a restaurant about a month or so ago but fortunately she didn't see me.

TEMPLE: (*Thoughtfully*) M'm.

PALMER: Now to get back to your question, Mr Temple. I did not provide Marian Faber, or anyone else, with a letter of Miss Millicent's. I did not

	dictate the contents of, nor suggest the sending of, a note to Roger Shelly.
TEMPLE:	Did you know that Shelly had received a note?
PALMER:	Yes. There was a paragraph in one of the papers which said he had received a threatening letter. It didn't say what the letter was about or who sent it.
TEMPLE:	Palmer, tell me: when you first discovered that Miss Millicent worked for Shelly did you realise that it was the same Shelly that your friend Miss Faber was friendly with?
PALMER:	I didn't know that Marian was friendly with Shelly – not until you told me.
TEMPLE:	Didn't Miss Faber ever mention him?
PALMER:	No. I never heard of Shelly until Miss Millicent told Mary that she was going to work for him.
TEMPLE:	Have you met Shelly?
PALMER:	Yes. I met him at Scotland Yard about a week ago. Inspector Eden introduced us.
TEMPLE:	I see.
PALMER:	Well – any more questions, Mr Temple? Or is the quiz programme over for this evening?
TEMPLE:	It's not quite over. Just one more question.
PALMER:	Well?
TEMPLE:	I'm a novelist, Palmer. I write detective stories.
PALMER:	Yes, I know. I've read them – they're very good.
TEMPLE:	Thank you. Well, if I was writing this story – the story of Miss Millicent and the mysterious Mr Vandyke – do you know what I should call you, Palmer?
PALMER:	No.
TEMPLE:	I should call you – Suspect No. 1.
PALMER:	(*Nervously, surprised*) Suspect No. 1?

TEMPLE: Yes.

PALMER: (*Quickly; rather angry*) Why? Why would you call me that? Just because I didn't tell you that Marian Faber was a friend of mine? Just because the cloakroom attendant at the Commodore Club lied to you about the attaché case? You know, Mr Temple, for a famous detective writer you're really rather stupid, aren't you?

TEMPLE: Stupid?

PALMER: (*Suddenly*) I'm sorry. I'm sorry – I lost my temper. I shouldn't have said that. It was awfully rude of me.

TEMPLE: (*Pleasantly; curious*) No, that's all right. Go ahead. Tell me, why exactly am I stupid, Mr Palmer?

PALMER: (*Laughing*) No. No, really, it was awfully rude. I'm sorry. I do apologize.

TEMPLE: No, please. Tell me …

PALMER: Well …

TEMPLE: Go on!

PALMER: (*Amused*) Well, surely, you of all people, ought to know that …

TEMPLE: Know what?

PALMER: That … Suspect No 1 … never turns out to be the villain …

TEMPLE: (*Quietly, watching PALMER*) There are exceptions, Mr Palmer.

FADE UP of music.

FADE DOWN of music.
FADE UP the sound of a car drawing to a standstill.
A car door opens.

STEVE: I'll drive the car round to the garage, darling.

TEMPLE: There's no need for that, Steve. I'll send Charlie down.

STEVE: Yes, all right.

In the background a taxi drives up to the kerb.
We hear the sound of the taxi door opening and closing.

TEMPLE: Don't forget your bag, Steve.

STEVE: Oh, yes.

TEMPLE: (*Suddenly; surprised*) Hello!

STEVE: What is it?

TEMPLE: Look who's here! It's Roger Shelly!

STEVE: Where?

TEMPLE: He's just getting out of that taxi!

STEVE: It looks as if he's going up to the flat, Paul!

TEMPLE: Yes. (*Calling*) Shelly! Shelly!!!!

STEVE: (*Quietly*) He's heard you, darling.

TEMPLE: By Timothy, he looks in a flap with himself, doesn't he? (*A moment: pleasantly*) Hello, Shelly! Were you just going up to the flat?

SHELLY: (*Excited: a shade overwrought*) Yes! Yes, I wanted to have a talk to you, Temple. I ... Oh, good evening, Mrs Temple! (*Breathlessly*) I'm so sorry, I'm afraid I didn't notice you, I ... Really, I'm quite at sixes and sevens! I just don't know whether I'm coming or going!

STEVE: Is anything the matter, Mr Shelly?

SHELLY: I've had the most devastating experience. I mean really devastating!

STEVE: Why – what's happened?

SHELLY: You know that note I received – the one I thought was a practical joke?

TEMPLE: Yes?

SHELLY: Well, I was wrong – quite wrong. Marian couldn't possibly have sent it.

TEMPLE: What do you mean?

202

SHELLY: Well, it turns out it wasn't a joke after all.

TEMPLE: (*Drily*) That's an interesting observation, Mr Shelly.

SHELLY: I don't think you understand. You see …

TEMPLE: Go on …

SHELLY: That note was a threat – a quite genuine threat. You see … (*Slowly; tensely*) … someone … tried … to … murder … me …

STEVE: (*Surprised*) Someone tried to murder you?

SHELLY: Yes.

TEMPLE: (*Quickly*) When?

SHELLY: Just over an hour ago. Oh, it was a terrible experience, Temple. My goodness, I never want to go through anything like that again!

STEVE: But why should anyone want to murder you, Mr Shelly?

SHELLY: That's the whole point, Mrs Temple! I don't understand – I just <u>don't</u> understand!

TEMPLE: (*Quietly*) What happened, Shelly?

SHELLY: Well, I got home from the office at about half past eight. I'd had a fairly heavy day and I wasn't feeling too good so I went up to my bedroom, changed into a dressing gown, took a couple of aspirins, and lay down on the bed.

TEMPLE: Go on …

SHELLY: Well, I suppose I must have been on the bed an hour or so – as a matter of fact I was dozing – when I heard a noise. I glanced towards the window and to my absolute horror I realized that a man had climbed the balcony and was actually in the room.

STEVE: Did you recognise him?

SHELLY: No, I'm afraid I didn't. I couldn't see very clearly but I'm pretty sure it wasn't anyone I'd seen before. I was petrified. I just didn't know what to do. I know it sounds highly melodramatic but it was just as if my body had turned to stone.

TEMPLE: Go on, Shelly.

SHELLY: (*Tensely*) I watched him. I watched him come closer and closer to the bed. He thought I was asleep. Suddenly, I saw him take something from his pocket. I couldn't see what it was – not at first – not until he was right on top of me and then …

STEVE: (*Tensely; interested*) What was it?

SHELLY: It was a knife. It was one of those squat little knives with a razor blade …

STEVE: (*Horrified*) Oh!

SHELLY: Suddenly, I remembered Queenie Edwards. I remembered your telling me what she looked like after … after …

TEMPLE: Go on, Shelly …

STEVE: What did you do?

SHELLY: There was only one thing I could do. I went for him. My God, how I went for him. He must have thought I was stark staring mad. I shouted, I kicked, I scratched. I fought like a demon. In the end he realised that the game was up and he made a dash for it.

STEVE: It must have been a very nasty experience, Mr Shelly.

SHELLY: It was horrible, Mrs Temple. Frankly, I'm exhausted. Mentally and physically exhausted.

TEMPLE: What was he like, this man?

SHELLY: He was tall, about your build, I suppose – but – I haven't the slightest idea what he looked like.

TEMPLE: Yes, well I'm afraid that's not very helpful, Shelly. By the way, have you told the police about this?

SHELLY: Not yet, but I intend to. Incidentally, I found this, Temple. It was on the floor near the bed.

STEVE: What is it?

SHELLY: It's a small buckle. I think I must have pulled it off his wristlet watch while we were struggling.

TEMPLE: Yes. Are you sure it isn't yours?

SHELLY: Oh, quite sure. What shall I do, give it to the police or …

TEMPLE: No, it's all right, Shelly, I'll take care of this. (*Pleasantly*) What are you going to do now – go back to your flat?

SHELLY: No, I couldn't possibly go back to the flat. I should be terrified! I'm spending the night with some friends. They've been very sweet and offered to put me up for the night. I shall probably go down to Marlow tomorrow.

TEMPLE: Yes, well, I'll have a word with the Yard about this, Shelly. Meanwhile – take care of yourself.

START FADE.

SHELLY: Well, I'll try. (*Wearily*) But, really! Goodnight, Mrs Temple.

STEVE: Goodnight, Mr Shelly.

FADE SCENE.

FADE UP.
TEMPLE is pressing the bellpush on the door of their flat: from within the flat we hear the sound of the buzzer.

STEVE: (*Thoughtfully*) Paul …

TEMPLE: Yes?

STEVE: Do you think Shelly was telling the truth?

TEMPLE: Well, the poor chap was overwrought. Yes, I think he was telling the truth, darling. (*With a thought*) He certainly looked as if he'd been in a fight. (*Pressing the button again*) What the devil's the matter with Charlie?

STEVE: Well, if you didn't forget your key every time you go out there wouldn't be any necessity for …

TEMPLE: (*Interrupting STEVE*) Here he is!

The door opens.

STEVE: We thought you'd gone to bed, Charlie!

CHARLIE: (*Unperturbed*) No, I've been listenin' to the wireless.

TEMPLE: Any messages, Charlie?

CHARLIE: Yes, a Mrs Desmond telephoned – as a matter o' fact she's phoned two or three times.

TEMPLE: Mrs Desmond?

CHARLIE: That's right. She said she wanted to see you. Blimey, she didn't 'alf sound in a stew!

TEMPLE: Is she phoning again?

CHARLIE: Well, I don't know. She said she was speaking from the Commodore Club. I think she wants you to go round there.

STEVE: What – to the Commodore?

CHARLIE: Yes.

TEMPLE: (*Faintly irritated*) What do you mean – you <u>think</u> she wants us to go round there?

CHARLIE: Well, she seemed so het up, it was difficult to understand half of what she was talking about. When I said you wasn't in she said – Tell Mr Temple it's urgent. I'm at the Commodore Club.

TEMPLE: (*Briskly*) If she phones again, Charlie, tell her we're on the way!

206

CHARLIE: Okedoke!
START FADE.
TEMPLE: Come along, Steve!
COMPLETE FADE.

Slow FADE UP of a dance orchestra.
Establish the dance music in the near background.
There is a slight background of voices.

STEVE: I don't see any sign of Mrs Desmond.

TEMPLE: (*Taking stock of his surroundings*) No, neither
           do I. I wonder if she's upstairs, Steve. I believe
           there's a ladies lounge on the first floor.

STEVE: Well, I hardly think she's waiting for us
           upstairs, darling, unless … (*She stops:*
           surprised)

McCALL: Hello, Mrs Temple! (*To TEMPLE*) Hello,
           there!

TEMPLE: Hello, McCall! What are you doing at the
           Commodore?

McCALL: I've taken over. Didn't Mr Droste tell you?

TEMPLE: Oh, yes! Yes, of course. I remember. The
           manager was taken ill or something.

McCALL: That's right. Appendicitis.

TEMPLE: Oh …

McCALL: (*Carefully*) Acute – appendicitis. (*Suddenly*)
           Well, I suppose you're looking for Mrs
           Desmond?

TEMPLE: (*Surprised*) Why, yes.

McCALL: She's been expecting you for the last hour or
           so. Boy, was she in a flap-doodle!

TEMPLE: Where is she now?

McCALL: She left about four or five minutes ago.

TEMPLE: Did she say where she was going?

McCALL: No, I'm afraid she didn't.

TEMPLE:	(*Thoughtfully*) I wonder if she's gone to the flat?
STEVE:	That's about what's happened, darling! We most probably passed her on the way here!
McCALL:	You've only just missed her.
TEMPLE:	(*Briskly*) Come on, Steve!
McCALL:	(*Suddenly, stopping TEMPLE*) Oh, Mr Temple!
TEMPLE:	(*Turning*) Yes?
McCALL:	This Mrs Desmond – is she the Mrs Desmond that was mixed up in the Miss Millicent case? The one with the baby girl?
TEMPLE:	Yes. (*Curious*) Why do you ask?
McCALL:	(*Vaguely*) Oh, I – wondered – that's all.

FADE UP of the dance music from the background.
Slow FADE DOWN.
FADE the dance music completely.

FADE UP a faint background of street noises.

STEVE:	I thought you parked the car here, darling.
TEMPLE:	No, it's just round the corner – don't forget we went in the side entrance.
STEVE:	Oh.

A pause.

TEMPLE:	Here we are, here's the car! (*He opens the car door*) Jump in, Steve!
STEVE:	No, I'll drive, Paul. You keep on the lookout in case we pass Mrs Desmond.
TEMPLE:	Yes, all right – move over.
STEVE:	Come round to the other side, darling.
TEMPLE:	(*Moving to the other side of the car*) I haven't got the key.
STEVE:	It's all right, I've got it.
TEMPLE:	(*Casually: opening the car door*) Is that your handbag on the back seat?

STEVE: Where? (*A sudden start of surprise*) Oh!
TEMPLE: What is it? Steve, what is it?
STEVE: (*Tensely*) Paul, it's that doll! The – doll – that –
            was in the attaché case!
TEMPLE: What? Are you sure?
STEVE: Yes. (*Softly: horrified*) Oh, Paul!
TEMPLE: What's the matter?
STEVE: It's – covered – in – blood!
FADE UP of music.

END OF EPISODE SIX

EPISODE SEVEN

STEVE ENTERTAINS

OPEN TO:

FADE UP a faint background of street noises.

STEVE: I thought you parked the car here, darling.

TEMPLE: No, it's just round the corner – don't forget we went in the side entrance.

STEVE: Oh.

A pause.

TEMPLE: Here we are, here's the car! (*He opens the car door*) Jump in, Steve!

STEVE: No, I'll drive, Paul. You keep on the lookout in case we pass Mrs Desmond.

TEMPLE: Yes, all right – move over.

STEVE: Come round to the other side, darling.

TEMPLE: (*Moving to the other side of the car*) I haven't got the key.

STEVE: It's all right, I've got it.

TEMPLE: (*Casually: opening the car door*) Is that your handbag on the back seat?

STEVE: Where? (*A sudden start of surprise*) Oh!

TEMPLE: What is it? Steve, what is it?

STEVE: (*Tensely*) Paul, it's that doll! The – doll – that – was in the attaché case!

TEMPLE: What? Are you sure?

STEVE: Yes. (*Softly: horrified*) Oh, Paul!

TEMPLE: What's the matter?

STEVE: It's – covered – in – blood!

TEMPLE: Covered in blood!

STEVE: Yes, darling, look!

During the following dialogue an ambulance can be heard rushing past the entrance to the mews in which TEMPLE has parked his car.

TEMPLE: By Timothy, you're right! I say, Steve, just look at the back seat of the car!

213

STEVE:	Why, it looks as if there's been a fight or something!
TEMPLE:	It looks remarkably like it!
STEVE:	Didn't you lock the car?
TEMPLE:	No, I didn't.
STEVE:	(*Puzzled*) Paul, what do you think has happened?
TEMPLE:	I don't know, Steve – unless Mrs Desmond decided to wait … (*Quietly*) Let me have a look at that doll.

A moment.

STEVE:	Is it the same one – the one that was left in the cloakroom?
TEMPLE:	Yes, it looks like it.
STEVE:	(*Suddenly*) Paul!
TEMPLE:	What is it?
STEVE:	There's an ambulance, darling!
TEMPLE:	(*Quickly*) Which way did it go?
STEVE:	It went round to the right.
TEMPLE:	That's the back of the Commodore Club! Stay here!

TEMPLE opens the car door and gets out of the car.

STEVE:	Where are you going?
TEMPLE:	I'm going back to the Commodore, Steve!
STEVE:	(*Suddenly*) Here's McCall!

BILL McCALL is running towards them.

McCALL:	(*Calling; running towards the car*) Temple! Temple, wait a minute! Wait a minute, Temple!!!
TEMPLE:	Hello, McCall! What's happened?
McCALL:	(*Breathlessly*) Gee, I'm glad I caught you! The guy on the door said that you … you …
TEMPLE:	Take it easy!
STEVE:	What's happened?

McCALL: One ... of ... the ... dance ... band ... boys ... found ... (*Unable to get his breath*) You'll have to excuse me! (*Slowly*) Boy, I must be out of condition!

A slight pause.

TEMPLE: Now, what's happened?

McCALL: One of the dance band boys strolled outside for a breath of air – he found Mrs Desmond in the mews at the back of the club – she was beaten up.

STEVE: Is she badly hurt?

McCALL: Yes, she's in a pretty bad way. We've sent for an ambulance.

TEMPLE: (*Quickly*) Come along, McCall! Take the car back to the flat, Steve. I'll see you later.

STEVE: What shall I do with the doll?

McCALL: (*Surprised*) The doll! Where did you find that?

TEMPLE: It was in my car.

McCALL: (*Puzzled*) In your car?

TEMPLE: Yes.

McCALL: That's very odd, isn't it?

STEVE: Have you seen it before, Mr McCall?

McCALL: Why, yes, of course! It belongs to Mrs Desmond.

TEMPLE: (*Quietly: watching McCALL*) How do you know?

McCALL: She had it with her – earlier in the evening, I mean. She told me that she was taking it down to Eastbourne for her little girl. But how the devil did it get into the car?

STEVE: (*Suddenly*) Paul, don't you see what happened? Mary Desmond got tired of waiting: she must have walked out of the Club just as we drove

215

up. When she found the car was unlocked she decided to wait for us. Unfortunately …

McCALL: Someone else spotted her and dragged her out of the car! Gee, that's just about it, Mrs Temple! That's just about it!

TEMPLE: (*Thoughtfully*) Yes. (*Suddenly*) Come along, McCall!

FADE.

FADE SCENE.

FADE UP the voices of a small crowd congregating near the ambulance.

TEMPLE: (*Surprised*) Hello, Inspector! It hasn't taken you long to get here!

EDEN: (*Turning*) Why, hello, Mr Temple!

TEMPLE: What are you driving these days – a stratocruiser?

EDEN: (*Laughing*) The matron of St George's happens to be a friend of mine. I was at the hospital when the call came through.

TEMPLE: Oh, I see.

EDEN: (*Grimly*) It's a nasty business.

TEMPLE: Is she badly hurt?

EDEN: Very badly, I'm afraid. It's a long time since I've seen anything like it. I'd like to get my hands on the swine.

TEMPLE: Is she conscious?

E£DEN: Just about.

TEMPLE: Do you think I could see her?

EDEN: Well –

TEMPLE: Actually, I had an appointment with Mrs Desmond.

EDEN: (*Surprised*) You did?

TEMPLE: Yes, that's why I'm here.

EDEN: Where did you arrange to meet her – at the
            Commodore Club?
TEMPLE: Yes.
EDEN: Did Mrs Desmond send for you, sir?
TEMPLE: Yes, she did. And she telephoned two or three
            times but unfortunately I was out.
NURSE: Excuse me, Inspector!
EDEN: Oh, yes, nurse?
NURSE: We're leaving now.
EDEN: This is Mr Temple. He wants to have a word
            with Mrs Desmond. Do you think he could
            travel back with you?
NURSE: Yes, I think that'll be all right, sir.
TEMPLE: Thank you, nurse. I'll see you at the hospital,
            Inspector!
NURSE: This way, sir!

*FADE UP the crowd voices and the sound of the ambulance
engine.*
FADE DOWN.
FADE SCENE.

*FADE UP of the ambulance travelling through the West End
of London.*
FADE DOWN slightly.
*CROSS FADE to TEMPLE, MARY DESMOND and the
NURSE inside the ambulance. Besides being very badly hurt
MARY DESMOND is tense and overwrought: she is trying
desperately hard to tell TEMPLE why she made the
appointment to see him at the Commodore Club.*
MARY: … I got tired of waiting that's why I … went
            … outside … I saw you drive up to the club so
            … I went to your car … I intended to wait for
            you in the car but he saw me … he saw me …
            and he … he …

TEMPLE: (*Quietly*) Who saw you, Mrs Desmond – Vandyke?

MARY: (*Tensely*) Yes … Yes, he saw me … He dragged me out of the car, he hit me … He hit me … (*Desperately frightened*) Don't let him hit me! Please don't let him hit me again! Please, don't! I swear I'll do what you want! I swear!

NURSE: It's all right, Mrs Desmond. No one's going to hurt you. We're taking you to the hospital. There's no need to worry – you'll be perfectly all right.

MARY: (*Bewildered*) To the hospital? You're … taking … me … to … (*Suddenly: suspiciously*) Who is that? Who is that sitting over there? Who is it?!

TEMPLE: It's me, Mrs Desmond – Paul Temple. Don't you remember – you wanted to see me.

MARY: (*Vaguely*) Temple? Oh, yes – yes, of course. I sent for you. I telephoned you, didn't I? I wanted to tell you about … about ... Miss Millicent …

TEMPLE: (*Softly*) Go on, Mrs Desmond … What about Miss Millicent?

MARY: (*With an effort*) Miss Millicent didn't know what she was doing … she didn't know what was in the package … We never told her, we never told her that … she … was … helping … to … distribute … drugs …

TEMPLE: (*Gently*) Go on, Mrs Desmond.

MARY: One day she opened one of the packages … it was intended for Mrs Droste … When she discovered what it was she wanted to go to the police. We told her that if she went to the

218

	police we'd say that … she … was … one … of … us …
TEMPLE:	You blackmailed her. Is that why she disappeared – why she took the child?
MARY:	Yes. She tried to turn the tables on us, she thought that if she had the child she could … force … us … to … change … our … mind …
TEMPLE:	What happened?
MARY:	We found her – and the baby. Vandyke found her. He sent for Queenie Edwards. He sent for Queenie Edwards because he knew that … that …
TEMPLE:	Because he knew that Miss Millicent had confided in her?
MARY:	Yes. When he discovered that Queenie worked at Madame Flaubert's in Mount Street he tried to … tried to … persuade … (*Weakly*) Oh, my head … (*Confused*) Don't touch my head … Please don't touch my head!
NURSE:	(*Quietly*) I'm afraid she'll have to be kept quiet, Mr Temple …
TEMPLE:	Yes, all right, nurse. Just one more question. (*Gently*) Mrs Desmond, tell me: who is Vandyke?
MARY:	(*Confused: in pain*) Vandyke? Vandyke is … (*Suddenly, desperately frightened*) Don't let him touch me! Please don't let him touch me! Please! (*Trying to force herself off the stretcher*) Please, don't hit me! Don't hit me again! Don't hit me …
NURSE:	(*Softly: soothing MARY*) It's all right, Mrs Desmond. Now it's perfectly all right. There's nothing for you to be frightened of … Just relax, Mrs Desmond.

MARY is breathing heavily: relaxing.

NURSE: Just … relax …

FADE UP of the ambulance racing through the crowded streets ringing its electric bell.

Dramatic FADE UP of music.

Slow FADE DOWN of music.

A door opens.

CHARLIE: Did you ring?

TEMPLE: Yes, Charlie. Bring me some more marmalade.

CHARLIE: O.K. Anything else?

TEMPLE: Yes, some toast and some more butter, Charlie.

CHARLIE: Blimey, you haven't half got an appetite this morning! What about coffee?

TEMPLE: No, we're all right for coffee. I expect Mrs Temple will want some more tea though.

CHARLIE: She's in the kitchen now – making it. Women are funny about tea, aren't they?

TEMPLE: They're funny about a great many things, Charlie. But don't let's go into that, not at this time of the morning.

The door opens.

STEVE: Good morning, darling!

TEMPLE: Good morning, Steve!

STEVE: Charlie, I've left the cooker on.

CHARLIE: Yes, all right, Mrs Temple.

TEMPLE: (*His mouth full*) Don't forget the toast, Charlie.

CHARLIE: (*Departing*) Okedoke!

STEVE: Paul, don't eat with your mouth full!

TEMPLE: (*Mouth full*) You mean don't talk with my mouth full.

STEVE: I mean don't – you know what I mean!

TEMPLE: (*Laughing*) Yes, dear!

A moment.

220

STEVE: Is that this morning's paper?

TEMPLE: Yes.

STEVE: Can I see it?

TEMPLE: Yes. (*He passes the paper*) There's a photograph of Mrs Desmond on the front page.

STEVE takes the paper.

STEVE: (*Surprised: faintly shocked*) Oh, Paul!

TEMPLE: Yes, it's pretty gruesome, isn't it. They must have taken it just as she was getting into the ambulance.

STEVE: (*Softly*) Oh, Paul, it's horrible!

TEMPLE: (*After a moment*) What are you doing this morning, Steve?

STEVE: Why?

TEMPLE: Well, I've got an appointment with Sir Graham at ten o'clock.

STEVE: Where is your appointment – at the Yard?

TEMPLE: Yes. Sir Graham phoned me about twenty minutes ago. Apparently they intend to ask Terry Palmer a few questions. After what happened last night it's not surprising.

STEVE: Do you think that Palmer was responsible for what happened?

TEMPLE: In other words is Terry Palmer Mr Vandyke? That's a leading question, darling – especially for this time of the morning. You can bet your bottom dollar on one thing though: whoever was responsible for what happened was under the impression that Mrs Desmond was dead, otherwise …

STEVE: Otherwise they wouldn't have left her.

TEMPLE: Exactly.

STEVE: (*After a moment; quietly*) Paul …

TEMPLE: Yes, Steve?

STEVE: (*Softly: seriously*) I'm awfully worried about this case.

TEMPLE: Why? Because of what happened to Mrs Desmond?

STEVE: Partly, and partly because I think – (*Seriously, obviously perturbed*) Well, if you must know, I think we're up against something we've never quite experienced before. I think that Vandyke, whoever he is …

TEMPLE: (*Quietly*) You think he's mad: you think he's a criminal lunatic, don't you?

STEVE: (*After a moment*) Yes. Yes, I do. Don't you? (*Suddenly*) Darling, you must do! After what happened to Mrs Desmond and Queenie Edwards how can you possibly think otherwise?

TEMPLE: (*Slowly: shaking his head*) Vandyke's cruel, sadistic, and utterly and completely ruthless, but he's not mad, darling. He's as sane as you and I. (*Suddenly; yet hesitating*) Steve, there's something I want to ask you.

STEVE: Yes?

TEMPLE: (*Hesitatingly*) You just said yourself that we're up against something we've never experienced before, so …

STEVE: Well?

TEMPLE: So …

STEVE: Paul, what is it?

TEMPLE: I want you to go away for two or three days – into the country – alone.

STEVE: Why?

TEMPLE: Well –

STEVE: You want me to go into hiding, is that it?

TEMPLE: Not exactly, but …

STEVE: Things are coming to a head, aren't they?

TEMPLE: (*A moment: seriously*) Yes, Steve, they are.

STEVE: (*Quite simply*) Well, I'm not going away.

TEMPLE: Steve, I wouldn't ask you to do this. I've never asked you before. We've always been together, but …

STEVE: Why are you asking me now?

TEMPLE: Don't you know why? (*A moment*) You know what happened to Queenie Edwards – to Mrs Desmond.

STEVE: It doesn't matter. I'm staying. (*Shaking her head*) I'm not going away.

TEMPLE: Steve, now don't let's be stupid about this.

STEVE: (*Emphatically*) Paul, I – am – not – going – away!

TEMPLE: All right. But promise me you'll be on your guard. Watch your step. If you receive a message check it – it doesn't matter who it's from, whether it's from me or Sir Graham or anyone else – check it and double check it.

STEVE: All right, Paul. (*A slight pause*) What happened last night? Was Mrs Desmond able to tell you anything?

TEMPLE: She was in a pretty bad state: by the time we reached the hospital she'd passed completely out. One thing she did do though, she cleared up the mystery of Miss Millicent. I always knew that Miss Millicent wasn't kidnapped.

The door opens.

TEMPLE: I told Inspector Eden several days ago that … Yes, what is it, Charlie?

CHARLIE: Excuse me, sir – but Mr Shelly would like to see you. I told 'im you was 'aving breakfast.

TEMPLE: Where have you put him, Charlie?

223

CHARLIE: I 'aven't put him anywhere, not yet, sir. I know where I'd like to put him.

TEMPLE: (*Smiling*) All right, Charlie. You'd better ask him in here.

CHARLIE: O.K., sir.

The door closes.

STEVE: What does Shelly want?

TEMPLE: Your guess is as good as mine, Steve.

STEVE: He's probably read about Mrs Desmond.

TEMPLE: Yes. Unless he's remembered something.

STEVE: What do you mean?

TEMPLE: Don't forget Mrs Desmond wasn't the only person to be attacked last night: someone went for Shelly.

STEVE: (*Thoughtfully*) I wonder.

TEMPLE: (*Smiling*) Don't tell me you doubt Mr Shelly, darling!

The door opens.

STEVE: Good morning, Mr Shelly! Come along in!

SHELLY: Oh, good morning, Mrs Temple! Oh, dear, have I interrupted your breakfast again?! How very tantalising! I'm so sorry.

TEMPLE: That's all right, Shelly. Delighted to see you. Have some coffee.

SHELLY: Well – may I? That's very nice of you.

TEMPLE: Well, how are feeling this morning?

SHELLY: I'm all right; a little stiff I suppose after that terrifying experience of mine.

TEMPLE: Well, you were very lucky, Shelly. Look what happened to Mrs Desmond.

SHELLY: (*Puzzled*) What do you mean?

TEMPLE: Haven't you seen the papers?

SHELLY: (*Surprised*) Why, no!

STEVE: Here we are, Mr Shelly – read this.

TEMPLE: (*Aside, to STEVE*) Pour Shelly a cup of coffee, darling.

A pause: during which STEVE pours the coffee.

SHELLY: (*Staggered*) But this is appalling! Mrs Desmond … Why, I can hardly believe it! It's – it's quite fantastic!

TEMPLE: (*Quietly*) Well, there you are, Shelly!

SHELLY: It says here that you were with Mrs Desmond – that you went to the hospital with her. Is that true?

TEMPLE: Yes.

SHELLY: Was she conscious?

TEMPLE: Part of the time.

SHELLY: (*Bewildered*) But this is dreadful! Really dreadful! (*Suddenly*) Let me have another look at that paper! (*A pause: softly horrified*) Oh, God, how awful …

TEMPLE: Now you know how lucky you were, Shelly.

SHELLY: (*Nervously*) Temple, do you think the person that attacked me was the same person that … nearly … murdered … Mrs Desmond?

TEMPLE: Yes, I do.

SHELLY: (*Tensely*) But why? Why should he attack Mrs Desmond?

TEMPLE: Well, I can understand that. But why should he go for you, Shelly – that's more to the point.

SHELLY: What do you mean?

TEMPLE: Well, after all, Mrs Desmond was mixed up in the Millicent affair: it was her baby that disappeared.

SHELLY: What do you mean?

TEMPLE: Do you know why I went to the Commodore Club last night? Do you know why Mrs Desmond was beaten up?

SHELLY: No.

TEMPLE: She wanted to see me. She sent me an urgent message asking me to meet her at the Commodore.

SHELLY: Why did she do that?

TEMPLE: Because she wanted to tell me the truth about Miss Millicent – about the mysterious Mr Vandyke.

SHELLY: And did she?

TEMPLE: Unfortunately she was too ill to say anything. She was in a very bad way – I'm afraid she still is.

STEVE: Here's your coffee, Mr Shelly.

SHELLY: Oh, thank you, Mrs Temple.

TEMPLE: I'll pass it, darling. (*Taking the cup: absent-mindedly*) Where did I put my lighter, Steve?

STEVE: I think you put it … Paul, look out or you'll spill the coffee!

TEMPLE: (*Turning*) What?

STEVE: (*Quickly*) Darling, look out!

The cup slips out of TEMPLE's hand and crashes on to the table: the coffee splashes across SHELLY.

SHELLY: (*Jumping*) Oh!

STEVE: Well, Paul – really!

TEMPLE: What a damn fool thing to do!

STEVE: (*Annoyed*) It's all over Mr Shelly!

TEMPLE: I'm most awfully sorry, Shelly!

SHELLY: (*Embarrassed*) That's all right. It's nothing … Really, it's nothing!

TEMPLE: (*Calling*) Charlie! Charlie!

STEVE: Here's a napkin, Mr Shelly.

TEMPLE: Look here, you'd better take your jacket off.

SHELLY: (*Drying himself*) No, really …

TEMPLE: Please …

226

SHELLY: It's really nothing, it's just … just … (*He continues to use the serviette*)

STEVE: Paul, what on earth were you thinking of?!

TEMPLE: (*Laughing*) Darling, I had the coffee in one hand and I was looking for … Look here, Shelly – do take your jacket off, please!

SHELLY: No, really, there's no necessity for …

TEMPLE: I insist, old boy!

SHELLY: (*Hesitating*) Well …

TEMPLE: I'll have it dry in next to no time if you take it off.

SHELLY: (*Laughing*) Yes, all right.

STEVE: Paul, you really are the limit!

The door opens.

CHARLIE: (*Brightly*) Did you call, Mr Temple?

TEMPLE: I did, Charlie!

STEVE: We've had an accident, Charlie. Just clear this up.

CHARLIE: O.K.

STEVE: Come along, Mr Shelly – we'll go into the drawing room.

TEMPLE: I'll be with you in a moment, Shelly. It won't take me long to do this.

CHARLIE: What about your coffee, sir? Will you take it with you or have you had enough?

SHELLY: More than enough, thank you!

They laugh.
FADE.

FADE UP.

TEMPLE: (*Pleasantly*) Here we are, Shelly. Here's your jacket. I think you'll find it's all right.

SHELLY: You shouldn't have bothered, Temple.

TEMPLE: It's very nearly dry.

SHELLY:	(*Putting on his jacket*) Yes, that's fine.
TEMPLE:	I don't think it'll mark.
SHELLY:	No. No, that's perfect. (*A moment*) Mr Temple …
TEMPLE:	Yes.
SHELLY:	I'll tell you what I dropped in about. After I left you last night I started thinking about – well – about what happened …
TEMPLE:	Go on, Shelly …
SHELLY:	Although I'm pretty sure that I wouldn't recognise the man again – the man that attacked me I mean – there was something that I think perhaps you ought to know about.
TEMPLE:	Well?
SHELLY:	When we were struggling I got hold of his wrist – I think it must have been his left wrist, the one with the wristlet watch on.
TEMPLE:	Go on …
SHELLY:	Well, it may have been my imagination but – (*With a little laugh*) – I think he was wearing a bracelet.
TEMPLE:	A bracelet?
SHELLY:	Yes. You know the sort of thing I mean. I used to wear one myself with an identity disc attached to it.
STEVE:	(*Suddenly, surprised*) Oh!
TEMPLE:	What's the matter, dear?
STEVE:	Nothing, I – was just thinking that's all.
SHELLY:	(*Watching STEVE*) Do you know anyone that wears a bracelet like that, Mrs Temple?
STEVE:	(*Confused*) No, I was just …
TEMPLE:	(*Frankly*) Well, do you, Steve?
STEVE:	(*A moment*) Yes. Yes, and you do, darling. Mr Droste wears an identity bracelet. He was

228

wearing it in Paris when we saw him at the restaurant.

SHELLY: (*Surprised*) Mr Droste!

TEMPLE: But Droste's in Paris, darling. He left last night.

STEVE: How do you know – did you see him leave?

TEMPLE: No, but he said …

SHELLY: I say, just a moment! Who is this Mr Droste anyway? Is he the millionaire – the man that owns the Commodore Club and the Wordsworth Hotel at Marlow?

STEVE: Yes.

TEMPLE: Do you know Droste?

SHELLY: Why, no. I've seen him about of course. (*Thoughtfully*) He's a rather thick-set swarthy individual.

TEMPLE: Yes, that's right.

SHELLY: (*Slowly: thoughtfully*) You know, that might have been Droste last night. I never thought of that …

TEMPLE: But you said the man was about my build?

SHELLY: (*His thoughts elsewhere*) Yes, I know I did but … (*Looking up*) What time did the plane leave?

TEMPLE: Well, I believe he caught the last plane.

SHELLY: (*Quietly: a note of tenseness*) Well, there you are!

TEMPLE: What do you mean – there you are?

STEVE: You mean that even if he did leave for Paris last night he could still have attacked both you and Mrs Desmond.

SHELLY: Precisely, Mrs Temple!

TEMPLE: (*Thoughtfully*) M'm. (*After a tiny pause*) Shelly, I think perhaps you'd better have a word with Inspector Eden about this. I've an

	appointment with Sir Graham at ten o'clock so you'd better come along with me.
SHELLY:	Well, it's nearly a quarter to ten now.
TEMPLE:	Yes, I know. Have you got your car here?
SHELLY:	No, I'm afraid I haven't.
TEMPLE:	Well, that's all right, don't worry. We can pick a cab up at the end of the road. (*To STEVE*) I don't know what time I shall be back, darling, but – don't forget what I told you.
STEVE:	I shan't.
SHELLY:	Goodbye, Mrs Temple. I'm sorry if I've made a nuisance of myself.
STEVE:	You haven't.
SHELLY:	Well – I hope I shall see you again sometime.
STEVE:	I hope so: only next time you drop in bring your umbrella.

SHELLY laughs.

| TEMPLE: | (*From the background*) Ready, Shelly? |
| SHELLY: | Yes, I'm ready. |

A moment.

STEVE:	(*Calling*) Oh, Paul!
TEMPLE:	(*In the background*) Yes, dear?
STEVE:	Here a moment.

TEMPLE returns to STEVE.

TEMPLE:	What is it, Steve?
STEVE:	(*For SHELLY's benefit*) You've forgotten your cigarette lighter again …
TEMPLE:	Oh …
STEVE:	(*Quickly: a serious whisper*) Why did you spill the coffee on him?
TEMPLE:	(*Innocently: the same tone as STEVE*) What?
STEVE:	(*The same whisper*) You heard me! Why did you spill the coffee on him?

230

TEMPLE: (*The same whisper*) Why, darling, don't be silly! You know me ...

STEVE: (*Puzzled: the same tone*) What do you mean?

TEMPLE: (*In a confidential whisper*) I come from a long line of coffee spillers! (*Raising his voice: brightly: in hasty retreat*) See you later, Steve! Take care of yourself!

FADE UP of music.

FADE DOWN of music.
FADE UP the sound of voices.
We are at Scotland Yard: TEMPLE, SIR GRAHAM and INSPECTOR EDEN are discussing the events of the previous night.
FADE IN of SIR GRAHAM's voice.

FORBES: ... I take it then, from what you say, Temple, that Mrs Desmond saw you drive up to the Commodore and decided to wait for you in the car?

TEMPLE: Yes, she probably suspected that Vandyke was watching her and she thought my car was a safe hiding place.

EDEN: In any case, she couldn't very well miss you if she waited in the car.

TEMPLE: Exactly.

FORBES: (*Thoughtfully*) You know, that swine must have actually dragged her out of your car and into the mews.

TEMPLE: No, it's my bet she put up a pretty stiff fight, Sir Graham, and made a dash for it. By the way, I don't know whether you've questioned Mrs Desmond or not?

FORBES: Mrs Desmond's dead, Temple. I've just had a message from the hospital.

TEMPLE:	Oh, I'm very sorry about that. Does Palmer know?
FORBES:	Yes, I told Eden to break the news to him.
TEMPLE:	Well, I had a word or two with Mrs Desmond in the ambulance and I'm pretty clear, in my own mind at any rate, as to how Miss Millicent fits into the picture.
EDEN:	That's more than I am!
TEMPLE:	Well, Miss Millicent was employed by Mrs Desmond as a sitter-in, but after she'd been with her a little while Mrs Desmond – or perhaps Terry Palmer – persuaded Miss Millicent to – well – run certain errands.
EDEN:	What do you mean?
TEMPLE:	She was asked to deliver packages – drugs of course – to certain people in the West End. Without thinking, and quite innocently, Miss Millicent delivered the packages. Then one day, no doubt by accident, she discovered …
EDEN:	She discovered what was in the packages and decided to have a show down!
TEMPLE:	Exactly! Miss Millicent told Mary Desmond that she intended going to the police. Mrs Desmond told her that if she did go to the police both she and Palmer would swear that Miss Millicent was part and parcel of the whole set-up. The old girl was distracted, she realised that this was tentamount to blackmail and she had no alternative but to carry on. Then suddenly she decided to confide in Queenie Edwards. Queenie was a lifelong friend and a pretty smart girl. Queenie advised Miss Millicent to play Mrs Desmond at her own game – in other words, fight back!

232

FORBES: So Miss Millicent kidnapped the child?

TEMPLE: (*Nodding*) Yes – she knew that the baby was the weak link so far as Mrs Desmond was concerned. As soon as the baby disappeared Mrs Desmond flew into a panic and contacted the police.

FORBES: Go on, Temple.

TEMPLE: Well, I don't think either Miss Millicent or Queenie Edwards quite anticipated the tremendous fuss which was made over the disappearance of the baby and the sitter-in. Anyway, Miss Millicent got frightened by all the publicity and told Queenie that she intended to return the child. Suddenly Queenie had a brainwave. She told Miss Millicent that before returning the child they would get their own back by throwing suspicion on to Terry Palmer.

EDEN: But how could Queenie Edwards throw suspicion on to Palmer?

TEMPLE: Well – (*Smiling*) I'll tell you, Inspector, if you'll promise that you'll do nothing about it.

EDEN: What do you mean?

FORBES: (*Quietly*) Go on, Temple.

TEMPLE: Queenie Edwards was friendly with Bert Walters, the cloakroom attendant at the Commdore Club. She discovered, through Miss Millicent, that Palmer was a member of the Commodore and she persuaded Walters to take the attaché case containing the doll. She obtained a cloakroom ticket from Walters which she intended to send to the police: in turn Walters promised that when the case was claimed he'd throw suspicion on to Palmer.

233

EDEN: (*Annoyed*) But look here, this is news to me about Bert Walters! We've had him here at the Yard – we've questioned him half a dozen times!

TEMPLE: (*Smiling*) I know you have, Inspector. You scared the pants off the poor little guy.

FORBES: When did you see him, Temple?

TEMPLE: Yesterday morning. It's surprising what a nice cigar and a cup of tea will do, Sir Graham.

FORBES: (*Significantly*) Yes! Well, go on, Temple.

TEMPLE: Well, everything was going pretty well true to form. Queenie was playing her cards very nicely and then suddenly – quite out of the blue – Vandyke played an ace!

FORBES: What do you mean?

TEMPLE: He found Miss Millicent and the baby!

EDEN: (*Quickly; anticipating TEMPLE*) That's why Queenie Edwards went down to Marlow! Vandyke sent for her! He told her …

TEMPLE: He told her that she was a very smart girl and he made Queenie a proposition: he said she either had to work for him or he'd inform the police that she'd been personally responsible for the disappearance of the baby. Queenie was frightened, she just didn't know what to do. In desperation she told Vandyke that she'd consider the proposition. Later that same night she reached a decision. You know what happened.

FORBES: She arranged to meet you at Paddington and sent you the cloakroom ticket.

TEMPLE: Yes. Obviously Vandyke – or someone else – overheard our conversation however, because –

234

	well – I don't have to remind you of what happened to Queenie.
EDEN:	McCall could have overheard that conversation: the phone call was made from the Wordsworth.
FORBES:	Yes.
EDEN:	Mr Temple, I don't dispute what you've told us, as a matter of fact is seems to make sense, but …
TEMPLE:	But what?
EDEN:	Well, it means we can cross Terry Palmer off the list, doesn't it? Obviously Palmer isn't Vandyke otherwise …
FORBES:	I don't agree, Inspector! Palmer may well be Vandyke! Don't forget, according to Temple's story, it was Vandyke that discovered the whereabouts of Miss Millicent and the baby. It seems to me that Palmer was in a better position than anyone else for tracking down Miss Millicent.
TEMPLE:	That's very true, Sir Graham!
EDEN:	(*Thoughtfully*) Yes, I suppose it is, sir.
TEMPLE:	Have you picked up Palmer?
EDEN:	Yes, he's in a pretty bad way, I'm afraid. This Desmond affair last night has certainly shaken him.
FORBES:	We'll have Palmer up here, Temple, and you can have a word with him.

FORBES clicks down the switch on the tele-communicator on his desk.

FORBES:	Bring Mr Palmer up here, sergeant.
SERGEANT:	(*On speaker*) Very good, sir.

EDEN: What do you make of Roger Shelly, Temple? You know, it seems to me he's not quite so naïve as he makes himself out to be.

TEMPLE: Did he tell you what happened to him last night?

EDEN: He certainly did!

FORBES: (*Dubiously*) Do you believe that story of his, Temple?

TEMPLE: Yes, I do, Sir Graham.

FORBES: Quite frankly, I think the fellow's something of an exhibitionist and he's simply trying to draw attention to himself. I must admit I can't imagine why.

EDEN: He seems to have got a bee in his bonnet about this fellow Droste.

FORBES: Yes. He can't really describe the man who went for him last night but on the other hand he seems convinced that it was Droste. Why should it be Droste when he admits he hardly knows the fellow?

EDEN: If you ask him why he suspects Droste he simply shrugs his shoulders.

TEMPLE: In any case Droste's in Paris, or at least he ought to be.

FORBES: We're checking on that.

There is a knock and the door opens to admit SERGEANT WRIGHTON and TERRY PALMER.

SERGEANT: Mr Palmer, sir.

FORBES: Oh, yes!

TEMPLE: (*Pleasantly*) Good morning, Palmer!

PALMER: (*Tensely*) Good morning.

FORBES: That's all right, sergeant – thank you.

The door closes.

FORBES: Will you sit down over there, Mr Palmer, please?

PALMER: If you don't mind I should prefer to stand.

FORBES: Very well. (*A moment*) Palmer, we understand that Mrs Desmond was a friend of yours – a very close friend.

PALMER: (*Tense and irritated*) Mary Desmond was a very dear friend of mine, you know that as well as I do! Now what's this all about?

FORBES: Mrs Desmond was murdered last night. It's our job – and our intention, Mr Palmer – to find out who exactly murdered her.

PALMER: (*Almost imprudently*) What do you mean who "exactly" murdered her?

FORBES: I mean that quite a lot of people, in one way or another, have contributed towards the death of Mary Desmond, but at the present moment we're concerned purely and simply with the identity of the actual murderer.

PALMER: Yes, well – I'm sorry I can't help you.

FORBES: I think you can help us, Mr Palmer.

PALMER: (*Angrily*) Now look here, let's get this straight. All I know about last night is what I've read in the newspapers. I've already accounted for my movements to Sergeant Reeton – or Reefer or whatever his name is – and there's nothing more I can tell you.

FORBES: In other words you refuse to help us?

PALMER: It isn't a question of refusing! If you really want to find out who murdered Mrs Desmond take your behind off that chair and stop asking a lot of fatuous questions!

FORBES: (*Quietly*) There's no need to be rude, Mr Palmer.

237

A moment.

PALMER: (*Tense, yet apologetically*) I'm sorry. I'm awfully sorry. I – I shouldn't have said that.

TEMPLE: (*Quietly*) Palmer …

PALMER: Yes?

TEMPLE: What happened after I left you last night?

PALMER: What do you mean – what happened?

TEMPLE: What did you do?

PALMER: I – I finished typing the article I was writing, mixed myself a drink and then went to bed.

TEMPLE: I thought you'd finished the article when I arrived?

PALMER: I didn't like part of it so I re-typed it.

TEMPLE: Did you receive any telephone calls?

PALMER: (*Hesitating*) No.

TEMPLE: Mrs Desmond didn't call you?

PALMER: Well, if I didn't receive any telephone calls Mrs Desmond couldn't have called me, could she?

TEMPLE: Palmer, I'm going to ask you a rather personal question. I hope you don't mind.

PALMER: I'm getting very used to personal questions. Go on …

TEMPLE: (*Quite casually*) How long have you worn an identity bracelet?

FADE UP of music.

FADE DOWN of music.
FADE UP of a piano: the piano is being played very casually.
STEVE is at the piano, playing and singing simply to amuse herself.
The door opens.
CHARLIE enters carrying a tea tray.
The piano stops.

CHARLIE: I've brought you some tea, Mrs Temple.

STEVE: Oh, thank you, Charlie.

CHARLIE: Where shall I put the tray?

STEVE: On the small table, Charlie.

A moment.

CHARLIE: Mrs Temple …

STEVE: Yes?

CHARLIE: Do you think I could pop out for an hour or so? I'll be back before dinner.

STEVE: Yes, that's all right. Don't be any later than six.

CHARLIE: O.K.!

STEVE: (*Suddenly*) Oh, there are two letters over there, Charlie.

CHARLIE: I'll see to 'em.

STEVE: I'd like the small one registered.

CHARLIE: O.K.

The door closes.

There is a long pause during which STEVE continues to entertain herself at the paino.

We hear the flat buzzer.

It continues.

STEVE stops playing and crosses to the front door.

STEVE opens the door and finds herself facing MARIAN FABER.

MARIAN: (*Pleasantly*) Good afternoon. Could I see Mr Temple, please?

STEVE: Well, I'm sorry but Mr Temple isn't in at the moment.

MARIAN: (*Disappointed*) Oh. Have you any idea when he'll be back?

STEVE: (*Hesitating*) Well –

MARIAN: (*Smiling: with charm*) Is it Mrs Temple?

STEVE: Yes.

MARIAN: (*With a pleasant little laugh*) Oh, I'm Marian Faber, Mrs Temple! I'm so sorry, I didn't recognise you.

STEVE: Oh, good afternoon, Miss Faber. I'm sorry but my husband's out at the moment, he won't be back till about five o'clock.

MARIAN: Oh, dear, what a nuisance, and I've come all the way from Chelsea. I suppose I ought to have telephoned really – it was stupid of me.

STEVE: Well, it's almost half-past four, Miss Faber, if you'd care to wait …

MARIAN: May I? That's very sweet of you, Mrs Temple.

STEVE: Do come in …

FADE.

FADE UP.

STEVE: Do sit down, Miss Faber.

MARIAN: Thank you.

STEVE: Would you like some tea?

MARIAN: Oh, really – I feel I'm putting you to an awful lot of trouble.

STEVE: You're not at all – it's here – ready. I was just going to have some myself.

MARIAN: Well, thank you, I'd adore a cup of tea.

STEVE pours out the tea.

A pause.

MARIAN: What a charming room, Mrs Temple. (*Suddenly*) Oh, I say, that's delightful! Who did that?

STEVE: It's by a French artist called Francois Raoul – he's not very well known, I'm afraid.

MARIAN: But it's charming! Did you buy it over here?

STEVE: Yes, we bought it from a little shop in Jermyn Street. Will you have milk, Miss Faber, or …?

240

MARIAN: Please …

STEVE: (*Handing MARIAN a cup*) Help yourself to sugar …

MARIAN: Thank you.

STEVE: (*Pouring herself a cup of tea*) What is it you wanted to see my husband about?

MARIAN: Well – I don't know whether Mr Temple told you what happened the other night, the night he came to the bungalow?

STEVE: Yes, as a matter of fact he did.

MARIAN: Well, I'm afraid I was very rude to Mr Temple and rather stupid into the bargain.

STEVE: Stupid – about what?

The telephone commences to ring.

MARIAN: Well, just as Mr Temple was leaving he noticed a photograph of … (*She stops speaking because of the telephone*)

STEVE: Excuse me! (*She crosses to the telephone and lifts the receiver: on the phone:*) Hello?

MAN: (*On the other end of the phone*) Could I speak to Dr Wilbur, please?

STEVE: I'm sorry, but I'm afraid you've got the wrong number.

MAN: Aren't you Mayfair 9763?

STEVE: No, I'm afraid not.

MAN: Oh, dear – I'm very sorry.

STEVE: That's all right. (*She replaces the receiver and returns to MARIAN*) What were you saying, Miss Faber?

MARIAN: I was saying – just as your husband was leaving he noticed a photograph of Terry Palmer.

STEVE: Yes – I understand Mr Palmer's a friend of yours.

MARIAN: Yes, although I'm afraid we don't see a great deal of each other.

STEVE: Go on …

MARIAN: Well, it occurred to me – after Mr Temple had left – that I might have given the impression that I was trying to throw suspicion on to Terry Palmer.

STEVE: Suspicion?

MARIAN: Yes. You see, your husband questioned me about a letter – a stupid letter I sent to Roger Shelly. The letter was written exactly as Miss Millicent would write it and Mr Temple was anxious to know how I was able to copy Miss Millicent's handwriting.

STEVE: Yes, I remember. You told Paul that someone gave you a sample of Miss Millicent's writing – you refused to tell him who it was.

MARIAN: Yes.

STEVE: And now you're worried in case he's jumped to the conclusion that it was Terry Palmer?

MARIAN: (*A little laugh*) Well, I don't want him to think that I was trying to throw suspicion on to Terry.

The telephone rings.

STEVE: You know, Miss Faber, if you take my advice … Oh dear, that wretched phone.

MARIAN laughs.

STEVE crosses to the telephone.

STEVE: (*Lifting the receiver: on the phone*) Hello?

TEMPLE: (*On the other end of the phone*) Hello – is that you, Steve?

STEVE: Oh, hello, Paul!

TEMPLE: Look, Steve, I doubt whether I shall be home much before six o'clock so I was wondering if you'd …

242

STEVE:	(*Interrupting TEMPLE*) Paul, Miss Faber's here – she's waiting to see you.
TEMPLE:	Miss Faber!
STEVE:	Yes, darling.
TEMPLE:	(*Curious*) Oh – How long has she been there?
STEVE:	About five minutes.
TEMPLE:	(*Quietly*) What does she want, Steve – do you know?
STEVE:	(*A little laugh*) No …
TEMPLE:	All right, I'll be home in twenty minutes.
STEVE:	Just a second, darling, I think you'd better have a word with Miss Faber. (*To MARIAN*) It's my husband. Perhaps you'd like to have a word with him.
MARIAN:	Oh, thank you.
STEVE:	(*On the phone*) Here's Miss Faber, Paul.
TEMPLE:	(*On the phone*) Yes, all right, Steve.
STEVE:	(*On the phone*) I'll see you later, darling.

A slight pause.

MARIAN:	(*On the phone*) Mr Temple?
TEMPLE:	(*On the phone*) Hello, Miss Faber!
MARIAN:	I'm afraid I'm making an awful nuisance of myself, Mr Temple.
TEMPLE:	That's all right. What can I do for you?
MARIAN:	Well – I did rather want to have a chat with you, but if it's at all difficult …
TEMPLE:	No, that's all right. I'd like to see you. (*Smiling*) I'd like to see you <u>very</u> <u>much</u>, Miss Faber. I'll be with you in about twenty minutes.
MARIAN:	Yes, all right.
TEMPLE:	See you later!
MARIAN:	Goodbye! (*She replaces the receiver: to STEVE*) Thank you, Mrs Temple.
STEVE:	(*After drinking tea*) Now where was I?

MARIAN: You were just about to give me a piece of advice.

STEVE: Oh, yes. I was going to say: if you take my advice, Miss Faber, you'll be perfectly frank with my husband and tell him all you know about this business.

MARIAN: I intend to be perfectly frank with him. To be truthful, that's why I'm here, Mrs Temple. I've done quite a lot of thinking since I last saw your husband. (*Suddenly*) I say, is anything the matter?

STEVE: This tea tastes awfully bitter – is yours all right?

MARIAN: Yes … (*She drinks*) … I think so.

STEVE: (*Drinking*) That's funny …

MARIAN: (*Drinks*) Mine's perfectly all right.

STEVE: (*Drinking*) M'm – perhaps it's my imagination.

MARIAN: (*After drinking*) Mrs Temple, do you mind if I ask you a very frank question?

STEVE: No.

MARIAN: What does your husband think of me?

STEVE: (*Innocently*) As an artist?

MARIAN: No. No, I don't mean as an artist, I mean – well – (*Frankly*) Does he think I'm mixed up in this Vandyke affair?

STEVE: Are you?

MARIAN: No. No, I told him when he came down to the bungalow – I'd never heard of Vandyke until he mentioned the name.

STEVE: I think Paul believes that it was Vandyke who gave you the Miss Millicent letter – that it was Vandyke who told you to write to Shelly.

MARIAN: Well, I'm sorry to disappoint Mr Temple. Believe me, after what happened last night, if I

244

	knew the identity of Vandyke I should go straight to Scotland Yard and …
STEVE:	(*Politely*) Last night?
MARIAN:	Yes. (*Incredulously*) The murder … Mary Desmond.
STEVE:	Oh – so you think Mrs Desmond was murdered by Vandyke?
MARIAN:	Well – don't you? It seems perfectly obvious to me that the same person … that murdered … that murdered … that … that … (*Faintly*) Oh, dear!
STEVE:	(*Quietly*) What is it?
MARIAN:	(*Puzzled*) I don't know. I – I suddenly felt very dizzy, I …
STEVE:	Would you like me to get some brandy?
MARIAN:	No. No, I shall be all right. I shouldn't feel like this, I … (*Trying to stand*) I … Oh, dear!
STEVE:	I shouldn't try and stand, Miss Faber.
MARIAN:	But I don't understand it, I shouldn't feel like this I … I … (*She tries to stand*)
STEVE:	I'm afraid it's no use – you can't stand – you'll have to sit down.
MARIAN:	But I've got to stand! This is stupid! I've got to stand … I've … got … to … Oh! (*She sinks back into the chair. Tense: drugged*) What's – what's the matter with me?
STEVE:	(*Slowly: watching MARIAN*) Don't you know, Miss Faber?
MARIAN:	What do you mean?
STEVE:	(*Slowly; tensely*) You didn't come here to see my husband. You didn't come here to talk to Paul about the Vandyke affair and what happened that night at the bungalow! You came

	because Vandyke sent you – you came here because Vandyke told you to kidnap me and …
MARIAN:	(*Brightened*) What – have – you – done?
STEVE:	I haven't done anything, Miss Faber – you've done it yourself. I knew that wrong number was a trick. (*A pause*) You put something into my tea while I was answering the phone, didn't you?
MARIAN:	Yes. But you drank it! You said the tea was bitter, you said …
STEVE:	I wanted you to think that the tea was bitter. I wanted you to think that everything was going according to plan – your plan, Miss Faber.
MARIAN:	What … do … you … mean?
STEVE:	(*Slowly*) Why do you think I asked you to speak to my husband?
MARIAN:	I … don't … know …
STEVE:	Don't you? You're not very bright, Miss Faber. While you were on the phone I changed your cup – for mine.
MARIAN:	(*Frightened*) No! No! I don't believe it! You couldn't – You couldn't have done! You couldn't!!!!
STEVE:	But I did, Miss Faber! I did!!!!

Quick, dramatic FADE UP of music.

END OF EPISODE SEVEN

EPISODE EIGHT

PRESENTING
MR VANDYKE

OPEN TO:

STEVE: (*Slowly; tensely*) You didn't come here to see my husband. You didn't come here to talk to Paul about the Vandyke affair and what happened that night at the bungalow! You came because Vandyke sent you – you came here because Vandyke told you to kidnap me and …

MARIAN: (*Brightened*) What – have – you – done?

STEVE: I haven't done anything, Miss Faber – you've done it yourself. I knew that wrong number was a trick. (*A pause*) you put something into my tea while I was answering the phone, didn't you?

MARIAN: Yes. But you drank it! You said the tea was bitter, you said …

STEVE: I wanted you to think that the tea was bitter. I wanted you to think that everything was going according to plan – your plan, Miss Faber.

MARIAN: What … do … you … mean?

STEVE: (*Slowly*) Why do you think I asked you to speak to my husband?

MARIAN: I … don't … know …

STEVE: Don't you? You're not very bright, Miss Faber. While you were on the phone I changed your cup – for mine.

MARIAN: (*Frightened*) No! No! I don't believe it! You couldn't – You couldn't have done! You couldn't!!!!

STEVE: But I did, Miss Faber! I did!!!!

MARIAN: Oh, my God! What's going to happen? Now what's going to … (*Desperately, rising to her feet*) I've got to go! Let me go …

STEVE: Sit down …

MARIAN: (*A note of determination*) Get out of my way! Let me go!

STEVE: Now don't be stupid! You can't walk! Sit down, Miss Faber!

MARIAN: I've got to go and … Oh, my head! My head's splitting!

STEVE: (*Suddenly*) Look out! Look out or you'll fall!

MARIAN falls forward: the tray is knocked off the small table. Quick FADE UP of music.

Slow FADE DOWN of music.
Slow FADE IN of MARIAN: she is breathing heavily and moaning …

MARIAN: Oh … oh, my head … I've got a splitting head …

TEMPLE: (*Quietly*) She's coming round …

STEVE: Yes.

MARIAN: (*Dazed: moaning*) Oh, my head … (*Confused*) What – what happened? Where am I?

STEVE: Here we are, Miss Faber – drink this.

MARIAN: (*Dazed*) What … happened …?

STEVE: Drink this …

MARIAN: (*Suddenly: alarmed*) No! What is it?

STEVE: It's all right – drink it.

TEMPLE: It's all right, Miss Faber, it won't do you any harm.

MARIAN drinks.

A pause.

TEMPLE: Well – are you feeling any better?

MARIAN: (*Slightly dazed*) Yes. Yes, it's my head, that's all … It feels like a lead weight. Do … you … think I could have a cigarette?

STEVE lights a cigarette.

TEMPLE: Yes, you can have one with pleasure but I don't know that it's a very good idea.

MARIAN: I'd like one, Mr Temple, if – if you don't mind.

STEVE: Here we are. I've lit it for you.

MARIAN: Oh, thank you. (*She takes the cigarette and inhales; a slight pause*) That's better … (*Trembling slightly*) What time is it?

TEMPLE: It's just gone six.

MARIAN: Good gracious, have … I … been … out … for … over … an … hour?

TEMPLE: Yes …

MARIAN: (*Hesitating*) Mr Temple …

TEMPLE: Yes?

MARIAN: (*A little frightened*) What are you going to do with me?

TEMPLE: Well, you know what I ought to do, don't you? Hand you over to the police. Unfortunately just at the moment, so far as you're concerned, Miss Faber, I'm rather at a disadvantage.

MARIAN: What do you mean?

TEMPLE: (*Quietly*) How long have you been working for Vandyke?

MARIAN: About six months.

TEMPLE: What happened? (*With contempt*) Do you take the stuff?

MARIAN: (*Quickly: tensely*) No! No, he had some letters of mine. He started to blackmail me, at first it was just money but later … he … made … me … work for him.

TEMPLE: I see. Tell me: what did you intend to do if my wife had fallen for this little trick of yours?

MARIAN: Vandyke told me to telephone him: we should have taken her away. I think he intended to hold Mrs Temple as a sort of hostage.

251

STEVE:	You bet he did!
TEMPLE:	Miss Faber, I don't think you realise it but you're a very lucky woman.
MARIAN:	Why do you say that?
TEMPLE:	Because I'm going to let you walk out of here, because I'm going to say nothing to the police about all this.
MARIAN:	Why? Why are you doing this?
TEMPLE:	I told you. I'm rather at a disadvantage.
MARIAN:	What do you mean?
TEMPLE:	Well – (*A moment*) I want you to do me a favour.
MARIAN:	(*Tensely: worried*) What sort of a favour? What do you want me to do?
TEMPLE:	(*Facing MARIAN: matter of fact*) I want you to write a letter, Miss Faber.

FADE UP of music.

Slow FADE DOWN of music.
TEMPLE and STEVE are having breakfast.

TEMPLE:	Pass the toast, Steve.
STEVE:	It's in front of you!
TEMPLE:	Where?
STEVE:	If you move the paper, darling – you'll see it!
TEMPLE:	Oh! Oh, yes, sorry. (*Munching: buttering some toast*) Absolutely nothing in the paper this morning.
STEVE:	Well, in that case do you think you could possibly tear yourself away from it for a moment or two?
TEMPLE:	In a second, darling. I'm just reading this speech by old what's-his-name. (*Delighted*) By Timothy, he's put his foot in it again!
STEVE:	Who do you mean – old what's-his-name?

TEMPLE: Thingamebob …
STEVE: Thingamebob?
TEMPLE: You know – the fellow who's always putting his foot in it. The chappie who said … er … you know!
STEVE: Darling, I don't know!

The door opens.

TEMPLE: Well, anyway he's certainly snookered himself this time! (*Looking up*) Yes, what is it, Charlie?
CHARLIE: Mr Droste's here, sir.
TEMPLE: Oh, yes. Tell him I won't be a minute, Charlie.
CHARLIE: O.K.

The door closes.

STEVE: (*Faintly surprised*) Did you expect Droste?
TEMPLE: (*Rising*) Yes, I phoned him. I want to have a chat with him. Here's the paper, Steve. The speech is on page two.
STEVE: Which speech?
TEMPLE: (*Surprised: seriously*) The one by old – thingamebob.
STEVE: (*Pulling TEMPLE's leg*) Oh, you mean old – you know?
TEMPLE: (*Seriously*) Yes.
STEVE: (*Laughing*) Gertcha!

FADE.

FADE UP of TEMPLE.

TEMPLE: (*Pleasantly*) Hello, Droste! Sorry if my phone call got you out of bed.
DROSTE: No. No, I'd been up for some little time.
TEMPLE: (*Taking out his cigarette case*) Will you have a cigarette?
DROSTE: Oh, thank you.

TEMPLE: Sit down, Droste. Sit down. It's all right, I've got a light! (*He offers his lighter to DROSTE*)

DROSTE: (*Lighting his cigarette*) Thank you.

A pause.

TEMPLE: When did you get back from Paris?

DROSTE: (*Hesitating*) I – I didn't go to Paris after all.

TEMPLE: (*Looking up*) Oh. What made you change your mind?

DROSTE: (*Not too sure of himself*) Well – I was terribly distressed about Vanessa and – my doctor advised me not to make the journey.

TEMPLE: (*Quietly: watching DROSTE*) I see.

DROSTE: I've got some very good friends in Paris so naturally everything's been … taken … care … of …

TEMPLE: Where have you been staying, down at Marlow?

DROSTE: No. No, at the flat.

TEMPLE: Were you there the night before last, the night that …

DROSTE: That Mrs Desmond was murdered? Yes, I was. That must have been a shocking business. Naturally, I heard all about it from McCall.

TEMPLE: Is McCall staying with you?

DROSTE: Yes, he is. I've put him in charge of the Commodore – for the time being at any rate.

TEMPLE: Mr Droste, tell me: how well do you know Roger Shelly?

DROSTE: Shelly? Is that the willowy young man: the one with a cottage near Marlow?

TEMPLE: Yes, that's right.

DROSTE: I don't know him – at least, not to speak to. (*Curious*) Why do you ask?

TEMPLE: Well, apparently, the night that Mrs Desmond was murdered someone else attacked Roger Shelly. It appears the assailant was about your build and wore an identity bracelet. I see ... you ... wear a bracelet, Mr Droste.

DROSTE: Yes. It belonged to my mother. It's not an identity bracelet. I've always worn it.

TEMPLE: I see.

DROSTE: My dear chap, why should I attack Roger Shelly? I've told you, I don't know the fellow. Besides, I can assure you, I'm not the sort of person that goes around attacking people – whether I know them or not.

TEMPLE: (*Casually: very pleasant*) Yes, well personally I'm quite prepared to accept your word, Droste, but of course unfortunately, I'm not Scotland Yard.

DROSTE: (*Frowning*) What do you mean? Are you suggesting that Scotland Yard think I attacked Shelly?

TEMPLE: (*With an evasive little laugh*) I merely said I'm not Scotland Yard.

DROSTE: (*Slightly annoyed*) Now, look here, Temple – let's get this straight. You know, as well as I do, that if anyone did attack Shelly then ten to one it's the same person that murdered Mrs Desmond.

TEMPLE: If anyone <u>did</u> attack Shelly? Do you doubt his word, then?

DROSTE: Frankly, yes!

TEMPLE: You hardly know the gentleman and yet you doubt his word? Isn't that rather a contradiction, Mr Droste?

A pause.

DROSTE: (*Quietly: subdued*) What is it you wanted to see
            me about?
TEMPLE: Ah, yes! (*Pleasantly*) Droste, I'm going to ask
            you to do something for me and I'm afraid – in
            view of your recent bereavement – you'll find
            it rather an unusual request. However, please
            believe me, I wouldn't ask you to do this if I
            didn't consider it very important.
DROSTE: Go on …
TEMPLE: (*Taking a piece of paper from his pocket*) I've
            got a piece of paper here – there are one or two
            names and addresses on it. I want you to make
            a careful note of them. Here we are.
DROSTE: (*Puzzled: reading*) "Marian Faber. Roger
            Shelly. Bill McCall. Sir Graham Forbes …"
            What's the point of this?
TEMPLE: Well – I want you to give a party, Droste.
DROSTE: (*Surprised*) A party!
TEMPLE: Yes.
DROSTE: When?
TEMPLE: Tomorrow night – at your flat. Eight o'clock.
DROSTE: (*Confused and puzzled*) But that's out of the
            question! I can't possibly give … Look! Do I
            understand you correctly? You want me to
            invite these people to my flat – tomorrow night
            – at eight o'clock – to a party?
TEMPLE: (*Pleasantly*) That's right.
DROSTE: (*Bewildered*) But, Mr Temple, it's only forty-
            eight hours since my wife …
TEMPLE: (*Interrupting DROSTE*) Yes. Yes, I know that,
            Droste, and believe me I wouldn't ask you to
            do this if it wasn't important.

A moment.

DROSTE: (*Suddenly*) All right – tomorrow night – my flat
               – eight o'clock.
TEMPLE: (*Nodding*) Thank you.
DROSTE: (*A little laugh*) But for the life of me I don't see
               the point, old man!
TEMPLE: You're not supposed to. You're just supposed
               to give the party.

DROSTE laughs: a nervous little laugh.
FADE UP of music.

Quick FADE DOWN of music.
*TEMPLE is dialling a telephone number: as he finishes
dialling we hear the number ringing out.*
A pause: during which the number rings out.
A receiver is lifted at the other end of the line.

PALMER: (*On the other end of the phone*) Hello?
TEMPLE: Terry Palmer?
PALMER: Yes – who is that?
TEMPLE: This is Temple here.
PALMER: (*Not too friendly*) Oh. What is it you want?
TEMPLE: (*Pleasantly*) I wanted to have a word with you,
               Palmer.
PALMER: You seem to spend your entire life having
               words with me! We spent an hour together this
               morning at Scotland Yard – surely that was
               quite sufficient to be going on with!
TEMPLE: (*Laughing*) Yes – I'm afraid I am making a
               nuisance of myself, but –
PALMER: (*Impatiently*) Well, what is it this time?
TEMPLE: (*A little laugh*) Palmer, I'd like to see you –
               tomorrow night if possible.
PALMER: (*After a slight hesitation*) Tomorrow night?
               What time tomorrow night?

257

TEMPLE: Well – eight o'clock would suit me best, if that's convenient?

PALMER: Yes – that's all right. Eight o'clock.

TEMPLE: Eight o'clock at your flat, Palmer. All right?

PALMER: (*Faintly puzzled*) Yes, that's all right. I'll be here.

TEMPLE: Good. Thanks very much. Look forward to seeing you. Goodbye.

PALMER: Goodbye. (*He replaces his receiver*)

TEMPLE replaces his receiver.

FADE UP of previous music.

FADE DOWN of music.

STEVE: (*Impatiently*) Paul, it's half past seven! If we're supposed to pick Sir Graham up and then be at Mr Droste's by eight o'clock …

TEMPLE: (*Rather on edge*) Yes, all right, darling! All right! I know the time! (*Irritated*) T't – t't, what the devil's keeping Charlie, he left here well over an hour ago!

The flat buzzer sounds.

STEVE: I should imagine that's Charlie now!

TEMPLE crosses to the front door and opens it.

CHARLIE: (*Breathlessly*) Sorry I'm late. I 'ad a bit of a job finding a taxi.

TEMPLE: (*Quickly*) Well – what happened? Did you deliver it?

CHARLIE: Yes …

TEMPLE: Just as I said?

CHARLIE: Yes – just as you said. I pushed it under the door.

TEMPLE: (*Worried*) All right, Charlie. Come in.

The telephone starts to ring in the background.

STEVE: (*In the background*) Paul, it's the phone!

TEMPLE: (*Quickly; pleased*) It's all right, Steve! I'll answer it!

TEMPLE crosses and lifts up the telephone receiver.

TEMPLE: (*On the phone*) Hello?

PALMER: (*On the other end of the line*) Mr Temple?

TEMPLE: Yes.

PALMER: Terry Palmer here.

TEMPLE: (*Brightly*) Oh, I was just leaving for your place, Mr Palmer!

PALMER: Temple. I'm sorry but I'm afraid I'll have to put you off!

TEMPLE: (*Apparently disappointed*) Oh, dear, what a nuisance!

PALMER: (*Thoughtfully*) I'm sorry, Temple, but I've been out all day and when I got back there was a message for me saying … Well, look here! Can't we make it some other time? Tomorrow morning perhaps?

TEMPLE: (*Pleasantly*) Yes, all right. Tomorrow morning.

PALMER: Twelve o'clock?

TEMPLE: Fine.

PALMER: Sorry about this, but …

TEMPLE: That's all right, Palmer. See you tomorrow.

PALMER: Thanks. Thanks awfully. Goodbye!

TEMPLE: Goodbye! (*He replaces the receiver*)

STEVE: Well, are you ready <u>now</u>, Mr Temple?

TEMPLE: Yes, Steve, I'm ready. I'm ready, darling! (*He is very pleased with himself: he whistles to himself – the tune of the Coronation Scot*).

FADE on TEMPLE whistling.
FADE SCENE.

Slow FADE UP of many voices.
We are now in DROSTE's flat.

TEMPLE, STEVE, SIR GRAHAM, BILL McCALL, MARIAN FABER, ROGER SHELLY and PHILIP DROSTE are all present.

There is a general buzz of conversation during the following dialogue.

McCALL: Won't you have one of these biscuits, Miss Faber?

MARIAN: (*Tensely*) No, thank you.

McCALL: Well, have an olive?

MARIAN: No, thank you.

McCALL: Gee, you must have something!

SHELLY: Do you mind if I have a biscuit?

McCALL: No, of course not. Help yourself, Shelly.

SHELLY: They're really quite delicious. You don't know what you're missing, Marian.

DROSTE: (*Rather nervous; forced jollity*) Would you like another drink, Sir Graham?

FORBES: No, thank you.

TEMPLE: (*Apparently in very high spirits*) May I have another martini, Droste?

DROSTE: Yes, of course. (*Calling to McCALL*) Bill!

McCALL: (*From the background*) Yes?

DROSTE: Another martini for Mr Temple!

McCALL: Coming up!

DROSTE: Now what can I get you, Mrs Temple?

STEVE: Oh, I'm fine thank you. I was just admiring your window, Mr Droste. I don't think I've ever seen such an attractive window.

The flat bell chimes.

DROSTE: Yes, most people seem to ... Will you excuse me, please?

STEVE: Yes, of course.

The general buzz of conversation continues.

The front door opens.

PALMER: Good evening, Droste! I understand you've
            finally … (*He stops dead: surprised*) What is
            this? What's happening here?

The conversation suddenly dies down.

There is a moment's pause, then:

TEMPLE: (*Extremely affably*) Why, hello, Palmer! By
            Timothy, it's a small world! Come in! Come in,
            old boy! (*To STEVE*) Darling, it's Terry
            Palmer!

STEVE: (*Brightly*) Hello, Mr Palmer!

PALMER: (*Entering the room: amazed*) Temple! Sir
            Graham! (*Astonished*) Marian!

MARIAN: (*Quietly*) Hello, Terry.

PALMER: What – what are you doing here?

MARIAN: Well, if it comes to that what are you doing
            here?

PALMER: But I was asked to come, I received a note
            saying …

SHELLY: But we were all <u>asked</u> to come, my dear boy –
            otherwise we shouldn't be here!

McCALL: (*Slowly*) Look here, Temple – don't you think
            you owe us an explanation?

TEMPLE: Me? But this is Mr Droste's party!

McCALL: (*Tough*) Look! Let's get this straightened out! I
            like parties – I like parties just as much as the
            next guy. But this isn't a party, brother – it's a
            gathering of the clan! Take a look around this
            room. D'you see who's here? (*A pause*) Mr
            Temple. I don't have many hunches but when I
            do get them believe me they're o.k. (*Quieter*)
            You're responsible for us all being here this
            evening, you're the guy behind this so-called
            party not Mr Droste. (*Simply, but determined*)
            Now what's it all about?

261

TEMPLE: (*Taking command: a note of authority in his voice*) I'll tell you, McCall. I'll tell you exactly what it's all about. The other night I had a talk – a very interesting talk – with Mary Desmond. She told me the truth about Miss Millicent, about the disappearance of the baby, and about Queenie Edwards.

McCALL: Go on …

TEMPLE: Mrs Desmond worked for a man called Vandyke. Vandyke was the English head of a drug smuggling ring: a ring which was controlled by a Parisian called Charles Marett. Marett had a shop in Paris on the Rue St. Lazare. Now Vandyke used to send people over to Paris in order to contact Marett and smuggle the drugs back to London. In order to establish their identity with Marett the people concerned used to carry a special pair of gloves: inside each glove was a small tab bearing Marett's name. Immediately Marett saw this tab he knew that he was dealing with an agent from London – one of Vandyke's people.

McCALL: I see.

SHELLY: Well, Mr Temple, tell me: how did that character De Wolfe fit into the picture? Did he work for Vandyke?

McCALL: De Wolfe? You mean the guy that was murdered down at my place?

SHELLY: Yes.

TEMPLE: No, De Wolfe was one of Marett's men: he came over here to see Vandyke. He'd never actually met Vandyke before: the receipt, which we found on him, took the place of a pair

262

	of gloves. You see, both the gloves and the receipt were purely a means of identification.
STEVE:	So that's why those gloves of Mrs Desmond's didn't fit?
TEMPLE:	Exactly! They'd been sent to her by Vandyke – the size was quite unimportant.
SHELLY:	Yes, but look here, Temple, this fellow De Wolfe was murdered. Why?
FORBES:	Well, I think it's pretty obvious why De Wolfe was murdered. You see, he came over not only to contact Vandyke but to find out exactly what he was up to. Marett was beginning to suspect that Vandyke was getting a little tired of playing second fiddle, he was in fact …
McCALL:	Getting too big for his shoes.
TEMPLE:	Exactly!
DROSTE:	But look here, Temple. My wife had a pair of those gloves, you commented on it yourself, so …
TEMPLE:	So, what, Mr Droste?
DROSTE:	Well – are you suggesting that Vanessa was an agent of Vandyke's?
FORBES:	You know perfectly well that she was – otherwise, why did you go to Paris?
DROSTE:	I told you why! At least I told Mr Temple. My wife was having an affair with Marett and I followed her …
FORBES:	(*Interrupting DROSTE: quietly*) She was having nothing of the sort! (*Seriously*) Your wife was a drug addict – you know that as well as I do, Droste. It's my guess that she was being blackmailed by Vandyke. It's my guess …

DROSTE:	(*Suddenly: tensely*) Yes! Yes, you're right! I was a fool, a stupid, damn fool! I ought to have told you this before. Vanessa did take drugs: there was nothing I could do about it! I tried! – but it was no use. One day she told me that Vandyke was blackmailing her. Although I never actually met Vandyke he sent a message through to me asking me to finance ...
PALMER:	(*Quickly: vehemently*) Shut up! Shut up, Droste! Keep your mouth shut!
MARIAN:	Terry!
PALMER:	If you say one word more, Droste, I'll ...
STEVE:	Paul, he's got a gun!
SHELLY:	Look out!
PALMER:	Stand back! Stand back, do you hear!?
TEMPLE:	Drop that gun, Palmer! Drop it!
FORBES:	Don't be a fool, Palmer!
PALMER:	(*Tense: strained*) I warn you, Droste! If you open your mouth just once more I'll ...
DROSTE:	(*Angrily*) If you think you can intimidate me, my friend, you've got another ...
McCALL:	(*Quickly: urgently*) Look out, Droste!!!!
STEVE:	Look out!!!
TEMPLE:	Get hold of him, McCall!!!!
MARIAN:	(*Throwing herself in front of PALMER*) Terry, don't!!!! Don't fire ...
STEVE:	(*Alarmed*) You'll hit Miss Faber!

PALMER fires and the bullet hits MARIAN.
A tense pause.

MARIAN:	(*Hurt*) Oh ...
PALMER:	Oh, Marian! Marian, I didn't mean it, I ...
STEVE:	I told you! I told you you'd hit her!!!!
MARIAN:	Oh, Terry, I ... I ...

MARIAN falls.

STEVE: Paul!!!!

FORBES: Get hold of her, Steve! Quickly!!!!

McCALL: (*Shouting*) Look out, he's going for the window!!!

PALMER makes a dash across the room.

TEMPLE: Stop him! Shelly, quickly!!!!

SHELLY: (*Trying to stop PALMER*) Now don't be stupid, Palmer, you simply can't …

PALMER strikes out and SHELLY receives a blow on the jaw …

FORBES: My God, he is going for the window!

TEMPLE: Palmer, don't!!!!

FORBES: McCall get hold of him!!!!

STEVE: (*Horrified*) Don't!!!!

TEMPLE: Palmer!!!!

There is a tremendous crash of glass as PALMER throws himself through the window.

STEVE screams.

Dramatic FADE UP of music.

Slow FADE DOWN of music.

FADE UP background noises of Paddington Railway Station.

TEMPLE: …I'll see you later, Sir Graham.

FORBES: Yes, all right, Temple.

TEMPLE: I think it's better this way, don't you?

FORBES: Yes. Yes, I agree.

PORTER: Come along, sir – we 'aven't much time.

FADE UP of station noises.

People are passing to and fro on the platform.

We hear the sound of carriage doors opening and closing.

PORTER: Here's an empty carriage, sir.

TEMPLE: No, I'll go further down if you don't mind.

PORTER: There isn't much time, sir.

TEMPLE and the PORTER continue down the platform.

PORTER: How about this one, sir?

TEMPLE: No, I'd rather … (*Suddenly*) Yes! Yes, that's all right. Put it in the non-smoker!

PORTER: Very good, sir.

The sound of the carriage door opening: TEMPLE and the PORTER enter the carriage.

TEMPLE: It's all right, I'll see to it now. Here we are.

PORTER: Thank you, sir.

The carriage door closes.

TEMPLE: Excuse me is this … (*Surprised*) Why, hello, McCall!

McCALL: (*Lowering his newspaper*) Why, hello, Temple! What are you doing here?

TEMPLE: I'm just going down to Maidenhead for two or three days. Sir Graham's taken a house there. But where are you off to?

The train starts and during the following dialogue gradually gathers speed.

McCALL: I'm going down to Marlow for the day – to The Wordsworth. I've still got to keep my eye on things you know.

TEMPLE: Yes, I expect you have.

McCALL: (*Hesitating*) Temple …

TEMPLE: Yes?

McCALL: I've – just been reading about last night.

TEMPLE: Yes. By Timothy, the papers have certainly gone to town on it, haven't they? (*Suddenly*) By the way, McCall, is Mr Droste on the train?

McCALL: Droste? Why, no! Why do you ask?

TEMPLE: (*Casually*) I thought I saw him, that's all. (*He sits back in his seat: almost a sigh*) Ah, well – we're off!

FADE UP of the train.

FADE UP of music.

266

Gradual FADE DOWN of music.

Train noises continue.

We hear the sound of the compartment sliding door being opened.

TEMPLE: (*Pleasantly*) May I come in?

SHELLY: (*Surprised: apparently delighted to see TEMPLE*) Hello, Mr Temple! I didn't know you were on the train!

TEMPLE: I thought I spotted you, Shelly, on the platform. Is this seat taken?

SHELLY: No … No … I'm delighted to see you. I think train journeys are the end – positively the end, don't you? Sit here, Mr Temple.

TEMPLE: They're not so bad when you've got company.

SHELLY: No, I quite agree. Is Mrs Temple with you?

TEMPLE: No, I'm travelling alone. Incidentally, McCall's on the train, did you know?

SHELLY: (*Surprised*) McCall?

TEMPLE: Yes.

SHELLY: Are you sure?

TEMPLE: Of course, I've just been having a chat with him.

SHELLY: Is he alone?

TEMPLE: (*Laughing*) Well, he says he is.

SHELLY: What do you mean?

TEMPLE: I could have sworn I caught a glimpse of Mr Droste.

SHELLY: Well, if Droste was on the train he'd be with McCall, surely? (*Indicating a newspaper*) I've just been reading about last night.

TEMPLE: Yes, it's in all the papers.

SHELLY: What an extraordinary person Palmer must have been.

267

TEMPLE:	(*Thoughtfully*) Yes. (*Suddenly; pleasantly*) I'm glad I bumped into you, Shelly, because I'd like to tell you a little more about that man De Wolfe.
SHELLY:	De Wolfe?
TEMPLE:	Yes, don't you remember? You were asking me about him last night.
SHELLY:	Oh, yes, De Wolfe. Yes, of course!
TEMPLE:	Well, De Wolfe went down to Marlow to contact Vandyke. It was all done very casually, of course – he struck up an apparently casual acquaintance with him – in the bar at The Wordsworth – and Vandyke invited him out to dinner.
SHELLY:	(*Amazed*) But I invited De Wolfe to dinner, don't you remember, I …
TEMPLE:	Yes! Yes, I know. But let me finish my story. Vandyke warned De Wolfe that there was a Scotland Yard man staying at the hotel called Sergeant Digby. The day that De Wolfe was due to go out to Vandyke's he discovered that Digby had left the hotel. De Wolfe telephoned Vandyke and told him this – he also told him that a Mr and Mrs Paul Temple had arrived.
SHELLY:	Go on …
TEMPLE:	When Vandyke received this call from De Wolfe he had a friend with him – another member of the ring – a lady called Marian Faber. Miss Faber was a great artist and – quite – a – gal – for – practical jokes!
SHELLY:	(*Tensely*) What do you mean?
TEMPLE:	Don't you know what I mean, Mr Shelly? She suggested that De Wolfe impersonate Digby and introduced himself as such to Mr and Mrs

	Temple. For obvious reasons De Wolfe liked the idea, he liked the idea very – very much.
SHELLY:	Go on …
TEMPLE:	Do you know what De Wolfe did when he impersonated Digby?
SHELLY:	No?
TEMPLE:	He threw suspicion on to you. You see, he'd already decided that you were a double-crosser and intended to advise Marett to get rid of you.
SHELLY:	My dear fellow, you're talking absolute nonsense! You know perfectly well that Terry Palmer was Vandyke so why …
TEMPLE:	Palmer was not Vandyke!
SHELLY:	(*Hesitantly*) What do you mean?

A moment.

TEMPLE:	(*Quietly*) Don't you know, Mr Shelly?
SHELLY:	(*A nervous little laugh*) Are you suggesting – Are you seriously suggesting that I'm Vandyke?
TEMPLE:	(*Slowly; watching SHELLY*) Aren't you?
SHELLY:	Why, of course not! I've never heard such utter …
TEMPLE:	(*Forcefully*) Aren't you, Mr Shelly?

A pause.

SHELLY:	You appear to be very well informed, Mr Temple.
TEMPLE:	I'm glad you think so. However, there are one or two points on which no doubt you can enlighten me.
SHELLY:	(*Quietly*) For instance?
TEMPLE:	Why did you start throwing suspicion on to Palmer? Surely Palmer was your right hand man?

SHELLY: I had no alternative. You see, I had to give Marett an explanation of the De Wolfe murder so I told him that Terry was responsible. From that moment I was instructed, by Marett, to throw suspicion on to Palmer.

TEMPLE: But you continued to throw suspicion on to him after Marett was murdered?

SHELLY: Of course, the police – to say nothing of a certain Mr Temple – already had their eye on Palmer. It was to my advantage that they should continue to suspect him.

TEMPLE: I see. And the café incident in Paris?

SHELLY: Well, that was unfortunate – most unfortunate. If that little incident had gone according to plan you wouldn't be here, Mr Temple, and the atmosphere, with all due respects, would be considerably less oppressive. (*Almost a sigh of regret*) However, it didn't, so there you are.

TEMPLE: What did you intend to do at the café – get rid of Mrs Droste and Marett, to say nothing of my wife and I?

SHELLY: Of course – that was the idea. I got Mrs Droste to arrange to see Marett at the café – unfortunately Marett got wise to what was happening and just didn't turn up. However, he was taken care of.

TEMPLE: By Franz?

SHELLY: Yes. Franz was an excellent fellow. I'm sorry you didn't get a chance of meeting him, Temple. (*A note of irritation*) What a pity he couldn't swim.

TEMPLE: (*Softly*) By Timothy, Steve said you were crazy!

SHELLY: Crazy? My dear fellow, do you know how
            much money I've made out of this little set-up
            of mine in the past eighteen months? (*Smiling*)
            Thirty-seven thousand pounds – free of tax.

A pause.

TEMPLE: (*Very quietly*) Shelly …

SHELLY: Yes?

TEMPLE: Tell me – just to satisfy my curiosity – did you
            murder Queenie Edwards, yourself, personally?

SHELLY: Yes. Franz overheard the conversation she had
            with you – actually he was watching her for me
            – and I followed her on to the train. Why do
            you ask?

TEMPLE: (*Slowly*) Because I saw Queenie. I saw her
            when they took her off the train at Paddington.

SHELLY: Oh. Oh, I see. Well, you mustn't be sensitive
            about these things you know. By the way, you
            might be interested to see the knife …

There is a sudden click: SHELLY has produced a knife.

TEMPLE: (*Softly: unpleasantly surprised*) Oh …

SHELLY: (*Tensely*) I'm glad you're suitably impressed,
            Mr Temple. (*With authority*) Now listen! And
            listen carefully! I'll tell you precisely what I
            want you to do. When we arrive at Marlow I
            want you to …

The sliding door of the compartment is suddenly thrown open.

SHELLY: Droste! McCall!!!!

DROSTE: Drop that knife! Drop it!!!!

The knife falls.

McCALL: O.K., Temple, relax!

TEMPLE: (*Relaxing*) Phew!

DROSTE: Pick it up, Bill!

McCALL: Don't worry – I'm picking it up!

271

SHELLY: (*Tensely: frightened*) Now listen, Droste! Don't
              be a fool! I'll make you a proposition. I'll tell
              you what I'll do!

DROSTE: You've already made me one proposition, my
              friend. One too many. Now stay where you are!
              Don't move!

TEMPLE: All right, Droste. Give me that revolver – I'll
              take over.

DROSTE: Just a moment, old man. Isn't Sir Graham on
              the train?

TEMPLE: Yes, he is.

DROSTE: Well, don't you think you'd better fetch him,
              after all – technically – it's a matter for the
              police. (*Smiling, quite simply*) We'll look after
              Mr Shelly.

McCALL: (*Slowly*) It's o.k., Temple.

TEMPLE: (*Slowly: watching DROSTE and McCALL*)
              Yes. Yes, all right. I may be a little while, of
              course, finding Sir Graham.

DROSTE: That's all right. That's all right, old man.
              There's no hurry.

SHELLY: (*Quickly: tensely*) Temple, don't leave me!
              Don't leave me!!!! Don't leave me with
              Droste!!!!

The compartment door closes.

SHELLY: (*Frightened*) Droste! Droste, what are you
              going to do? (*A pause*) I didn't mean to kill
              Vanessa! I swear I didn't! It was an accident!

DROSTE: (*Calmly: almost as if he hasn't heard him*) Get
              up. Get off that seat …

SHELLY: Droste, what are you going to do? Tell me –
              what are you going to do to me …?

DROSTE: Open that door …

SHELLY: Which – which door?

DROSTE: The carriage door. Open it.

SHELLY: But the train's moving, you can't … No!!! No!!!

DROSTE: All right, Bill. Open it.

The carriage door is opened.

FADE UP slowly the sound of the train.

SHELLY: Droste, what are you going to do?

DROSTE: Give me the knife, Bill …

SHELLY: No!!! Droste, no!!! Listen to me!!!

DROSTE: (*Vehemently: advancing towards SHELLY*) You little swine! You've asked for this!

SHELLY: Droste, don't touch me! Don't come near me!!!! Don't!!!! (*Terrified*) Droste, don't! I'm near the door!!! Droste, please … Don't!!!! Droste, I'm slipping!!!! For God's sake get hold of me!!!! Get hold of me!!!! Droste!!!!

SHELLY clutches wildly and over-balances.

There is a wild shriek as he falls.

Quick FADE UP of the noise of the train.

Hold train noises for some little time.

Slow FADE DOWN.

The compartment door opens.

FORBES: (*Quickly: excitedly*) Where is he? Where is Shelly?

DROSTE: I'm sorry, Sir Graham. There's been an accident.

FORBES: An accident! What do you mean?

McCALL: He opened the carriage door and made a jump for it. Short of shooting him in the back there was just nothing we could do about it.

DROSTE: It was unfortunate. Most unfortunate.

TEMPLE: Most unfortunate, Mr Droste!

FADE UP of music.

FADE DOWN of music.

FADE UP the sound of water lapping against the side of a punt: there's a slight background of country noises.

TEMPLE, STEVE and SIR GRAHAM FORBES are in a punt on the river near Marlow. SIR GRAHAM and TEMPLE are relaxing.

STEVE is punting.

TEMPLE: (*Lazily*) What a delightful afternoon.

FORBES: (*Relaxed*) So peaceful …

TEMPLE: (*A sigh of content*) I could sit here for hours.

STEVE: (*Faintly exasperated*) Yes, well you're not going to sit there for hours! It's about time one of you characters took a turn with this pole.

TEMPLE: You're doing very nicely, Steve – very, very nicely.

FORBES: (*Relaxed*) Couldn't do better if I tried, my dear.

STEVE: Yes – well, you're not trying!

A pause.

FORBES: What are you going to do, Temple – now this Vandyke affair is over?

TEMPLE: (*Vaguely*) Oh, take things easy, I suppose. As Sam Dodsworth would say, I shall sit back with my feet on the …

STEVE: Listen! One crack about Sam Dodsworth and putting your feet on the mantelpiece and you've had it, Mr Temple!

TEMPLE: What do you mean?

STEVE: You know what I mean – Old Man River!

TEMPLE: Darling, you wouldn't dare!

STEVE: Wouldn't I!

FORBES laughs.

A long pause.

The punt slows down.

TEMPLE: Are we stopping, Steve?

STEVE: Yes, we are.

TEMPLE: (*Disappointed*) Oh …

FORBES: (*Also disappointed*) Oh …

STEVE: (*With heavy sarcasm*) Only for a moment, gentlemen, while I flex my muscles.

FORBES: (*Thoughtfully*) Temple, I've been thinking. You know, there's something about the Vandyke affair I don't quite understand.

STEVE: There's quite a lot I don't understand!

TEMPLE: Oh, Lord – I thought we were going to skip this! The good old post-mortem!

FORBES: No, but, Temple – seriously. I don't understand why Shelly persuaded Marian Faber to send that note.

TEMPLE: Which note?

FORBES: The one he sent to himself – the one that was supposed to have been written by Miss Millicent.

TEMPLE: Well, Shelly was very sure of himself and he made up his mind that he was going to get rid of Marett and take control of the Paris organisation. The note served a dual purpose. Firstly, Shelly was under the impression that if he produced a threatening note apparently written by Miss Millicent we would jump to the conclusion that Miss Millicent was in hiding and was actually the mysterious Vandyke: secondly, he was convinced that once we discovered the identity of De Wolfe we would very quickly …

FORBES: Catch up with Marett?

TEMPLE: Exactly, Sir Graham.

STEVE: But when you saw Marian Faber she admitted quite frankly, that the note was a practical joke?

275

TEMPLE: Of course she did! Don't forget it was Shelly that told us that Marian was an expert forger. When I visited Marian she said precisely what Shelly had told her to say: she made him sound like a silly young man who deserved to have a practical joke played on him.

FORBES: She also, by means of the photograph, threw further suspicion on to Palmer.

TEMPLE: Yes. You see, Steve – once the police discovered that Miss Millicent was dead – and therefore couldn't possibly have written the note – Shelly was in a spot, he simply had to think of some explanation.

STEVE: Well, if Shelly didn't actually receive a threatening note – a genuine note I mean – why was he attacked and who attacked him?

FORBES: Well, obviously Droste attacked him. Droste knew perfectly well that Vandyke, alias Shelly, had been responsible for the death of his wife.

TEMPLE: Curiously enough, I'm quite convinced that it was you, Steve, that first persuaded Shelly that he'd been attacked by Droste.

STEVE: You mean when I mentioned the identity bracelet?

TEMPLE: Yes. Shelly threw suspicion on to Palmer, of course, but he knew perfectly well that it wasn't Palmer. He just didn't know who it was.

FORBES: I had a talk to Droste, Temple – it appears that Vandyke was not only blackmailing his wife but he was trying his damnedest to blackmail Droste as well.

TEMPLE: Yes, I guessed as much. I think he had some scheme or other that he wanted Droste to finance. He did everything he could to get a hold over Droste: he even tried to influence McCall. When he realised that McCall wasn't having any, but intended to play the game by his chief, he got Franz to plant the cigarette lighter …

STEVE: In the hope of getting McCall convicted for the Marett murder?

TEMPLE: Exactly.

STEVE: Now, darling, tell me: why did you spill the coffee on Shelly?

TEMPLE: Well, although I suspected that Shelly was Vandyke I was still rather suspicious of Palmer. I spilt the coffee on Shelly, however, for the simple reason that I wanted to have a look in his wallet. I took his jacket away – ostensibly to dry it, of course – and …

STEVE: Went through his wallet …

TEMPLE: Exactly. Inside the wallet I found part of a letter – a quite unimportant letter – written by Shelly himself. This was exactly what I wanted. Later I gave Marian Faber this letter and told her to copy the handwriting.

FORBES: (*Puzzled*) You told Miss Faber to copy …?

TEMPLE: Yes – I told her to write a letter to Palmer – in an exact copy of Shelly's handwriting. The letter simply said: "Droste has agreed to co-operate. Meet me at his flat tonight at eight. Vandyke."

FORBES: But I don't see the point of that?

TEMPLE: Don't you? I think you will, Sir Graham. Having got that letter I then made an appointment to see Palmer the next evening at eight o'clock. During the course of that particular afternoon, however, I made certain that the note was delivered to Palmer. Palmer immediately cancelled our appointment – thus confirming the fact that he thought the handwriting was Shelly's and was under the impression that he had received a genuine note from Shelly alias Vandyke. I knew then that if he turned up at Droste's …

FORBES: You knew that if he turned up at Droste's Shelly was Vandyke!

TEMPLE: Exactly!

STEVE: Well, I think that was very clever of you, darling. Very clever.

TEMPLE: Thank you, Steve.

FORBES: (*A sigh*) Well, that's the finish of the Vandyke affair, Temple.

TEMPLE: Yes.

STEVE: And frankly I can't say I'm sorry.

TEMPLE: Yes – By Timothy, he wasn't exactly a pleasant customer, was he, Steve?

A pause.

FORBES: My word, we've had some adventures since we first met, haven't we, Temple?

TEMPLE: By Timothy, yes! (*Thoughtfully*) The Knave … The Front Page Men … The Marquis … REX …

STEVE: Valentine … Mr Gregory … Dr Belasco …

FORBES: Curzon … Madison …

TEMPLE: And Vandyke …

A pause.

FORBES: What are you going to do now, Temple – write another book?

TEMPLE: I'd like to. I'd like to, Sir Graham, but curiously enough I feel pretty tired. (*Seriously: without really realising what he is saying*) Do

278

you know – I think I shall take a rest. I think I shall sit back with my feet on the mantelpiece and, as Sam Dodsworth would say, think of nothing more exciting than the temperature of the beer.

Suddenly: the punt is rocking to and fro – wildly.

TEMPLE: Here, Steve! Steve!! Steve!!! Steve!!!!

There is a tremendous splash.

STEVE: By Timothy, I warned you, Mr Temple! I warned you!!!!

SIR GRAHAM starts to roar with laughter.

FADE UP of music.

THE END

Press Pack
Press cuttings about Paul Temple and the Vandyke Affair ...

Radio Roundabout by James Mack

Francis Durbridge's new Paul Temple serial, The Vandyke Affair, on Mondays, brings Kim Peacock and Marjorie Westbury together again in a detective adventure which follows the usual pattern, but is none the worse for that.

The author is an expert scatterer of red herrings, and by now listeners have come to expect wonders from Paul and Steve and can accept the incredible without even a 'tut'.

The manner in which the private detectives of fiction are consulted by the police always amused me, but one can tolerate the unlikely for the sake of a good story, and I think the creator of the omniscient Temple can be relied upon to hold the interest.

Martyn C. Webster has produced so many thriller serials that he has the technique off pat with the result that his productions are very easy on the listeners.

Unknown publication

Another villain in the current Vandyke Affair has just been drowned with superb assistance from the effects staff, and Paul Temple is nearing the climax of a further crisis in his not-inactive life.

The great appeal of a Temple saga, which like the Cromwell Road in London, has no end, lies in the ingenious plot-capacity of author Francis Durbridge, the no-holds-barred production by Martyn C. Webster, and the acting of a cast – headed by Kim Peacock – who revel in every gory glory. Shuddering, we await every 'next instalment' baffled and excited.

To scrape one small particle of gilt off the gingerbread, I feel Mr Durbridge is cramming too many characters into his works and laying so many false, though plausible, trails that the listening brain is overstretched. Next time I'd welcome a smaller *dramatis personae* and have all the villains elude death or arrest until the final chapter.

Then let loose a holocaust beside which the penultimate act of *Hamlet* would seem but a cosy tea-party at the vicarage.

Unknown publication

With *The Vandyke Affair* drawing to a close (it has been another Paul Temple triumph), devotees of that kind of thing seem to be in for rather a thin time. I wish Francis Durbridge would write one Paul Temple adventure to be given in its entirety on a Saturday night or, failing that, why not revive the first serial at one sitting?

www.ingramcontent.com/pod-product-compliance
Lightning Source LLC
Chambersburg PA
CBHW020233260626
47156CB00002B/659